SOLDIER HOLLOW

A novel by Richard Hooton

1st WORLD PUBLISHING

SOLDIER HOLLOW

A novel by Richard Hooton

© Richard Hooton 2008

Published by 1stWorld Publishing
1100 North 4th St., Fairfield, Iowa 52556
tel: 641-209-5000 • fax: 641-209-3001
web: www.1stworldpublishing.com

First Edition

LCCN: 2007943707
SoftCover ISBN: 978-1-4218-9850-6
HardCover ISBN: 978-1-4218-9849-0
eBook ISBN: 978-1-4218-9851-3

This material has been written and published solely for educational purposes. The author and the publisher shall have neither liability or responsibility to any person or entity with respect to any loss, damage or injury caused or alleged to be caused directly or indirectly by the information contained in this book.

The characters and events described in this text are intended to entertain and teach rather than present an exact factual history of real people or events.

Cover photography by Heather Crowe

Amelia,

Thanks to a fellow
writer for the
conversations and
for providing the
insperation for
some of my story.

Kindest regards -
Richard Hooton

THE CONTENTS

PROLOGUE

In the farmlands of Scotland during the time of the *"clearances"* in the mid-nineteenth century, it became common practice for many landholders to evict tenant farmers in order to make way for large sheep farms, thus depriving the humble shepherds of the means to raise livestock and care for their families. Many immigrated to America, setting sail for a vast new land and an uncertain future.

> And then went down to the ship,
> Set keel to breakers, forth on the godly sea, and
> We set up mast and sail on that swart ship,
> Bore sheep aboard her, and our bodies also
> Heavy with weeping, and winds from sternward
> Bore us onward with bellying canvas,
> Crice's this craft, the trim-coifed goddess,
> Then sat we amidships, wind jamming the tiller,
> Thus with stretched sail, we went over sea till day's end.
> Sun to his slumber, shadows o'er all the ocean,
> Came we then to the bounds of deepest water,
> To the Kimmerian lands, and peopled cities
> Covered with close-webbed mist, unpierced ever
> With glitter of sun-rays
> Nor with stars stretched, nor looking back from heaven.
> Swartest night stretched over wretched men there.

Ezra Pound

CHAPTER ONE

FOLLOWING HOPE

Holy Island, North Wales—1856

Fort Holyhead was cloaked in early morning darkness when the old Scotsman roused from his troubled sleep, shivering from the damp cold, and feeling uneasy from the lingering remnants of a bad dream. The fleeting apparition of his little daughter's pale countenance faded from memory as he became fully awake. Unrelenting winds off the Irish Sea had blown throughout the night to deliver freezing rain and penetrating, bone-chilling misery.

The old man gathered his belongings and emerged from his temporary sleeping spot in the doorway of St. Gybi's Church. He made his way past the gravestones that lined the sides of the path leading out of the churchyard. No light shone through the windows of the old Anglican Church, nor were there any signs of life from within the tiny stone schoolhouse that stood next to the church inside the walls of the ancient fort. Abandoned centuries earlier by the Roman soldiers who built it, Fort Holyhead now sheltered the Anglican Church and tiny school, and provided a burial place for generations of families who had lived and died on the island.

The Scotsman paused briefly to look back, pulled his broad-brimmed hat tightly onto his gray head, and leaned into the wind. He turned his collar up against the cold and began his trek down the narrow lane toward the harbor. The clacking and tapping sounds from his hobnail boots and shepherd's crook on granite cobblestones echoed off the stone-clad buildings with their icicled eaves.

He had walked most of the miles to North Wales from his home in the Scottish Borders near the village of Dun. He slept in barns along the way, and built fires by the roadside to keep warm whenever wood was plentiful. His clothing smelled of rain-soaked hay and wood smoke. He tried to make steady progress during his southward trek, and kept to the main roads to avoid trouble with landowners who were easily agitated by trespassers. When he stopped at night to rest, he was unable to avoid the constant thoughts of his wife and daughter. He sorely missed them, but no longer had a reason to turn back.

He kept up his steady pace down the hill. Lying just inside the north inlet of Holy Island, the natural harbor was ideal for deep-hulled vessels. As the man felt the descending pavement begin to level at the bottom of the lane, he stopped abruptly and lifted his head to listen for sounds that might guide him closer toward the harbor and docks. It took a few moments to set his bearings straight in the dim light.

A soft whine came up from the furry shadow that crept low to the ground alongside him. "It's all right, lad. It won't be long now," he spoke in a soothing tone. The black dog padded silently beside him, reassured by its master's voice. The man peered ahead into the darkness, listened carefully, then turned and strode along the dockside, pausing occasionally to search the silhouettes in the harbor for the tall shape of the sailing ship that was sure to be lying at anchor or moored along the heavily-timbered docks.

The smell of kelp and salt air filled the man's nostrils. Sea birds heralded the coming of the new day, piercing the early morning air with their noisy bickering as they scavenged along the shore and squabbled over breakfast.

He passed by a long sloop that rested low in the water, heavily laden with cargo. There was no movement on the decks, nor any light or sound coming from the interior of the vessel. The ships in the harbor seemed deserted so early in the morning. A few steps more and he could make out the shape of a larger ship, tied off against the dock with thick mooring line.

The old Scotsman stopped and looked up, squinted in the dim light and read the word that was carved into a wooden name plank mounted high up on the ship's stern. He could just make out the bold, chiseled letters in brightly painted red and gold. *Cumbria.*

"This is it," he said aloud. He gazed down the length of the tall, three-masted ship. She was a sturdy barkantine, built to withstand the elements, and suitable for carrying passengers and cargo safely across the ocean. It was a craft capable of navigating through the fierce storms that often rose up in the North Atlantic, but he hoped the weather would be favorable for the crossing.

Voices, faint and indistinguishable at first, drifted down from the main deck. The light from a bulkhead lantern was barely visible through the early morning mist. He made his way along the dock to the ship's gangplank, grasped the thick hawser handrail, and mounted the heavy planks that led to the main deck.

"Stay with me, dog," the man urged in a soothing, low-pitched voice. The dog hesitated, but did not disobey, and would not be left behind. It moved up the inclined plank in an instant and took its place alongside its master, crouching low on the deck to hold its balance as it felt the gentle rocking of the ship against the pilings. There was nothing familiar about the sights and smells of this strange place, and the dog did not like it, but it was his master's will that brought them to the ship, and the dog trusted its master. The man had given him work, provided food and shelter, and had done him no harm. He would stay with his good master.

Arrived on the deck, the old Scotsman stopped and stared at the back of a finely uniformed man, tall like himself, and with good bearing and posture. He was obviously a man of importance. He was engaged in conversation with a passenger, a small man burdened with several large pieces of baggage. The passenger's wife and young daughter stood close behind him, and all three listened intently to instructions from the uniformed man.

"Ye had best be going below now, sir, and get your family settled. I am afraid all the best bunks are taken, but there should be space for you up forward, near the bow." The man gestured toward an open forward hatch, his outstretched arm pointing the way. As the new passengers turned to go, he dropped his chin slightly and offered a courteous nod to the man and his wife. His other hand lifted, respectfully, to touch the brim of his cap.

"And mind your step on the ladder. It's quite steep," he called after them.

Captain William Norman Gillespie had been master of the *Cumbria* for more than ten years. He had served as first officer for nearly three years, and assumed command after the ship's former captain took ill and succumbed to a bout of consumption. He heard the footfall of a man's approach behind him on the deck.

Few things ever escaped the Captain's attention aboard the ship that he had come to know so intimately over the years. From his quarters in the stern he could hear a gull making itself comfortable on a mast, or a rat scurrying up a mooring line in the middle of the night. Experience and the years had honed his senses. He turned to face the man, clasped his hands behind his back and braced his feet a good distance apart on the deck, a posture which helped him maintain his balance on rough seas.

Each man waited for the other to speak, as each one assessed the other man's size and bearing. The old Scotsman held a steady gaze with the Captain for a moment, and then wisely capitulated.

"Good morning to you, sir. My name is Stewart." A quick nod was the only response from the Captain.

"I'm told this ship is bound for America, sir. I'd like to book passage, if you'll allow it," he continued.

Captain Gillespie looked the old Scotsman over carefully. It was a simple thing to recognize the man was a shepherd. A long shepherd's staff was grasped firmly in his left hand, fashioned from smoothed hardwood and topped with a finely-carved ram's horn crook. Stewart's long woolen coat hung loosely over his large shoulders, upturned collar protecting his neck from the chill wind. The well-worn garment bore dark stains from many years of gathering soot and soil, and the faint odor of lanolin from sheep's wool still lingered in the weavings.

"We have precious little space remaining, sir," Captain Gillespie replied, dismissively. He glanced down at the man's dog, and continued his explanation.

"We must put into port in Ireland to take on more passengers and cargo. Arrangements were made for them in advance. Perhaps we can find one extra bunk, but you cannot bring the dog in any case," the Captain stated flatly, gesturing with his chin at the rough-coated black collie crouched at the man's feet.

"Oh, he'll nae be any trouble, Sir," Stewart assured him.

"I cannot allow it," the Captain said, with a tone of finality. "You travel alone, or not at all."

"He'll nae be trouble," the old Scotsman repeated. "It's an obedient dog that he is, and he stays by me side, always," he explained. "Reconsider, sir. Please," he implored. "This dog is the reason I am making the journey to America. I can nae go without him."

The Captain looked down at the dog again, admiring the animal's fine bearing and obedient nature. He had transported many domestic farm animals on his crossings to America, and this dog did have the appearance of a keen working dog. Stewart sensed the Captain was wavering, and took advantage of the moment of uncertainty.

"I'll pay double the fare—full passage for both of us," he bid. It was an extremely generous offer for any thrifty Scotsman to make.

Captain Gillespie listened patiently, allowing the man a moment to plead his case. "The dog cannot go below. There is scarcely room enough for passengers," the Captain explained.

"We'll stay on the deck. We've nae need of a bunk," Stewart insisted, raising a hand to touch the bedroll slung over his shoulder. "A piece of canvas sheeting to keep the rain off our 'eads will do fine."

The Captain was, among other things, a fiscally prudent man. It could do little harm to post two more fares in the ship's passenger log. He acquiesced. "Do you have your payment in full, sir?"

"I have it here," Stewart offered, enthusiastically. He produced a leather pouch from an inside pocket of his heavy coat and held it up for the Captain's inspection.

"Very well. Give your name to the First Officer when he comes on deck," the Captain instructed. "And see that you keep your dog out of his way. Mr. Trent has no fondness for dogs." He turned and walked away toward the stern, toward the large ship's wheel, where two seamen had already positioned themselves and were busy with preparations for the voyage. Looking back over his shoulder, the Captain offered one last admonition. "You had best keep a lead on your dog, and do not let him foul my deck. Be quick to collect any baggage you have ashore. We sail in one hour."

Stewart smiled and patted his bedroll. "I have it all here, sir. Thank you." He turned and looked for a quiet spot, a place out of the way of the seamen and the masts and the busy hatchways. He looked for a place where he and his dog could rest, undisturbed. "Stay with me, lad," he said softly to his dog as he lay down on the deck behind the main hatchway. It was still early morning, but his energy was depleted from his long journey on foot, and exhaustion granted him sleep.

Stewart awoke to the sound of hard rain pelting the canvas under which he had taken refuge. His black dog lay quietly against his leg. They both felt the ship moving, pitching in the open water. The ship had slipped its mooring and was already at sea. Time was difficult for the man to measure on the open sea, and he could not discern the hour, or guess how long he had been asleep. He reached down to gently stroke the dog's ruff. A faint whine escaped its throat, and it trembled slightly under its master's comforting hand.

"I know, lad," the man reassured. "It's all right. This is all strange to me, too."

He lifted the canvas coverlet just enough to peer out through the falling rain. He could see the faint light of a beacon shining from a whitewashed tower in the distance. The South Stack Lighthouse was barely visible, perched atop a rocky little isle and separated from the western shore of Holy Island by not more than a few yards. The ship had cleared the harbor and moved out onto the Irish Sea. He could not have been asleep for more than a few hours. The ship was at full sail, and a following wind carried the barkantine along at a fair clip toward its next port of call in Ireland.

"We've just begun, lad. A few more weeks, now, that's all. We've come this far," he said as if to reassure the dog, but meant as encouragement to himself.

As he watched the rocky coast of North Wales slowly fade away in the distance, he began to feel something wrong with his equilibrium. A queasy feeling quickly overcame him, and without warning, he doubled over and emptied the meager contents of his stomach onto the deck of the ship. Stewart suddenly lost interest in the retreating horizon, and gave up on being a sightseer. He was now a miserable, seasick passenger. The stories he had heard about seasickness sprang to mind with new relevance.

Then he remembered the Captain's earlier warning not to allow his dog to foul the deck, and set aside his nausea for the moment to search for a bucket. Never mind the possibility that his dog might foul the deck; he needed to erase the evidence of his own weakness from the wooden planks before the Captain or one of the crew discovered his failure as a seafarer.

Huddled under canvas, Stewart concentrated his efforts on keeping dry and warm, and he pulled his dog close for added warmth. The dog trembled as it lay close to its master, from fear as much as the cold. The dog did not like the movement of the ship. Stewart covered himself with his thin wool blanket and pulled the dog closer. Sleep, he thought. Just sleep. It will get better.

When he woke, it was still daylight—or was it the light of a new day? He could not tell how long he had slept. The sky was overcast and the wind was reduced to a light breeze. His nausea was replaced with hunger. He sat up and rummaged through his small pack, breaking some bread away from one of the loaves that the Anglican priest at St. Gybi's Church had given him the day before.

"Meals may be scarce," the priest had warned him. "Take what food you can, and buy what you can afford before you leave Ireland."

The kindly priest had allowed him to spend the night in the covered entrance to the church, even though dogs were not allowed on the hallowed grounds.

"It's a miserable night, to be sure" the Priest had acknowledged. "Stay out of the rain and do not wander about the churchyard or cemetery. It's not likely we will have any visitors before morning, but you must be gone with your dog before the sun."

Stewart took inventory of his pack. Some dried salmon, cheese, and the priest's gift of bread. A few hens' eggs he had purchased at a farmhouse on his way into Holyhead were wrapped up in a shirt. He took the time to inspect them, and found one cracked. Stewart broke the cracked shell open and offered the raw egg to his dog.

"Here, lad. You'd better eat something." The dog hungrily accepted, lapping the rich liquid from the shell. Stewart ate a little cheese, and shared a piece of bread with his dog. It was enough to sustain them both for a time.

Stewart pulled himself to his feet and steadied against a side rail. Gazing off in the distance in the direction they were sailing, he tried in vain to make out any shape on the horizon that might be Ireland. There was nothing but clouds, sky and water. He was unable to measure time on the open sea with the sun covered by clouds. There were no lengthening shadows of trees or familiar landmarks to line up with the rising and setting sun. This briny expanse was not to his liking. "I'd prefer to feel the earth beneath my feet, wouldn't you, lad?" he asked, stroking the dog's head. The dog gave a soft, plaintive whine in reply. The feel of the ship was not to the dog's liking either.

Memories of home and family began to intrude upon Stewart's conscious thoughts. Unable to resist, he reached into his coat pocket and lifted out a tarnished gold locket—his wife's only valued possession when they first met. He opened the clasp and gazed at the trimmed ovals cut from photographs of his wife and daughter.

Marjorie was posed in her plain gray Sunday dress with a white lace collar. Her auburn hair was combed smooth and pulled back into a tight bun, and a faint smile graced her lips. His sweet daughter's frail image was frozen in time, preserving her flawless, pale skin and patrician features. She had her mother's eyes and hair color. Her little head was topped with luxuriant auburn hair and adorned with a satin ribbon. She had worn a new white lace dress to pose for the photograph, a dress crocheted by her grandmother just for the occasion.

Stewart and his wife had married without the benefit of a lavish ceremony. He had no ring to give her, and she came into the marriage with no dowry—only the locket and chain he now held in his hand.

Stewart closed the locket and lowered it back into its hiding place inside his heavy coat. No outward emotion was visible on his stern, weathered face. His gray eyes stared off into the distance, lost in a memory. All the tears he had to give had already been given. He covered himself with his blanket and went back to sleep.

The sound of lighthearted laughter woke Stewart from his troubled sleep.

"Come here, boy. I won't hurt you," he heard a child's voice coax in a soothing tone.

He sat up and lifted a corner of his makeshift canvas shelter—a piece of sail cloth draped over two oaken water barrels and held in place on top by a heavy coil of hawser. He had crawled in between the barrels and held onto the lower edge of the canvas, tucking it under his prone body to prevent it from flapping in the wind.

A little girl of not more than eight or nine years of age was patting his dog gently on its head and stroking its soft, black fur. The dog sat quietly for the girl as she lavished it with love and attention. Its white-tipped tail dusted the deck as it wagged, and its pink tongue lolled contentedly as the girl patted and praised.

"You're a pretty dog, aren't you?" she cooed, stroking the dog's ears and neck with both hands.

The dog looked very much like a black wolf, except for the white tip of its wagging tail and a few white whiskers on its muzzle. The black dog heard its master stir and turned its head to look toward the old Scotsman for approval. Stewart smiled at the sight of the little girl fawning over his dog. She reminded him of his own sweet Mary, who always came out to greet him when he arrived home from his day's work in the pastures. She would kneel to hug the sheepdog before escorting it to a dish half-filled with stale bread and some rabbit meat or mutton left over from the previous day's meal.

"You were snoring," the girl observed, without criticizing. "Why do you sleep up here?"

"The captain will nae allow my dog to go below," Stewart replied, "and I can nae leave him up here alone."

"What's his name?" she asked, as she continued to fondle the dog's neck and ears.

"Roy," he answered. "His name is Roy."

The girl lavished more affection on the dog. "You're a fine dog, Roy. Yes, you're a fine dog." Abruptly, the girl got to her feet and turned to rush off. "I have to get back to my mother and father now."

Stewart watched as the girl crossed over to the opposite side of the ship and moved forward along the railing toward a man and woman who were standing with their backs to him, looking across the sea. He recognized them as the English passengers who were speaking with the captain when he came aboard the ship at Holyhead.

"Land!" the cry came from high up on the mainmast. "Land to starboard."

Passengers and seamen gathered at the ship's rail, necks strained and eyes searching the horizon for the green hilltops that would mark the town of Cobh, the cove of Cork. A chorus of excited voices followed when the southern tip of Ireland came into view from the main deck.

The Irish port town of Cobh was a welcome sight. Stewart could not remember if it had been three days or only two since he had embarked from the seaport in North Wales. He turned his attention to the approaching harbor, not thinking about the weeks that it would take to cross the North Atlantic.

More than a dozen cargo and passenger vessels lined the docks, preparing to set out for America or to destinations on the European continent. It was to be the last stop for the *Cumbria* before it would enter the vast expanse of the Atlantic Ocean.

The wharf was alive with dock workers and vendors offering their wares.

The mooring lines were not yet secured before a portly man in a flour-dusted apron began to hawk his baked goods to the ship's passengers. "Fresh bread!" the baker called out from the dock below. A rather scrawny, bandy-legged man pushed by him and ordered a nearby seaman to open a gate in the ship's rail to receive the gangplank.

"Keep your mongrel out of the way!" a harsh voice commanded Stewart.

"Stay with me, dog," Stewart said quietly, as he stepped back out of the way. The dog growled a low, distrusting growl in the direction of the bandy-legged little man.

"Whist, keep quiet now, lad," he whispered, waiting patiently for an opportunity to go ashore for provisions.

Stewart remembered the Captain's admonition to stay clear of the ship's First Officer, warning him of the man's dislike of dogs. He fashioned a short lead from a length of twine and kept it on his dog when people were about. Roy had never been constrained except by his master's voice. He was unaccustomed to the lead, but readily succumbed to his master's bidding.

Mr. Trent had glared at the dog on the day Stewart paid the fare and signed his name to the passenger list.

"See that you keep the cur on a short line," he ordered, when he first encountered Stewart. "If it bites, or even threatens, I'll have it put over the side, and it can swim with the fish."

Stewart nodded his assent without remark. He knew it would not pay to cross this man.

Both man and dog watched as new passengers boarded the ship and went below to locate their sparse accommodations. Cargo was loaded, including several small pens of sheep and cages of chickens. Roy watched the process intently, eager to be a part of it. Stewart took the opportunity to go down onto the dock for provisions.

Vendors on the wharf pushed carts or set up makeshift counters with wooden planks laid across barrels to display their eggs, fish and salted pork. Some of the prices were high, but Stewart recalled the advice of the Anglican priest at St. Gybi's Church to prepare for the voyage with as many provisions as he could afford to buy. He bought bread and cheese, some dried fish and salt pork. Fresh eggs and chicken were costly. He would have to make do with what was affordable.

Stewart marveled as a large, steam-powered ship moved slowly out of the harbor in the early afternoon, black smoke erupting out of the stacks from the coal furnaces deep in the ship's belly. Unheeding of tides or prevailing winds, the power-driven ship moved past the breakwater and onto the open ocean. Cobh had become a busy seaport during this time of famine and evictions. More and more immigrants were bound for America, leaving behind a life of suffering, starvation and oppression for a life of uncertainty in a strange new land. Most had few possessions to carry with them; nearly all held the hope of a bright future for their families in America.

The *Cumbria* slipped its mooring lines and was away on the following day before the sun, catching the ebb tide and a fair wind out onto the Atlantic. By the time passengers began stirring from their bunks and climbing the ships ladders to the main deck, the southern coast of Ireland was already behind them and nearly out of view.

A woman stood alone at the ship's railing and wept silently as she saw her homeland grow smaller in the distance and disappear into the low hanging clouds. Stewart watched her, somberly, but said nothing. No words of comfort would make a difference, he thought. He felt his own grief again, a weight pressing down on his chest.

He reached inside a deep pocket in his coat and retrieved the letter from the bottom, wrapped carefully inside a woolen scarf.

"*Dear brother*", it began. He had read it countless times.

"We have survived our trip across the Atlantic and are in the Port of New Orleans. Margaret has given birth to a healthy boy. We named him James. He appears quite healthy, and his big sister adores him and loves to hold him. Margaret is pleased, as she is still not fully recovered and she appreciates the help. Walter misses home, but tries to keep himself occupied, and he is looking forward to seeing our new home in the West. He speaks of you often.

As soon as mother and child can travel, we will go up river to Missouri and join one of the wagon trains bound for Utah. Large parties are leaving for California and the Utah Territory every year until late spring. It is our hope to reach the Utah Territory before the end of summer. I have learned that harsh cold and deep snow make the western lands and mountain regions impassable late in the year, so we must be away before the end of May or I fear we will have to wait in St. Joseph through the winter.

We hope you can meet us there before we begin our trek west. Bring your best collie dog if you can. It seems there are few good herding dogs to be found in America. A good dog should prove to be quite useful."

Your brother, James

There is nothing to keep me in Scotland, Stewart remembered thinking when his brother's letter arrived. It only took a day for him to write and post a letter in reply.

"I'll sell every earthly possession," he wrote back to his brother, "and be on board the first ship that will take us."

"The sheep were sold when the eviction was served, though they did not fetch a fair price. I believe there is still enough coin to make the journey."

"I'll bring Roy," he continued. "He's young, but shows good promise. I've never seen a dog as keen, or with such herding instinct. He has nerve, and a powerful eye, so he'll prove valuable on a farm, I'm certain."

Stewart left for Wales before he knew if his brother had received his reply. Once he arrived in America, he decided, he would make his way to St. Joseph as quickly as he could. For now, he languished on the deck of the barkantine, marking off the days. At night he wrapped in his blanket and lay under the canvas sheet to fend off the cold, and during the day he battled with boredom. It was no place for a working man, someone who was accustomed since childhood to long hours in the fields, seeding and harvesting crops or herding and tending to livestock. He could not remember a day in his life when he was allowed to sit idle, not even when he was ill. Work had to be done, and neither crops nor sheep would wait on a farmer's recovery from sickness or bouts of laziness.

The little girl's voice penetrated the boredom and raised him out of his sullen mood.

"May I play with your dog again," she asked politely.

Stewart turned to look at the fair-haired child who reminded him so much of his own Mary. His dog had already taken its place in front of the girl, sitting obediently as its tail mopped the deck planks. A furry paw was raised in invitation, swiping the air until the girl took it in her small hand and began to stroke the dog's upturned head with the other.

"It appears Roy already gave his permission," he said, smiling.

"Father said that I might have a dog when we get to Salt Lake, if it can learn to work," the girl announced with pride in her voice. "I want a dog like Roy. He's a fine dog."

Roy's head cocked to one side when he heard his name spoken, and he reached again with his paw to ask the girl for more attention. Bright, brown eyes fixed attentively on the girl and his one pricked ear seemed to listen for the familiar praise he once heard from his own little girl.

"A dog like Roy is a lot of work, child," Stewart said. "Are you sure you want one like him? Perhaps a wee dog would make a better companion."

"I'm sure," the confident little girl replied quickly. "I don't want a small dog. I want one with some life in him, too—not a lazy sack of bones," she explained. She seemed certain of the kind of dog that would be her match.

Stewart spied the girl's mother and father on the other side of the ship, talking with another small group of passengers.

"Is that not your mother and father, child?" he asked.

She turned to look in the direction Stewart had gestured. "Yes", she answered simply. She got to her feet and hurried off to be with her family, leaving Roy with one more loving stroke of his ruff.

The wind was rising and the sky darkened as evening fell. Rain was coming. Old Stewart huddled under his piece of canvas as the cold rain broke over his makeshift shelter, dousing the ship and running in rivulets down the sloped fabric to join the sheets of rainwater rushing across the deck planks, through the gunnels and back into the sea. The ship pitched and rolled in the heavy seas and the rain began to find its way under the canvas and into the man's clothing and bedding. A strong gust ripped the flapping material from his grip and hurled it out into the night. Roy huddled closely, trembling. Stewart was soaked and miserable before the last light of day passed from the ominous western sky.

Gale force winds ripped at the unfurled sailcloth in the masts throughout the night, and the angry sea lifted the vessel to the crest of twenty foot waves, then drove it down before it into the trough of frothy seawater.

Stewart kept one arm wrapped around a length of hawser, the other held tightly to his dog. On his knees between the barrels that were once his shelter, he bowed his head against the wind and rain, pulling his dog in tightly against his chest. He made no attempt to offer calming or encouraging words to his dog in the face of the storm.

The hours were an eternity in the cold dark of night on the raging sea. Stewart opened his long coat and pulled Roy inside to keep the shivering dog warm against his body. They were both wet and trembling, sharing what warmth their bodies would provide. He could no longer tell whether he had been sleeping or had simply lost consciousness when he awoke to a hand on his shoulder, vigorously shaking him awake.

"You must come below, sir," a man's voice yelled against the howling wind. "You'll catch your death up here in the freezing wind and rain."

Stewart tried to rise to his feet, using his shepherd's staff to support his weight. He fell to the deck, unable to feel his legs. Roy whined, nuzzling under his master's forearm.

"Let me help you," the other man said, taking Stewart's arm and pulling him to his feet. "Steady yourself on me."

Stewart walked with him, taking small, shaky steps as he let the man guide him toward a hatchway. He was numb with cold. Feeling began to return to his limbs as he walked.

Blinding spray from the wind and sea lowered a watery veil between the men and the forward hatch, making it nearly impossible to find their way. They stumbled over the hatch door before they saw it. The Samaritan lowered Stewart to the deck and opened the hatch cover, climbing onto the steep ladder before helping the rain-soaked Scotsman down after him.

"Oh, the poor man," the passenger's wife whispered, as her husband lifted the half-frozen Stewart off the bottom step. "He looks near death."

"I told you, Mama," the little girl said to her mother. "I told you he stayed outside with his dog all the time."

"Hush, Sarah," the woman said quietly. "There's no need to wake the others." She helped her husband pull the rain-soaked woolen coat off the man's shoulders and wrapped him with a dry blanket.

"But where's his dog?" the girl asked, with emphasis on the dog's name. "Where's Roy?"

Suddenly reminded that he had forgotten the dog during his rescue of the man, Sarah's father started back up the ladder and came face to face with the wet dog, lying with its head half inside the open hatch, looking down at its master and the little girl. It crouched low to the deck as the man came through the open hatchway.

"Come on, boy," he coaxed. Roy wasn't sure of the man, but he wanted to be by his master's side, so he lay still and permitted the man to pick him up. With the dog under one arm, he moved down the ladder and pulled the hatch cover closed. Sarah met them at the bottom step and took over from her father.

"Oh, Roy!" she cried plaintively. The dog sat for her, shivering. "You're all wet, you poor thing."

Sarah found a piece of sackcloth and used it for a towel, stroking the dog's coat repeatedly to remove as much water as she could from its black fur. Roy watched his master being helped into a small bunk and covered with another blanket, eyeing the people carefully to be sure there was no mistreatment of his human protector.

"Come back to bed now, Sarah," her mother urged. "The dog will be all right. You leave him with Mr. Stewart."

Sarah gave the dog a final stroke with the sackcloth and led it over to the bunk where it could be near its master. She laid the cloth on the deck next to the bunk and gave the dog a hug.

"You stay here, Roy," the girl whispered, as though the dog might have been inclined to move from the spot. She made her way back to the curtain-draped bunks where her mother and father prepared to get back into bed.

"That was a good thing you did, Sarah," her father said. "The wind and rain are wicked cold tonight. Mr. Stewart might have perished had he stayed out in that tempest through the night."

He climbed into the bunk and pulled covers snugly up under his chin, still shivering from his own brief battle with the storm. Sarah had squeezed in next to her mother and was already asleep, wrapped in the peaceful slumber granted only to the innocent.

Stewart awoke to the smell of hot tea and cooked oatmeal. The storm had abated, and sunlight streamed through an open hatch. Passengers were up and moving about, some climbing to the main deck for fresh air. He sat up and looked around for his boots.

"Will Bradley is my name, Mr. Stewart," Sarah's father introduced, extending his right hand in friendship.

"You've had a miserable night of it, I'm afraid." He offered a bowl of oatmeal with his other hand. "This should help to warm you up."

Stewart accepted, gratefully. "Thank you kindly, Mr. Bradley," he said. "I can pay you for the meal. I have money."

"It's not necessary." Bradley dismissed the notion of remuneration. "There's plenty for all the passengers. Didn't they tell you?"

Stewart shook his head, sullenly, and spooned the warm oatmeal into his mouth. "No," he said, as he chewed and swallowed. "No, they did not." He disliked the First Officer more now than he did the day before.

"Surely you didn't think they would let us all starve, did you, Mr. Stewart?" Bradley asked, with a look of mild amusement, as he watched the gray-haired Scotsman gulp his food.

"I thought they might," Stewart replied matter-of-factly, talking into his bowl. He scraped the last few specks of oatmeal from the bottom and sides of the bowl and licked them from the spoon.

"I can nae remember the last time I had a hot meal. I'm obliged. I best see to my dog, now," Stewart said, pulling himself to his feet. "He'll be hungry, no doubt."

"My daughter has seen to your dog, Mr. Stewart. The last I saw her she was going in his direction with a tin of biscuits.

"She's a fine lass, your daughter." Stewart praised. "A kind heart in her, too."

"Yes, she's my pride," Bradley answered, nodding agreement. "It was she who told us you were spending every night on deck with your dog, and were likely to be out in that hellish storm last night," Bradley explained. "Insisted that I go up to look for you and the dog, she did."

The two men heard a commotion from the direction of the hatchway.

"Papa, help!" Sarah shrieked.

Stewart and Bradley reacted simultaneously, rushing forward in time to see First Officer Trent disappear down a passageway toward the bow. A burly seaman climbed the ladder, dragging Roy up behind him by the twine lead wound about his neck.

"Papa, they're going to throw Roy to the fish!" The child was frantic, her face ashen with fear.

"No!" Stewart bolted toward the hatchway, pulled himself up the ladder and clamored onto the deck, finding his balance as he looked around frantically for his dog. He spotted the bulky seaman towing the struggling dog across the deck toward the port rail. Roy fought against the line that was knotted tightly about his neck, twisting and tugging to free himself. His toenails scraped across wooden deck planks as he whined and growled, crouching and pulling backwards against the noose in a vain attempt to thwart his executioner.

Stewart rushed toward the man, determined to stop him in any that way he could. The seaman turned and looked back with cold, merciless eyes. Stewart stopped, frozen in place with arms outstretched at his sides, palms up in a gesture of supplication. He did not want to goad the man into action.

"Do nae hurt ma dog, please, sir," Stewart pleaded. He took one tentative step forward, then another, in an attempt to close the space between himself and his dog. Measuring the distance to the rail, he calculated whether he could cross the deck in time.

The burly man opened his mouth and revealed a toothless grin. "He's done now," the seaman chortled in a tone filled with sadistic pleasure, as he pronounced final sentence upon the dog. He tightened his grip on the line and lifted the dog over the ship's railing by its neck to seal its fate.

"Belay that, Mister Walker!" Captain Gillespie bellowed, as he appeared out of nowhere. "What mischief are you about?"

"Just following orders, sir," the seaman said. "Mr. Trent found the dog below in passengers' quarters. Says it attacked him and he told me to put it over the side." The dog struggled to free itself again, tightening the line on its neck.

"Set the dog on the deck and leave it be, Mr. Walker," the captain calmly ordered in a stern voice. He stepped toward the seaman. *"Quickly,"* he repeated in a harsh, threatening tone.

The seaman released his grip on the struggling dog. Roy dropped to the deck and lay flat, eyes casting about for his master as he gasped for air. "Just following orders, sir," the man said again, defending his actions.

"You'll follow my orders now," Mister Walker. "Go on about your duties. If you trouble this man or his dog again, it will be you who swims with the fish." The seaman vanished down an open hatch, with a respectful "aye, sir" to his captain.

Will Bradley stood by the ladder, watching the scene unfold as he held his breath. He exhaled with a sigh of relief and approached the Captain.

"Captain Gillespie, the fault is mine. I took Mr. Stewart and his dog below during the storm last night. They were in true misery, and I did not think it would cause any harm."

"The fault is mine," the Captain assented. "Perhaps I should have made allowances in view of the foul weather, and arranged better protection for Mr. Stewart and his dog."

"I will be glad to take an apology to Mr. Trent," Bradley offered.

"It won't be necessary, Mr. Bradley," the Captain said. "I'll deal with Mr. Trent. Perhaps you should see to your friend." He gestured in Stewart's direction.

Will Bradley turned to see Stewart kneeling over his dog, and hurried to his side. "Is he all right?" he asked, with genuine concern.

"He'll be fine," Stewart said, removing the last of the knotted line from around Roy's neck. "I should never have tied this accursed garrote around his throat. He is nae accustomed to constraint. It's the sound of my voice that he heeds, not the tug of a line." Stewart stroked Roy's rough black coat, allowing the heavily panting dog to steady its breathing and recover from its ordeal.

Will Bradley kneeled beside the older man and his dog. "He'll be needing some water, I expect," Bradley said, smiling.

"Thank you, Mr. Bradley," Stewart said, looking the younger man in the eye. "I'm deeply indebted to you."

The days passed uneventfully for the next two weeks. Will and Martha Bradley were pleased that their daughter had been delivered from boredom by the many hours she spent with Roy, while they got better acquainted with Stewart.

Stewart's gray eyes clouded over when Martha Bradley asked about Mrs. Stewart, reflecting sadness from deep in his soul.

Will Bradley sensed that something was wrong. "Perhaps Mr. Stewart would rather not talk about his family, Martha."

"I'm sorry if I offended you, Mr. Stewart," Martha apologized. "I just thought..."

"It's all right, Mrs. Bradley", Stewart interrupted, looking solemnly off in the distance in the direction of his homeland. "I suppose you should know something about me—and why I make this journey alone. I'm truly obliged for your kindness." He lifted the tarnished gold locket from its hiding place in the deep pocket of his coat lining and opened the clasp.

Will and Martha Bradley listened respectfully as the old Scotsman told his story and explained how he planned to re-unite with his remaining family in Missouri. Martha thought she should say something to demonstrate her understanding and concern.

"I'm very sorry for your loss, Mr. Stewart," Martha said quietly. "I expect we are all following our own hopes and dreams for a new life in America."

Sarah looked up from her blanket on the deck where she had been enjoying a picnic of biscuits and honey with Roy, who had become the grateful recipient of the girl's affections. She listened attentively as Mr. Stewart quietly recounted for her mother and father the events of his wife's lingering illness and death during the last winter, and the tragic disease that claimed his little Mary just six months later.

"Are they in heaven now, Mr. Stewart?" Sarah asked innocently. Will Bradley did not attempt to quiet his inquisitive daughter.

"Yes, child, I believe so," Stewart answered softly, nodding his head. "Tis sure that they are. They've gone to glory."

The last days at sea passed quickly as the passengers grew more accustomed to daily routine, and busied themselves with small tasks to while away the hours. Stewart obtained a small block of pine from the ship's carpenter and took up his favorite pastime of whittling. After a few days of carving away the pieces of wood that didn't resemble a dog, he had a good likeness of Roy. He gave it to Sarah, along with the promise that he and Roy would see her again in Utah.

"Here, lass," Stewart said. "You keep this carving to help you remember Roy until you see him again."

Sarah proudly showed the wooden figure of the dog to her father, who told her what a fine likeness it was of Roy.

"Don't forget, Sarah," he reminded his young daughter. "It will take a lot of work to train and care for a dog of your own." He knew that Sarah would be devoted to the task. The girl loved animals with an uncommon passion.

After nearly four weeks at sea, the call was finally heard from high up in the mainmast that land had been spotted to the southwest. A loud cheer went up on the deck from passengers and crew alike.

"At last," Stewart whispered to his dog. "We can put our feet on solid ground again."

The *Cumbria* sailed south along the coast for the better part of a day before turning into Boston Bay. Scores of tall-masted ships lay at anchor in thick clusters across the bay.

"Have you ever seen the like?" Martha Bradley marveled to her husband. Will Bradley put his arm around her shoulder and pulled her close. Looking out across the tops of the ships toward the city, he voiced his optimism to his pretty wife.

"We're halfway there, Martha. We've made it to America. Nothing can stop us now."

Sarah stood with her parents at the railing for a time, studying the many ships and various buildings along the wharf and on the hill above the waterfront, then turned her attention back to Roy.

Arrived on the dock with all their possessions in hand, Will and Martha Bradley made a last effort to persuade Stewart to join them.

"We'll be taking a train as far as Iowa City, and from there it becomes a more arduous overland journey to Utah. You will probably join your brother and his family sooner," Will said.

Stewart declined. "He's expecting me in St. Joseph," he said. "He may already be waiting there for my arrival."

Sarah gave Roy a good supply of farewell hugs and promised that she would see him in Utah in the fall.

The Haymarket District was a bustling center of commerce near the docks. It appeared that every imaginable cargo must pass through the busy marketplace. Livestock, farm produce, fish, tobacco, tea, linens, and sundry products of every size and description were offered for trade. Carpenters, coopers and tinsmiths lined the long aisles, and shoppers inspected the wares and bargained for merchandise.

Across the way, the streets were lined with buildings occupied by merchants and solicitors. Cobblers, hatters and clothiers had set up shop in the busy district to keep the inhabitants of Boston well-attired.

Stewart went in search of warm food and a bed. The Lantern Inn marked its entrance with a carved wooden sign suspended over the doorway of the two-story brick building near the Haymarket District. It was a welcome sight. Stewart stepped inside and found a small table near the door. Roy dropped to the floor and rested quietly at his master's feet. A portly woman came to the table and took Stewart's meal order.

"We have lamb stew and fried cod," the woman said. The tempting aroma of cooked meat and potatoes drifted from the kitchen.

"I'll have the stew," Stewart asked politely, removing his hat. Roy would appreciate a taste of meat, too, he thought.

"And some hot tea, if you please. Do you have beds available?"

"Sure, see the innkeeper," the round woman said, pointing a chubby sausage finger in the direction of the bar before turning to waddle off to the kitchen. Stewart looked up to see a man in a white apron who was standing behind the compact mahogany bar, talking animatedly with two of his patrons. He decided to wait until after his meal, rather than interrupt the proprietor's conversation.

The dining room was nearly full, mostly with merchants, farmers and seafarers. A warm fire crackled in the open hearth. He recognized two seamen from the Cumbria at a table near the fire. They were looking in his direction as they whispered to each other. He had made an impression on the crew as the man whose dog had been saved from certain death by the ship's captain.

The door swung open and the First Officer from the Cumbria strutted through on his bandy legs, demanding service as he came. "A pint of ale, publican, and be quick," the irascible little man demanded from across the room.

Roy saw him first. The fur on the dog's neck bristled and his lip curled. Stewart's shoulders tensed when he heard Trent's voice, but he sat quietly, hoping to be ignored.

"Put up a pint for me, innkeeper, and don't keep me waiting," Trent ordered again, as he pushed his way past the crowded tables. He caught a glimpse of the Scotsman and his dog out of the corner of his eye and abruptly changed his course.

"Well, well," the scrawny replica of a human being chided. "If it isn't the dirty shepherd and his mongrel."

Stewart fixed his steely eyes on the little man, but said nothing. It was provocation enough for Trent just to see him seated comfortably at the table with his dog, awaiting food and drink.

"You caused me a fair amount of trouble with the Captain," Trent complained. The revelation pleased Stewart, but he saved his smile for later.

"You caused your own trouble," Stewart corrected. "Perhaps you would be happier in a different line of work," Stewart said, tightening his grip on the Hazelwood crook he held just under the table.

Trent flew into a fury. He was not accustomed to being spoken to in this manner by someone he considered to be beneath him.

"Do not presume to tell me what is good for my career, Scottie. You do not enjoy the Captain's protection here," the unlikable man threatened, drawing back his booted foot to aim a kick at the dog.

"Nor do you, sir," Stewart responded instantly, springing to his feet to confront the smaller man. The old Scotsman's tall, rugged frame loomed over his adversary and his smooth ram's horn crook found a snug fit under Trent's chin. He nestled the shepherd's crook firmly up under the little man's jawbone as he gripped his coat lapel with his free hand. It took all the self-restraint Stewart could muster to keep himself from cracking the man's skull. Roy crouched low to the floor, not from fear, but in readiness. The dog inched forward as its master spoke, never taking its eyes off the little man with the raised foot.

"I would nae offer my boot to the dog if I were you," Stewart warned, staring into the little man's face from just inches away. "He may misunderstand, and think the foot is his to keep as well."

He released his hold on Trent's coat, and the scrawny man toppled backwards onto the floor against the entry door. Roy stayed where he was, eyes fastened onto the prone man, awaiting his master's command.

"I believe you've found the way out, sir," the innkeeper called out from across the dining room, speaking to the troublesome ship's officer. "I've had enough of your bad manners over the years, and so have my good customers."

Trent righted himself, straightened his coat and barged out through the door, red-faced and furious.

The portly serving woman returned with a tray and placed a large bowl of stew in front of Stewart, along with fresh bread and a tall mug filled with hot tea.

"You must let me know if you'll be wanting more bread or tea, sir. There's plenty more."

Roy lifted his head and sniffed under the edge of the table next to his master's knee, excited at the prospect of a tasty reward for his good behavior.

Stewart settled into a warm, dry bed for the first time in more than two months. His belly was full, and he was clean from a warm bath. He could not remember the last time he felt such comfort. He was in America, at last. He pulled the blankets up under his chin, laid his head back on the down pillow, and felt a harsh cough come from deep in his chest.

Roy curled himself comfortably onto the oval hook rug beside the bed, released a deep, stress-relieving sigh and closed his eyes.

CHAPTER TWO

THE STOCK HANDLERS

Train fare to Peoria used up nearly all of the money left in Stewart's purse. The trip from Boston was a series of rides on loosely-connected railroads across Massachusetts, Pennsylvania and Ohio, then further west through Indiana and Illinois. He would have to travel by foot and by riverboat the rest of the way into St. Louis. The journey to America and the several days spent in Boston gathering information and advice on the best routes and transportation methods to the far west had cost more in time and currency than he expected. Paying another fare to bring Roy aboard the ship in Holyhead was an expense he had not anticipated, but leaving the dog behind was never an option to be considered. He regretted having lingered in Boston for so long.

It rained for most of the trip downriver on the riverboat to St. Louis, but that did little to dampen Stewart's spirits. Man and dog sat on the foredeck amid the stacked cargo of whisky barrels destined for St. Louis and New Orleans from the distillers in Peoria. It seemed there must be a lot of thirsty men downriver, he mused. The next stop was the gateway to the west, and he vowed that this would be his last boat ride. He intended to plant his feet on firm ground and keep them there.

A few fields and farmhouses began to appear along the river, and riverboat traffic in both directions became more frequent. St. Louis couldn't be far away.

"Have you ever seen such a mighty river, lad?" Stewart said idly, gazing in awe at the Mississippi. Roy sat close to his master, wiggled and whined at the sound of his master's voice, then continued to fix his stare on the slowly passing scenery along the riverbank and the occasional glimpse of sheep and cows. Roy shared his master's desire to feel the earth beneath his feet.

Roy trembled with excitement and stared ahead as his keen senses alerted him to the presence of livestock. The docks on the east side of St. Louis were not yet in view, but the dog could smell the stockyards and the familiar odor of cattle and sheep. It smelled like work.

Stewart sought out an eatery as soon as they disembarked and brought out a meaty beef rib for Roy before stepping back inside to fill his belly with beef stew and bread. The proprietor was a jovial Irishman who prided himself on taking good care of his regular patrons from the docks and stockyards, serving hearty food and large portions. Stewart paid the man and stuffed some bread into his pocket for later. There was no telling when he might afford another meal.

Roy was lying near the door, happily gnawing on the stripped beef bone when his master reappeared.

"Come on lad, bring your bone with you," Stewart invited. "What we need is some wages."

The pair followed their noses down the side streets past the livery stables and feed barns to the stockyards. It was a busy livestock center, the likes of which Stewart had never seen. Business appeared to be good at every store front along the street. There were blacksmith shops and a saddlery—even a wagon maker. A dry goods store occupied a large corner building next to a saloon.

Stewart stepped inside and asked the storekeeper about the job situation in town. "Do you know of anyone who's lookin' for an able pair of hands and a strong back to help them out?" he queried. "I can work afore the sun and 'til after dark, without sittin' down."

"Try Benson's Livery Stable," the storekeeper answered amicably. "He knows just about everybody who's looking to hire extra help around the yards."

Winkler Benson was unloading sacks of grain from a wagon when Stewart walked into his stables. He left Roy just outside the barn door so he wouldn't spook the stalled horses. Benson heard Stewart's footsteps behind him as the man approached, but didn't pause to look up from his task.

"What can I do for you?" Benson asked. "You need to board a horse, or hire one?" He laid the last sack of grain on the stack before he turned to look at the tall, gray-haired Scotsman. "Or maybe you need a horse and wagon?" he said, pausing to catch his breath.

"The man at the dry goods store said you were the man to talk to about findin' work." Stewart held his hat in his hand as a polite gesture toward the man he was asking for help. "He said you knew just about everyone in the yards."

"You work with cattle?" Benson asked.

"Cattle and sheep," Stewart replied. "Mostly sheep."

"Well, hang on a minute while I get my hat," Benson said. "I'll take you down to the yards. There's plenty of work for them that's willin' and able."

Benson turned and called out to someone in the hay loft as the two men walked out into the street. "Tom, you get down here and rake out these stalls, you lazy sack of bones! I know you're up there. I'll be back in half an hour."

Roy fell in behind the two men as they strode quickly down the street in the direction of the livestock odor.

"Who's this?" Benson asked, looking down at the black dog that followed closely at his master's side.

"He's my helper," Stewart replied with no small amount of pride in his voice.

"Charlie, this man's lookin' for work," Benson said as the two men approached a corral where a man was sitting astride the top rail, watching two younger men struggle to move a few head of uncooperative cattle through a gate and into a small loading pen. Stewart thought he could see a family resemblance between the liveryman and the stock pen boss. They were both big men with stocky builds, and they shared the same jaw line, nose, and hair color.

The man climbed down and stuck his hand out in greeting. "Who do you have here, Wink?" the man asked.

"Stewart's my name," the old Scotsman interjected, grasping the offered hand in a friendly shake. "I understand you might be able to use some help."

"I'm Charlie Benson," the man answered, looking Stewart squarely in the eye. "This big oaf who brought you down here is my little brother," he explained, with a mock punch aimed at Wink's arm. "You know how to work cattle, Mr. Stewart?"

"I can work them," Stewart affirmed with a nod.

"It's hard work, even for a young man," Charlie Benson warned. "We go all day until the last boat is loaded and the sun goes down, or until the last drover comes in with stock. We rest and eat when we can."

"I'll give you a day's work and no complaints," Stewart assured.

Charlie Benson looked the gray-haired Scotsman over once more, wondering whether the man could stand the physical work. He noticed the black dog for the first time, lying quietly under the bottom rail of the corral fence, with its eyes fixed on the cattle that were circling around the fence line to avoid the open gate into the loading pen.

"What does he do?" Benson asked.

"He helps me."

"Well, get in there and see if you can help those boys to pen a cow or two. Just tell them where you want them to stand."

"It's better if they stand out here with you and watch," Stewart said. "I think we can manage a few cattle."

"Have it your way. Sam! Matthew! You boys climb on out of there. You've exercised those cows enough for one day. This man thinks he can show you something."

Two grateful, sweat-soaked young men climbed the fence and perched on the top rail next to the burly Benson brothers. "Sorry, Mr. Benson," young Matthew Chisholm said to his boss. "I never saw such stubborn cows."

The four men all settled onto the top rail and watched as the old Scotsman climbed into the corral, shepherd's crook in hand, and called his dog in with him.

"Come on lad," Stewart urged in a low, soothing voice. "Let's go to work."

Roy lowered his shoulders and haunches to slip easily under the bottom fence rail and into the corral, taking his place close to his master. The dog dropped and lay still while Stewart sized up the cattle. He could read livestock as well as any herder from the highlands to the borders.

The dog remained perfectly still, one pricked ear raised as if to listen for its master's command; eyes riveted on the bony range cattle at the far side of the corral. The stubborn animals all stood facing in the direction of the man and dog. The two in front lowered their horned heads, watching the dog carefully for any sign of sudden movement. Roy fixed a steady stare on the animals and prepared to move into action on his master's command.

Stewart could see that the cattle were not accustomed to being worked by a herding dog. They were agitated, and beginning to turn this way and that, searching for an escape route.

"Wait, lad," the old Scotsman said in a whisper, as he took a few slow and measured steps toward the pen gate at the far left side of the corral. "Let them settle down a bit."

Roy dropped his chin to the dirt and waited. The cattle turned their attention to the man, as he walked slowly toward the pen gate and pulled it open in a steady, fluid movement so that his actions would not startle the animals. Holding the edge of the gate in one hand, Stewart turned and raised his shepherd's crook, pointing the tip in a direction just behind his dog. Roy raised his head, waiting for the next signal.

Stewart pursed his lips slightly, pushed his tongue against the back of his teeth, and blew a shrill whistle in Roy's direction. The instant the sound reached the dog's ears it was on its feet, moving wide to the right. Slowly, carefully, and without ever taking his eyes off the cattle, Roy moved in a wide arc, balancing the cattle between himself and the open gate. His shoulders and haunches low, head and tail down, Roy moved cautiously around to the far fence line before changing course directly toward the cattle waiting near the center of the corral.

The dog's approach unnerved the cattle, but they still refused to give way, only backing up a step or two. Roy dropped to the ground and gave the livestock a little time to consider their options. The cattle backed up warily, heads and horns lowered, and eyed this dog that looked like a black wolf. Almost in unison, they raised their heads and turned to look toward the man and the open gate. It didn't look so much like a trap any longer. It appeared more like a safe haven—a place to be away from the dog with the wolf eyes.

"Roy, get up," the dog's master invited in a soft voice. The dog rose carefully and took one measured step toward the cattle, then another. That was all the added encouragement the cattle needed. They turned and walked briskly past the shepherd and into the pen. Stewart followed the last cow, swinging the wooden gate closed behind it as he dropped the wire loop fastener over the fence post. The two young men on the fence rail both let out a whoop, waving their hats in the air.

"Did you ever see anything like that, Mr. Benson?" young Matt Chisholm said to his boss. "That dog barely moved."

"No, I never did, Matthew," the stock boss said to his young cow hand, with quiet admiration in his voice. "I never did."

Wink Benson slapped his older brother on the shoulder and climbed down from the fence. Charlie watched the man and his dog walk back toward the top end of the corral, appearing as though they had just finished a simple, routine chore.

"You can thank me properly at the Stockmen's Saloon later, Charlie," Wink Benson called back over his shoulder toward his big brother. "I may feel a little parched."

The Benson brothers had worked with livestock their entire lives, doing most of their chores on foot or by horseback. Both men were impressed by the old man and his herding dog.

Charlie Benson jumped down from the fence and waited for the Scotsman and his dog to approach. He didn't want to appear too eager. He looked down to admire the black dog with one pricked ear, and made his offer of employment.

"I'll pay four bits a day for the dog and another dollar a day for you to make sure he gets to work on time," Charlie offered.

One day followed the next, with little change in routine through the fall and early winter. Stewart worked six days a week with the younger stock hands, moving cattle and sheep from corral to pen and into the loading chutes.

He stayed in the loft at Benson's Livery Stable until the weather grew too cold in November, then moved into a small bunk shack a short distance from the stock yards. He shared the cramped space with Matt Chisholm and Roy. Matthew had become fond of Roy, and never tired of watching him work with the livestock.

"Do you think I could learn to work a dog like Roy, Mr. Stewart?" Matthew asked one morning as they took the brisk walk up the dirt road toward the stockyards.

"It just takes time and patience, lad," Stewart replied. "And the right dog. You can't expect just any dog to do the work Roy does. He's been bred for it. It's mostly due to instinct, and with a little help from training. Besides, I don't think you have much time for training dogs, lad. I've seen that young lady you've been wooin' on Sunday afternoons down at the café."

Matt Chisholm's face turned a bright shade of scarlet. "Aw, she's just a waitress I talk to sometimes," the young man defended. He cast a quick sidelong glance at the older man to see if his brief explanation had been believable.

Neither man spoke for another minute or two as they walked to work. Stewart finally broke the silence and responded to the young suitor's remark. "I expect she's quite pleasant to talk to." Stewart wore a faint smile, remembering his own courtship days.

Matt didn't look up. The men finished their walk to the stockyards in silence. Roy had to pause every few seconds to look back and wait for the two men who were moving so slow. Roy didn't understand why the men didn't move faster—cows were waiting to be sorted and penned.

Stewart taught Matt how to work with his dog, instructing him on the proper voice and whistle commands, and how to position himself inside the corral to assist the herding dog with its work.

Matt could never get enough of working with Roy. He looked forward to the day when he could have such a dog, and train it to work with livestock.

Christmas neared and nothing had changed much around the stockyards. Livestock was moved in and out, on its way to markets in the east and downriver. Roy was a contented dog, working nearly every day and going to sleep well fed and on a warm rug. Except for the streams and green pastures of Scotland, nothing was missing from the dog's life. He had work and he had his master to care for him—a master who was saving every spare dollar so that he could afford to make the trip west to Utah, where he could meet up in the spring with the only family he had left. The last letter Stewart had received from his younger brother had been posted in New Orleans and arrived in Scotland more than nine months ago. He was certain they had made it to the Utah Territory by now. There was no way to contact his brother unless he sent a letter by general delivery to Salt Lake and trusted that it would eventually find its way into his brother's hands.

Matt began spending more time around the café and had even become bold enough to wait until closing time so that he could walk Millicent Fielding home in the evenings. Every day after work he would rush back to the bunk shack and clean up so he could get to the café before closing time. He sat near the kitchen door to be close to Millie as she made her rounds from the tables to the kitchen and back again.

Later, on the mile and a half walk to her aunt's house, Millie would talk about anything that popped into her head, and Matthew always listened intently, just happy to be walking next to her. Matt and Millie grew closer every day, and were soon to become inseparable.

Stewart lay in his bunk most of the day on Sunday, coughing uncontrollably from deep in his chest. Roy lifted his head to nuzzle his master's hand every minute or two, seeking reassurance from his master.

"It's all right, lad," Stewart rasped between coughs, stroking the dog's head to assure it that nothing was wrong. He attempted to suck large breaths of air into his lungs to replenish the oxygen his body was lacking, but the fits of coughing made it impossible. His chest ached and his breathing was painful.

Stewart finally dozed off, his chest aching from the constant coughing. He was still sleeping peacefully when Matthew returned from walking Millie home. Matt slipped into the bunk shack quietly so he wouldn't disturb Mr. Stewart and went straight to bed. He awoke early the next morning to the sound of harsh coughing. Stewart was usually up and dressed before the sun, but on this morning he lay in his bed, shivering and sweating, coughing and struggling for air. Roy whined and pushed his muzzle against Matt's hand, asking for help. He hurried from his master to Matthew and back again, anxious for the old man to get on his feet and behave normally.

"Mr. Stewart, are you very ill?" Matt questioned, lightly shaking Stewart's shoulder to gain the man's attention. Stewart raised one hand slightly and tried to nod his head, a feeble attempt to assure the younger man that he would be all right. He made a clumsy attempt to stand, but fell back onto the cotton-stuffed mattress, too weak to rise.

"I'll go get Mr. Benson. He'll fetch the doctor. Don't try to move, Mr. Stewart," Matt insisted. The old Scotsman shook his head and tried to voice a protest, but could only cough more.

Matt pulled on his trousers and boots, grabbed his coat and hat from the wooden chair next to his bunk, and turned to assure Stewart that he would hurry. "Don't try to move, Mr. Stewart. I'll be back as soon as I can."

The dog was already on its feet and ready to follow Matt out the door. "You stay here, Roy. Stay here."

Matt's legs carried him as fast as he had ever run. He couldn't find his boss at the stockyards. That was uncommon for a Monday morning. He kept running until he reached Benson's Livery Stables, and rushed inside, gasping for breath.

"Mr. Benson, old Stewart is terrible sick. He's coughing and he can't catch his breath. He looks real bad." Matt bent over, out of breath himself. Both hands were braced on his knees as he gulped air into his lungs.

Wink Benson tossed the last of his coffee out of the tin cup that was doubling as a hand warmer. He had not seen this usually level-headed boy so agitated. Wink didn't waste any time with questions. He had lived through the typhus epidemic that wiped out nearly a tenth of the population of St. Louis in the last decade, and knew that some illnesses were deadly killers. He hadn't seen the old Scotsman miss a day of work in four months.

"You go back and stay with Stewart. I'll fetch Doc Carson," Benson instructed as he hurried out through the open door of the livery. "And don't let him get out of bed."

Matt rushed back to the bunk house on legs that were beginning to wobble from fatigue. He arrived at the shack to find his elderly friend sleeping, or at least appearing to sleep. He was still shivering and sweating. Matt soaked a washcloth in cold water and mopped the older man's face, then folded it and pressed it over the man's forehead. He pulled a chair over to Stewart's bed and sat next to him.

"Wink Benson is going for Doc Carson. I'm sure they'll be here right away. Will you drink some water?" He got up and fetched the water pitcher and a cup.

"This man has pneumonia," Doctor Carson diagnosed aloud to the other men after examining his new patient. "He needs undisturbed bed rest. No physical work or exertion of any kind," he added. "Make sure he stays warm. Keep wood in that stove, cover him with an extra blanket, and get some hot soup into him. There's not much else that can be done. I'll be back in a few days to look in on him."

Matt took one of the blankets off his own bed and spread it over his elderly friend and mentor. "I'll be sure to do everything you said, Doc," the young man assured.

Wink Benson knew this man was a valuable asset to his brother's business. "You stay here with him," he instructed Matt. "I'll let Charlie know you won't be at work today."

The bunk shack warmed a little after Matt added some firewood to the old wood stove. Old Stewart's coughing subsided and the shivering stopped. Stewart slept as his black dog lay quietly on the wooden plank floor next to the bed.

Matthew sat on a chair by the wood stove and watched the gray haired Scotsman sleep. He worried that the winter chill blowing through the cracks of the hastily built bunk shack would make it harder for Stewart to recover. Matt thought about his mother and father. Both had succumbed to typhus during the epidemic that ravaged St. Louis not so many years ago. He was only thirteen when he lost his parents. He took odd jobs around the mercantile to keep himself fed, and occasionally delivered bundles of laundry to the boarding houses for Mr. Chan. When he was fifteen, Charlie Benson gave him a real job at the stockyards.

He thought about moving his elderly friend to a boarding house for a couple of weeks, but quickly decided that no one would allow the sick man in his current condition. Matt would just have to take care of him as best he could.

Nearly a week passed with no change in Stewart's condition. The harsh coughing did not subside, and his breathing was raspy and labored. Matt watched over the old man day and night, making certain he was warm and well fed. He left the bunk shack only to bring food and to let Mr. Benson know how the old man was doing. He brought meat for Roy from the café every night, even though the dog's appetite was poor.

When it appeared that the old Scot was beginning to recover, Matt was able to take a little more time walking Millie home after work. He never tired of spending time with the fair-skinned girl. He thought his heart would bust right out of his chest every time he looked at her. Her radiant face was angelic and her voice was music. He wondered what her answer would be when he finally got up the nerve to ask her to marry him.

He was never quite sure what interested the pretty girl the most, so he talked mainly about the men he worked with every day, and about how clever old Stewart's dog was when he moved livestock around the pens.

"You should see Roy sometime, Millie," he boasted. "He does the work of ten men, and never gets tired." It was Matt's way of avoiding conversation about himself. He was a bit self conscious and did not think he had much to offer the girl. Millie had already heard about

Roy's talents many times, but always listened as though it were the first. She intended to marry this young man, and believed it was important for a woman to listen to her husband, even if he was a little boring at times.

It was windy and bitter cold when Matt returned to the bunk shack that night. He closed the door hurriedly behind him, and banked the fire in the wood stove with a couple of pieces of firewood before he got ready for bed. Roy was lying on the oval rug close to Stewart's bunk. The dog's chin rested on the floor as his eyes moved furtively back and forth from his master to Matthew, pleading with the young man to help. There was nothing to be done. The old man's body lay cold and still.

"Walter Stewart—Died February 12, 1857" read the simple inscription on the plain wooden grave marker. Matthew wasn't exactly sure how old the man was, but he reckoned the old Scotsman had lived a hard life and looked much older than his years.

Millie went with Matt to the cemetery, not because she knew Mr. Stewart well, but because she didn't want Matt to be alone in his grief for the loss of his good friend and mentor. The Benson brothers were both there—Charlie and Wink. So were a couple of the boys from the stockyards. Millie said what a shame it was that Mr. Stewart didn't have any family to pray over him. None of the men spoke. They just stood with their hats in their hands and stared at the pine coffin being lowered into the ground.

Millie recited the Lord's Prayer. "It's not right to send a man into the next life without a word to his maker," she said.

Matt nodded in agreement. "The last thing he asked of me was that I promise to take care of Roy and never let any harm come to him," he said to Millie as they turned away from the graveside and began the walk back into town.

He turned and called to Roy, who lay unmoving by his master's open grave.

"Roy! Here Roy," he called. "Come on lad," he mimicked Stewart's frequently-used call to the dog. Roy started in Matt's direction before turning back to lie down beside the wooden box in the ground that held his master's body. Matt beckoned again, whistling for the dog to come as he continued to walk away. Roy refused to move, but simply watched as Matthew moved further and further away. Finally, seeing the distance between them grow, Roy yielded to the whistles and reluctantly trotted off to join his new master, pausing once or twice to look back and wait for the old Scotsman to catch up with them.

CHAPTER THREE

THE GLORY TRAIL

"Iowa City, end of the line. Iowa City," called out the moustached conductor in his vested blue suit.

Passengers began to rouse themselves as the black locomotive slowed for its final stop at the station platform and relieved its pressure with a hissing belch of pent-up steam. After hours of watching the countryside go by or dozing to the clickity-clack rhythm of heavy wheels rolling on steel rails, people began to stir and gather their belongings. The railway station sat at the edge of town, next to the stockyards and livery stable, and just across the road from a busy lumber yard. Along the rutted dirt road were blacksmiths, wagon makers and a dry goods store.

The late afternoon sky was pale, made gray by a thin layer of clouds. It was colder than usual for the time of year. The station employee who pushed the baggage cart was bundled up in a heavy coat and mittens, and every person in town except the blacksmith was dressed in warm woolens.

Sarah Bradley stepped off the train ahead of her mother and father, and came face to face with a man carrying the biggest rifle she had ever seen. She thought the man's enormous coat must have been made from some shaggy animal, dark brown and thicker than sheep's wool, and his large hat had a band around the crown adorned with colorful beads. His ruddy face was wrinkled and cracked like an old saddlebag from time he had spent outside in the harsh weather, making him appear much older than his years.

"Are you a cowboy?"

"No missy," the man answered, smiling down pleasantly at the inquisitive girl. "Where have you come in from?"

"We're from England," Sarah replied proudly. "But we're going to the Utah Territory. My father is going to have a farm, and we're going to raise cattle and sheep."

The leather-faced hunter smiled and nodded. "Good luck to you," he said. "And be careful along the trail."

"Have you been to Utah?" Sarah asked, as the man turned and strode away down the platform.

"Yes, I have, child," he called back to her. "I'm going back there soon."

"Sarah, you stay with us," Martha Bradley insisted, as she followed her husband out of the vestibule of the train, dragging baggage along with her.

Sarah followed her mother and father, carrying her share of the baggage across the road and around a corner toward a small hotel a short walk from the station. Will Bradley thought his family deserved at least one night in a bed before they began their journey west.

Will Bradley left his wife and daughter at the hotel and set off to find a blacksmith. No better place to begin than to ask a smithy about available wagons, he supposed. He walked into the shop and approached a big man in a leather apron who was swinging a heavy hammer down against an anvil, beating a red hot piece of metal into submission as he turned his heavy tongs and continued to shape his creation. His bare arms and sweaty brow were blackened with soot from his fire, and he did not look like a man interested in idle conversation. Will Bradley asked where he might find a good wagon and team.

"Go over to the livery stable," the blacksmith pointed with his chin, scarcely looking up from his anvil. "You'll find out who has wagons and horses for sale. Or oxen, if that's what you want," he finished.

Will thanked the soot-covered man, who grunted in response and kept swinging his heavy maul down against the hot metal being fashioned into a rim for a wagon wheel.

Richard Hooton

He carefully inspected a number of canvas covered wagons and teams, thinking about what would best suit their needs before making his decision. He arrived back at the hotel in mid-afternoon to tell his wife what transport he had obtained for their journey west.

"I've never seen the like, Martha," he said excitedly, gesturing with outstretched arms and upturned palms to give emphasis to what he believed was an inadequate description of the large size and capacity of the covered wagons.

"It has more than enough room for everything we own. The wagons are built especially for the journey across the plains," he explained. "Prairie schooners, they call them. But the cost is dear. I met another man who is making the journey with his wife and son. If we travel together, we can afford a wagon and two teams of oxen. We may very well need a spare animal or two for the journey, and there will be more than enough room in the wagon for all our belongings. They say it's more than a thousand miles from Council Bluffs to the Utah Territory."

Martha looked a little pale, but determined to finish what they had begun. "When will we leave?" she asked.

It was well past noon on the day that Will Bradley and James Pierce loaded their small families and all their belongings into the wagon and began the journey west. It was certain to take them two weeks or more to cross the state to Council Bluffs and the Nebraska border. Each man took his turn walking alongside the ox team, keeping them moving steadily west at a slow and plodding pace. Neither man possessed any skill as a teamster, but they were confident they would gain all the experience they needed after a couple of weeks on the trail. As it turned out, they both felt like old hands at driving an ox team before they reached Council Bluffs. Will Bradley was proud of himself. He had become a bone fide bullwhacker. Not much of a stretch from an English farmer, but still, he felt he was becoming as one with the American West. They traveled nearly twelve miles on good road their first day, and spirits were high when the families camped for the night in a grassy spot alongside a clear stream. There was good grazing for the oxen, and plenty of fresh water.

Sarah and the Pierce boy began to explore along the stream for a short distance, careful not to stray out of sight of the camp. They waded barefoot in the water, dredging smooth pebbles from the creek bottom to skip across to the far side.

Their mothers sat beside each other next to the camp fire and spoke of the journey ahead. They agreed that with a good wagon and team, and strong men to protect them, the hardship would be minimal on the journey west.

"Others have made the trip before us," Dora Pierce said to her new friend and traveling companion. "There is always safety in a large wagon company and with good people to help out if we encounter a problem with the wagon."

Martha Bradley agreed. "I'll feel better when we join a large wagon company in Council Bluffs," she said.

The two women busied themselves with the evening meal. Martha heated water for soup in a large black kettle and Dora unwrapped some of the biscuits they had bought in Iowa City.

"I fear that time will be against us," James Pierce said quietly to Will, not wanting to upset the women. "They say we should have started out a month ago," he continued in a near whisper. "We risk bad weather and poor grazing on the open prairie, and some of the streams will be dried up this late in the year."

"I wouldn't worry too much, James," Will said, with an air of confidence. "I heard that hundreds of people are still leaving for the west every week out of Council Bluffs."

Will Bradley felt an enormous sense of relief when the wagon pulled into Des Moines on the evening of the third day. Their wagon had been tested on the open plains and found trail worthy. They stopped to replenish provisions for the journey to Council Bluffs and to have repairs made to one of their wagon wheels, then pushed on past the neat rows of buildings to find a suitable camp site on the western edge of town.

"Another week or so should put us into Council Bluffs," Will said. "Provided we have good weather and don't get bogged down on a muddy trail."

"Don't invite hardship into our lives with your negative thinking, Will Bradley," Martha cautioned. "Let's be content with the heat and the dust."

It was well past the middle of July when the Bradley-Pierce wagon rolled laboriously into Council Bluffs, Iowa. Sarah was still enjoying her adventure, fascinated with the new sights they had encountered along the way. She pointed out to her mother every animal, bird, brush and flower that was new and unfamiliar to her. The time went by quickly, and Sarah was becoming comfortable with her new and ever-changing surroundings.

Council Bluffs was just what Will Bradley had expected. The town was buzzing with the activity of immigrants making ready to travel to the west. Council Bluffs and the neighboring town of Omaha, Nebraska across the river were the last real vestiges of civilization along the Mormon Trail that led west across Nebraska and Wyoming, and on into the Utah Territory. There would be re-supply stops at Fort Kearney and Fort Laramie, but for the most part, the hardy pioneers that journeyed the high plains were on their own.

Will Bradley asked around town to learn when another wagon company might be forming to make the journey to the far west, and learned that all the immigrants with any sense had already left weeks ago. There were still a few latecomers like themselves who were searching for enough wagons to make up a large enough company to travel safely. There were few experienced guides who knew the way and the land, and fewer still who might be willing to set out so late in the year. They needed a man with courage—one who would make a capable leader and a suitable captain for a small wagon company.

Over the next week they were able to locate only sixteen more wagons of immigrants who were preparing to make the journey to the far west. Most were dissuaded from making such a late start, and had already determined to wait out the winter in Council Bluffs. Two more precious weeks were lost in convincing enough hardy people to take the risk this late in the year, and the job of locating a willing wagon boss proved even more difficult. They found a big Swede named Magnussen in a local saloon—a man who favored whisky over sobriety, but who had traveled the trail to the west three times before. All the members of the small wagon company agreed that the Swede gave them their best chance of success, given his confident nature and his knowledge of the trail.

The real truth was that the man was broke. He needed the money badly and there was no work for him in Council Bluffs to keep him through the winter, or even to buy his next drink of whisky. He agreed to remain sober for as long as he was in charge of the wagon train. They would leave for the West the following morning.

Will was confused by what he saw when they reached the western edge of town. He counted a company of more than four hundred men, women and children, pushing and pulling at least a hundred wooden handcarts slowly west on the road to Nebraska. Men and women alike leaned into the wooden crossbars and strained against the weight of their loads. The odd-looking caravan plodded steadily forward as it converged into a single line along the dusty road that stretched westward out of town. The carts were fully laden with possessions, and no one rode except small children and the very elderly. Several of the men and older boys walked behind a herd of around forty cattle, keeping a steady pace with the handcarts.

"Did you ever hear of anything like it?" Will asked.

James Pierce stared, slack-jawed, and said nothing. His mind had not yet fully comprehended the vision before him. There were only two ox-team wagons in the rear, probably loaded with extra provisions. It could not be possible that these ill-equipped people would be traveling far on foot, pulling open wooden carts no more than four or five feet in length. Why were there so many traveling together, he wondered.

James finally broke his silence. "What do you think, Will?"

"I don't know what to make of it, James," Will answered, just as baffled as his friend. "They don't have wagon teams to carry them on a long journey—only one or two in the rear. Maybe they're only going as far as Omaha."

"They're Mormons," Magnussen said to Will Bradley in answer to his question, overhearing the conversation between the two men. "Two or three companies of handcarts already left for Utah in the spring. Another left ahead of this one not more than a week ago. I don't know if either of them will make it very far. I expect we'll overtake that last company before they get out of Nebraska."

When the Mormon handcart company had first been formed, a meeting was held and a vote taken. Overwhelmingly, the pioneers elected to make the late trek across the plains to Utah, emboldened by the illusion that they would be protected by their great numbers, and believing that God would see them through. None of them had ever experienced the kind of hardship that lay in wait for them on the vast prairies of the American West.

Eleven families from the company turned back after the first two days on the trail, and returned to Council Bluffs to become Iowans. A few vowed half-heartedly that they would try again in the spring.

They experienced little else but misfortune and hunger on their long trek to the West. Beyond Fort Kearny, it became difficult to find fresh water or grazing along the trail for their few pitiful cattle. Many of the small, seasonal streams had dried up before the end of June. Grass became brittle and turned a dirty brown, clad with dust and lacking in nutrients. No rain had fallen for days. It seemed as if God had forsaken them, giving them up to the harsh, unforgiving land that tested their resolve with every step.

Halfway across Nebraska, an enormous herd of buffalo appeared on the horizon early one morning and by late afternoon the herd was still passing them by, stretching for miles across the prairie. Most of their cattle defected to the buffalo herd, seeming to accept the prospect of better grazing by joining the shaggy wild beasts. Efforts to catch them proved futile. All the men were too weak to run, and it would have made little difference if they could.

They reached the Platte River in western Nebraska in mid-September. The group that left Iowa with more than four hundred determined immigrants had already seen its numbers reduced when a few of their members died from illness and old age. They were tested by hardship and peril with each new day, aggravated by food shortages and the lack of proper shelter. They had a few moldy biscuits, enough flour to ration ten ounces per day for each adult, and no meat. When they stopped to make camp for the night, a few optimistic men and boys tried to catch birds or rabbits to roast on a fire or to make a soup. Most of the time they were unsuccessful, even when they were lucky enough to spot game near their camp. Most nights their supper was an uncooked watery gruel of flour stirred in a pot and eaten cold. None of them had imagined that life on the trail would be this difficult.

There was no such thing as unseasonable weather in the northern plains. The territories might be visited with snow or rain or sleet or hail on any day of the year. A blinding blizzard halted the handcart company on an early afternoon during the first week of October, forcing the immigrants to make camp and wait out the storm. Many of their party were unable to pitch tents in the driving wind, or even drive tent pegs into the frozen ground. They huddled in and under their handcarts, covering themselves with blankets and canvas sheeting to shelter them from the foul weather. Buoyed only by their inextinguishable faith, they struggled on.

The wagon train made steady progress across Nebraska, guided by the capable wagon boss Magnussen, who knew the trail well. They crossed into Wyoming by early fall.

Sarah Bradley's keen eyes spotted a low silhouette hunched over in the snow a quarter mile up the trail.

"Papa, what is that?" she asked.

Her father had already seen it. The shape moved slightly, low to the ground, but he still couldn't make out what it was. "Maybe a dog," he answered.

Sarah frowned a little, never taking her eyes off the dark form as they came nearer.

"What's it doing, Papa? Do you think it has a rabbit?"

Will Bradley brought the team of oxen to a halt. "Sarah, get in the wagon," he commanded.

She obeyed, climbing quickly up into the front bench seat and turning to ask her father again. "What is it Papa?"

The wagon boss spotted the wolves, and lifted his rifle free of its saddle scabbard as he approached carefully, keeping his eyes riveted on the grisly scene ahead of him. He nearly missed seeing the two gray wolves a few yards away from the trail, a short distance from the wolf the Bradley girl had spotted earlier. The wolves were eating something. At first, he couldn't see what prey the pack of hunters had caught, but as he got closer, one of the wolves saw him and picked up its meal to carry it a safe distance away. He was able to see clearly the shape of a human hand and forearm. He turned his attention back to the black wolf and saw that it was feasting on a man's torso.

Clothing had been ripped and tugged away from the body to expose the flesh. Magnussen brought his rifle up and fired. He spurred his horse, yelling as he galloped toward the wolves.

"You get away from there! Go on, get away!" The wolf gave up the remainder of its meal without a fight. It had already eaten well.

Magnussen kept the wagons moving. They needed to cover at least fifteen miles a day and they were already taking a big risk by attempting to cross the plains and make it through the Rocky Mountains this late in the year. He didn't want any unsettling incidents to cause further delay. The sight of the dismembered body did little to unnerve the big Swede. He had witnessed death on the trail before, and was familiar with the nature of the wolf. If live prey was scarce, they would readily scavenge an easy meal. Several men were already gathered around the remains when Magnussen rode back to where the bodies lay, and the men could tell by his expression that he had seen this kind of tragedy before.

Magnussen didn't want to stop, but he soon realized that several of the men would not continue on until they had provided a decent burial for the unearthed human remains. He organized a few men to collect what scattered body parts they could find and returned them to their graves. The men dug deeper in the frozen ground and placed as many large rocks as they could gather on top of the dirt mounds to discourage further digging by carnivores. Judging from the length and width of the mound, the wagon boss was certain that at least seven or eight bodies had been placed side by side in the shallow grave. There was good reason why the bodies would not have been laid to rest in a deeper grave. The ground was frozen too hard, and the survivors who dug the hole were probably too weak, or maybe they had no time.

Magnussen had seen the narrow wagon tracks in the trail for several days. The ruts were not deep, which meant the loads were not especially heavy. Not like the big ox-drawn wagons. They had to be close behind the handcart company.

"They can't be more than a day ahead of us," Magnussen said. "But they're moving faster than I ever believed was possible."

Will Bradley couldn't understand what accident could take so many people at one time.

"Why would so many die like that?" he asked. "Do you suppose they became afflicted with a disease?"

"It's the handcart company, Mr. Bradley. They've been on foot for several hundred miles, and pulling their carts the entire way. I expect the cold took some them, and exhaustion or illness took the rest. Maybe a few others were just too old to withstand the journey."

Magnussen also wondered to himself if the handcart company had ample food supplies for the long journey. The carts were small—not more than four or five feet long. They had to carry their belongings and enough provisions for a two or three month journey. He was amazed that they had come so far in such cold weather. He had seen no hoof prints from cattle along the trail for more than a week, and no animal bones in the campfire ashes. There were no remnants of broken handcarts left behind. Likely as not they had used the cart wreckage for firewood. He was sure that he would learn the truth in the next day or two. He spurred his horse into a gallop and moved to the front of the wagons.

"Let's go," he called out to the lead wagon. "We can't do any more good here. We're losing light."

Drivers cracked their whips, and oxen strained against their yokes, pulling the wagons slowly west along the prairie trail. Wooden wheels and axles creaked under their heavy loads. All eyes were turned toward the grave site as each wagon rolled by in turn. Spirits were low. Sarah Bradley strained to see the grave as their wagon moved past, then quickly climbed toward the back of the wagon so she could get a better view, peering out at the ghostly sight. It was a lonely place to die, she thought. She gazed at the gravesite and beyond, across the windswept prairie. It

Richard Hooton

was a cold and desolate sight.

"There's nothing more to see, Sarah," her mother said. "Come sit down."

The wagon company moved another two or three miles along the trail and stopped for the night. The mood was somber among the wagon party, and there was little conversation as campfires were lit and the evening meal prepared. Most were thinking about what they might discover on the trail the next day.

Magnussen counted more than twenty white plumes rising above the western horizon. A sure sign that damp wood was being burned in the campfires. It had to be the handcart company, he thought. He decided it would be wise to halt the wagons and set up camp, even though they had scarcely covered ten miles on the day. It was early afternoon, and the freezing cold had penetrated every living thing. They could get a fresh start the next morning and catch up with the handcart company before nightfall. No one questioned why they had stopped early. They were glad to be able to build fires and rest.

"Are they the ones who buried those people by the trail, Papa?" Sarah asked her father, as she stood looking toward the smoke plumes in the western sky.

"They may be, daughter," her father answered quietly. "They may be. We'll find out for sure tomorrow. Go and help your mother now."

Sarah helped her mother and Mrs. Pierce get the cooking pans out of the wagon, then sat on a camp stool and began to peel potatoes for their supper. She looked up every minute or two and watched the campfire smoke in the distance.

Will Bradley walked beside the lead wagon, driving his team of oxen forward over a knoll. The wagon boss had gone ahead of them, and was now out of sight. No one had seen him for the better part of an hour. Will reached the top of the rise and his stride became easier. The ox team rolled the wagon easily over the crest and down the gentle slope toward the small valley stretched out below them.

In the distance he could see a long line of handcarts, strung out in single file along the trail, and moving toward a tall, narrow gap in the steep hillside at the west end of the valley. A small number were gathered at the rear, busying themselves with collecting rocks and placing them on an earthen mound.

Magnussen rode up the hill toward the wagon train at a gallop, waving an arm high in the air as a signal for the drivers to stop where they were. Will Bradley stopped his ox team and rushed toward the wagon boss.

"What is it, Mr. Magnussen?" Bradley asked.

"It's the handcart company we saw leaving Council Bluffs," the wagon boss said. "They lost more of their party during the night. We'll need a few men to help gather rocks to protect a grave site."

Magnussen rode back along the wagon train and found two men with saddle horses. He asked each of them to come, and to bring another man with them. He turned his horse and rode back down the hill toward the immigrants at the gravesite. He arrived to find several men and boys piling rocks onto the burial mound. They all appeared to be weak and malnourished.

"I've asked more men to come and help," the big wagon boss said to no one in particular, climbing down off his horse. "They should be here soon."

No one responded. They didn't even look up to acknowledge his presence. A young boy of about twelve or thirteen with dirty, tear-stained cheeks carried a large rock to the grave. His shoulders were stooped and his frail body trembled, but the boy remained on his feet and continued to gather rocks, walking them back to the mound in silence. Magnussen wondered if any of the bodies in the grave were from the boy's family. He thought it best to say nothing, but went to work picking the heaviest rocks he could find and placing them atop the smaller rocks already piled on the burial mound.

Only the heaviest rocks could keep out the wolves that had been scavenging the gravesites. The survivors had set the bodies in one shallow grave. They were too weak to dig deeper in the frozen ground, and had no time to give their deceased the dignity of separate graves.

Will Bradley arrived at the burial site, riding double behind one of the men who owned a saddle horse, and two others came up close behind. He jumped down and rushed over to where Mr. Magnussen was hard at work, prying a boulder-sized rock out of the frozen earth.

"We need to find the heaviest rocks we can lift," Magnussen explained. "Something the wolves can't dig up or push aside to get at the bodies."

Will Bradley helped to pull the rock free. Together they rolled it toward the mound, pushing it up onto the smaller rocks already in place. The men all worked for the better part of an hour, doing what they could to protect the interred bodies from the hungry grave robbers that were waiting unseen, somewhere off in the prairie, for the funeral party to leave so they could attempt to exhume a free meal.

The men of the handcart company stood around the grave, hats removed and heads bowed, and offered one last prayer for the deceased. The young boy stood close to the grave with his head down, his body racked by uncontrollable sobs as he shivered in the chill wind. Will Bradley noticed the youngster for the first time. He saw that the boy wore no gloves, and his knuckles were bleeding from digging rocks out of the frozen ground with his bare hands. A shock of black hair hung across his forehead, nearly covering one tear-filled eye. The boy's feet were wrapped with woolen strips tied around his ankles with leather to fashion a sort of moccasin-like boot. The threadbare coat he wore was a few sizes too small, unfastened in the front and with sleeves that reached just below his elbows.

Will looked around at the others and realized they were all half clothed and ragged. Their boots appeared to have been worn out for the past hundred miles or more. The man who had been praying looked up at the others and announced that they should all hurry to catch up with the handcart company before they lost any more daylight.

One of the other men put a hand on the young boy's shoulder and tried to offer some solace.

"I'm sorry Benjamin," the man said quietly. "I know this is hard for you, but we have to keep moving. We'll lose sight of the others if we don't go now."

"I've got no place to go now," the boy said numbly, without lifting his eyes off the ground. "I've got no one left." The boy lost consciousness and collapsed face down onto the frozen dirt. He didn't feel Will Bradley's strong hands lift him up from the cold ground.

Martha Bradley washed the unconscious boy's dirt-smeared face and hands before she dressed his knuckles with ointment and wrapped them with clean strips of cotton cloth to keep out infection. Dora Pierce helped to remove the woolen wraps from his feet and treated the sores and blisters with the same care. They covered him with a warm blanket and left him to sleep, undisturbed in the back of the wagon as they went about preparing supper by the campfire.

Sarah kneeled by Ben's side and watched over him while he slept. "Sarah, you come on now—you let him sleep. You can't do anything more for him," her mother said. Sarah reluctantly climbed down out of the wagon and stood next to her father.

"How is the boy doing?" Bradley asked his wife, as he returned to camp with an armful of sagebrush firewood.

"He'll be fine, Will," Martha answered. "His feet are frostbitten, and he needs to rest and get some food in his belly. He's thin as a rail and looks as though he hasn't had a proper meal in a month."

"What's going to become of him, Mother?" Sarah asked. Martha ignored her daughter's question, wondering the same thing herself.

Martha grasped her husband's arm, standing close so that she could speak to him in a whisper. "How could these people have left on such a long and difficult journey, so ill-equipped and unprepared?" she asked. "What is it that's driving them? They've lost so many people to the cold."

"They've gone to glory," Sarah whispered reverently, as she listened to her mother's question. She reached into her pocket and held tightly to the wooden carving of the sheepdog. "They've all gone to glory."

No one spoke during supper. Sarah watched her parents silently as she ate her bread and soup, wondering whether the boy would be well enough the next day to return to the handcart company. After supper, she overheard her father explaining to Mr. Pierce that the men from the handcart company said the boy had been orphaned that very morning when his mother became the last of his family to succumb to the cold.

The boy's father and older sister had both died two days earlier. His seventeen-year-old sister had walked away from camp onto the cold, snow-covered prairie to search for firewood two nights ago, but didn't return. His father had searched for her throughout the night, and the next morning some of the other men discovered her stiff, frozen body crouched behind a cluster of tall sagebrush, a few pieces of firewood still clutched in her arms. It had been too much for Ben's father to bear. He refused to eat, and surrendered his own life to the cold that very night.

Their bodies were laid beside several others in a shallow grave, scratched out of the snow and frozen earth with cooking pots and broken shovels. In their starved and weakened state, seven more immigrants had failed the cruel test of the thirteen hundred mile journey that led to their promised land. The dreams of a new beginning in the western territories now belonged to the surviving family members and fellow pioneers.

News that the boy from the handcart company had been brought back to the wagon train had circulated around the camp and a few people, both the curious and the concerned, had stopped by the Bradley-Pierce wagon to ask about him.

The wagon train caught up with the handcart company the next afternoon on the far side of the Sweetwater River. Passing through the tall and narrow gap known as Devil's Gate, they saw a number of handcarts on the opposite bank.

Pulled by mules and oxen, the wagon train experienced little trouble fording the river, but the handcart company had not been so fortunate. Several carts had been lost, bogged down in the mud with broken wheels or swept downriver, unable to be saved by the men and women who tried in vain to push and pull their carts across the swift water while they fought to keep their footing. One frail, middle-aged man had attempted to cross with a small boy in his arms, but he stepped into a deep eddy, slipped beneath the surface of the water and never came up. Several men walked downriver for nearly a mile, but found no sign of the man or the child.

The wagon train made camp for the night a short distance from the river. It was their chance to water their animals, wash their clothing and fill the water barrels. Magnussen and a few of the men rode to the handcart encampment to see if they could offer any assistance, and discovered misery and hunger among the large group of determined travelers. Some of the nearly four hundred handcart immigrants had feet and hands blackened from frostbite. Others were in a state of near starvation, their weakened bodies unable to sustain themselves on their meager rations of flour.

Even the hardiest among them appeared gaunt and malnourished. The soles of their shoes had been worn completely away from the thousand mile trek from Iowa, and some covered their feet with rags. The company had been caught on the trail too late in the year, and the weather had been unforgiving. Their situation was dismal.

"Isn't there something we can do to help?" Will Bradley asked the wagon boss. "We still have a good supply of wheat and potatoes."

"There may be too many of them for us to do much good," Magnussen replied somberly. "Wait until I can speak with their captain, then we can go back and talk it over with the others."

He rode off to find who was in charge, leaving the rest of the men to learn what they could from the few stragglers who had fallen behind and were struggling to catch up with the rest of their party.

The men were astonished to learn that the entire company had been subsisting on nothing but a few ounces of flour per person each day. The handcart immigrants had long since depleted any meat or rice that was part of their original provisions, and they had no livestock. A few had been able to barter for a little bacon, butter, and rice at Fort Laramie, but it only lasted a few days. No one expected the journey would take so long, or that it would be fraught with so many difficulties and delays.

The company was forced to stop frequently to repair handcarts, originally built from green timber and fitted tightly, but now falling apart as the wood dried out and the spokes loosened from the wheel hubs and rims. Bad weather had halted them for two or three days at a time on more than one occasion. They confessed to leaving Iowa late in the year, but insisted that they had no choice. Having no means to survive through the winter in Council Bluffs without work or a place to live, they took what little they had and began the journey west to Salt Lake.

Will Bradley was determined to leave as much food for these people as could be spared from their wagon. He knew that Martha would agree, and he was sure that James Pierce and his wife would feel the same way.

Their wagon boss came back before long, and gathered the men for a meeting. "We can't leave these people with nothing," Magnussen insisted of the large group of men gathered by the river. "They're in a wretched situation, and with nothing but flour rations to eat. If you can find it in yourselves to spare some of your provisions, it could go a long way toward keeping them alive. They've had no meat for some time now, and every day they spend out on this prairie puts them one day closer to dying."

There was little hesitation or resistance to the notion of helping the unfortunate handcart immigrants. Their only concern was that they keep enough food and provisions for themselves to complete the two or three week journey into the Salt Lake Valley.

Sarah walked alongside the wagon as they hurried to catch up with the handcart company. The determined handcart pioneers had already packed up and left before dawn, stoically driving forward in the face of overwhelming hardship to reach their destination.

She reached inside her coat pocket, feeling for the carving of her sheepdog while she marched along the trail, marking her steps with a short, crudely fashioned shepherd's crook as she kept pace with the wagon. Young Ben Thompson rode quietly in the back of the wagon. His damaged feet were beginning to heal, but his heart ached from the loss of his family.

"Sarah, don't get ahead of us," Martha Bradley called out to her daughter. "You stay close to the wagon. I don't want to have to look for you."

"I will Mother," Sarah called back. She picked up her pace a little, stretching her stride to cover more ground.

"Sarah!" Martha Bradley's stern voice reached out and caught her daughter mid-stride. Sarah slowed her pace a bit, without looking back at her mother.

"She's a stubborn one," Martha said to her husband. "I'm sure I don't know where she gets it."

"I'm sure I don't know," Will said. He was proud of Sarah for her independent nature and sense of self-reliance.

"I've been thinking about the Thompson boy, Will," Martha said. "He's lost his family, and he's in no condition to walk, much less push a handcart. I wish you would talk to someone and convince them to let him ride with us to Salt Lake."

Will nodded silently, thinking of what he might say to convince the captain of the handcart company to leave the young Thompson boy with the wagon train. In his condition, the boy would only slow them down, so it seemed a reasonable request to ask that they keep him until they reached the Salt Lake Valley.

Sarah heard a cry from one of the forward wagons. "There they are!"

Ben sat up in the wagon and peered through the canvas cover. He felt downhearted at the prospect of being left with the handcart company again. He had no possessions, and his only family had been buried in unmarked graves along the trail. He pondered what he might offer the Bradleys and the Pierces to convince them to let him stay with the wagon train. He was a good worker, and thought the kindly people might agree to let him work to repay their generosity if they would allow him to ride with them to Salt Lake. The boy was exhausted from worry and grief. He lay his head down again and fell into a deep sleep. When he awoke hours later, the wagon train had overtaken the hand-cart company, and was already several miles ahead. He wondered if he had been forgotten.

For several days the wagon train crossed wide stretches of snow-covered ground as it climbed in elevation into the Rocky Mountains. Sarah was cold, and out of breath, when she climbed into the wagon and sat between her mother and Mrs. Pierce to keep warm, and still be able to maintain a good view of the trail ahead. She watched as her father kept the team of oxen moving steadily along behind the wagon ahead of them. Mr. Magnussen criss-crossed the ground on horseback ahead of the lead wagon, looking carefully for signs of soft or muddy soil that could bog a wagon wheel in the muck.

Whenever there was something interesting to see, Sarah didn't want to miss it. If there was an elk or a coyote along the trail, she wanted to see it. This vast new land fascinated her, and she was sure that she would love her new life in the West. There was something about the clean, crisp air and the high, tree-covered mountains and wide valleys that made her feel like she belonged here.

She saw the wagon boss rein in his horse and raise a hand to shade his eyes from the sun, leaning forward in his saddle as he strained to see something that was moving on the trail ahead. At first it appeared as two small dots on the horizon, but it was moving at a rapid pace, and directly toward them. Magnussen wheeled his horse around and rode back to the lead wagon.

"Rider coming in," he shouted. "Hold up for a minute. Hold up," he said again, as he rode past the second and third wagons.

The dark shapes became more distinguishable as a horse and rider came clearly into view, with a second horse being led behind. Sarah stood up in the wagon seat and tried to steady herself on her mother's shoulder to get a better look as the wagon slowly creaked to a halt.

"Sarah, sit down!" her mother ordered. "Whoever it is will be here soon enough."

The wagon boss turned his horse and rode out to meet the rider, and Sarah watched with curious interest as he approached the rider in the distance. She strained to see what was happening as the rider reined in his horses and approached Mr. Magnussen. The two men reached across to each other from their saddles and shook hands, then rode together back toward the wagons.

"Mama, I saw that man at the train station," Sarah said excitedly, as she stood up again to watch the wagon boss ride up with the rider in the shaggy brown coat.

"That's not possible, Sarah. Sit down."

"It's him, Mama! He had that big rifle, and the coat, and the big hat with the colored beads on the hat band. It's him." Sarah waited anxiously as the men rode up and stopped by the lead wagon. The wagon boss spoke to the people at each wagon before riding on to the next. He rode up with the stranger and stopped by the Bradley-Pierce wagon.

"Will, this man has been sent to find the handcart company we passed on the trail. If you can spare a little salt and a couple of potatoes for him, it would help a great deal. He's a hunter, and he's come to shoot wild game to help feed those people. He has no time to stop and hunt to feed himself."

"Of course we can spare something. That's good of you to do this, sir," Will said. "Those people desperately need your help."

Sarah stood up in the wagon again and waved her little hand at the hunter to get his attention. He looked up and smiled broadly, his weather-worn face showing the deep wrinkles etched by the sun and wind.

"Well, hello again, missy," the man said. "It appears you've found the right trail to Utah after all."

"Yes, sir," she answered, delighted that the man remembered her. "We'll be there soon."

"You're there already, child. You've probably been in Utah for the past two days," he said, as he dismounted and changed his saddle over to his other horse.

Sarah reached into her pocket, withdrew her carving of the sheepdog and held it out proudly for the hunter to see. "I'm going to have a dog like this when we get a farm," she said. "Mr. Stewart is going to help me train it after he arrives."

"I'm sorry my daughter is so talkative," Martha Bradley apologized, as she handed a small sack of salt and three potatoes to the hunter. "I hope she hasn't bothered you."

"No bother, ma'am. She's a bright girl. Seems to know her own mind. You should be pleased." He pushed the salt and potatoes into a saddle bag. "Thank you kindly, ma'am. I won't forget this." He mounted his fresh horse and prepared to leave. He needed to cover a lot of ground before nightfall, and had no time to lose.

"My name is Sarah," the outspoken little girl said, as she pushed her wooden carving back into her coat pocket.

The hunter wrapped the lead line of his spare horse around his saddle horn, reined his tall chestnut mare around and spurred it to a gallop.

"I'm proud to know you, Sarah," he called back to her as he rode away. "My name is Ephraim."

Nearly two weeks had passed since the wagon train left the ill-fated handcart company behind on the trail beyond Devil's Gate near the Sweetwater River. The determined Mormon immigrants continued to trudge ahead in their effort to cover distance across the frozen ground. They buried more dead almost daily, and prayed that the frozen bodies would not be uncovered and defiled by predators. The depth of their suffering was unfathomable.

Another young woman's husband had died during the night, the life in his body robbed by cold and hunger. His grieving widow cried most of her tears in the hours after she discovered her husband's still, breathless body. She covered his lifeless form with a blanket and loaded the stiffened corpse into a handcart with the help of two other women. In a vain attempt to protect it from predators and scavengers, the women wrapped the body tightly in a woolen shawl and struggled to raise it up to a large tree branch, securing it with tight knots high above the ground, and hopefully out of the reach of scavenging wolves.

"Perhaps another wagon train will come through soon, and they will take the time to give your husband a proper burial," the young woman's friend comforted. The pregnant young widow would not be consoled. She kneeled in the back of the handcart, hunched over and sobbing as the two other women took the crossbar and pushed to catch up with the rest of the company. A gust of cold wind tore the woolen scarf off her head and sent it flying, unnoticed, across the prairie.

Bitter tears rolled down her pale cheeks as she wept, falling onto cold hands that lay folded in her lap. "He said he would always be there for us," she lamented quietly. "He promised to be there when our son was born."

CHAPTER FOUR

THE ORPHAN TRAIN

Missouri—1860

Matt Chisholm was full of hope. His small family was about to begin a new life upriver in the town of Hannibal, Missouri. Millicent was excited about the move, too. She always dreamed of having a place of her own someday, big enough to raise her boys and to give them room to grow without getting into trouble.

St. Louis was a thriving town, but it had grown too big for Millie. She yearned for a more rural setting and hoped that the farmlands west of Hannibal would provide it.

They followed the road north, with all their worldly possessions roped down in the buckboard wagon and pulled along the road by an odd team of horses Matt had purchased for a few dollars from Wink Benson. Benson's Livery Stable would often get overcrowded with horses left behind by owners who never came back to pay the boarding charges. Wink would sell them after a month if the owners didn't show up to claim them. Chief was a big Belgian draft horse, second only to a mule for its strength and ability to pull a plow, while Maggie was a small saddle horse. She was a sturdy little paint, no more than fourteen hands high. Together, they made a durable pair, and Maggie tried to keep pace with the larger horse, doing her fair share to pull the loaded wagon. A Jersey dairy cow tethered to the back of the wagon was forced to keep up, and was lucky enough to get a rest break every few miles.

Roy trotted alongside, sometimes taking a break and accepting

Matt's invitation to ride in the wagon, perched atop the canvas-covered load of furniture and household goods. The dog had a fine view of the passing countryside as they made their way north.

A few months earlier, Matt heard about a forty-acre farm for sale a mile or two west of Hannibal. It had water, a small orchard, and good pastureland—everything they needed to keep a few milk cows and sheep, and plenty of room for a garden and chickens. More importantly, it had room for his family to grow. Matthew had no farming experience, but he had come from a long line of stockmen. He believed he could make it work.

Matt was a thrifty young man. Everything he had saved since he first began working for wages was enough to buy the farm, with a little help from the bank who administered the estate of the previous owner, who was now deceased.

As the mismatched team of horses pulled the wagon steadily north, Millie chattered about her plans for decorating their new home with bright gingham curtains and an oval hook rug in front of the fireplace, and furnishing it with her aunt's rocking chair and kitchen table, even though she had never set eyes on the house. All they had was the description in the banker's letter. Millie knew it would be perfect.

Matt was mostly concerned about whether he could sell enough apples and eggs at the farmer's market in Hannibal to provide them with what money they might need. He was sure that he could grow enough food to keep his small family well fed. After all, if you had apples, eggs and milk, he thought, they probably wouldn't starve.

Their two boys kept entertained by watching the black stockdog detour off the road every fifty yards or so to chase a rabbit down a hole or a squirrel up a tree. Roy never seemed to tire of hunting and exploring, and only rode in the wagon when Matt commanded him to get aboard the wagon so he could rest. Matt, Jr. was the spitting image of his dad, right down to his big feet. Even at two and one-half years of age, the boy had ceased hanging on to his mother's skirts, and was more interested in the things his father did. He shared his mother's talkative nature, a trait that often made his father wish that it was time for the boy to take a nap. His baby brother didn't talk yet, but squealed excitedly and pointed a chubby little finger at every bird and squirrel along the road.

Little Matt wanted to drive the team of horses. "Can I drive, Pa?" he asked, reaching for the reins.

"Just hang on a minute, Matt," his father said. "Let me steer us around this next bend in the road, then you can take over for me."

Matthew had let the boy hold the reins a few times, but never with such an oddly matched pair of horses in the harnesses. It was a little tricky to keep Maggie moving in pace with the larger draft horse so they wouldn't veer off the road or go around in circles. He decided it would be a good time to take a break and give the animals a rest, and Millie needed to feed the baby.

He let little Matt take hold of the reins just as they approached a clearing, so it wouldn't matter if Maggie slowed a little. Just as Matthew expected, Maggie slowed down and the big draft horse turned the wagon off the road and came to a stop after a few steps into the clearing.

"Good job, son," Matthew praised, taking the reins from his boy. "Now let's have something to eat." He knew that food was the only thing that would take his son's mind off the fact that he had only been allowed to drive the team about fifty feet. The little teamster was satisfied, and confident that he had done well.

Millie laid out a blanket in the grassy clearing and fetched the wooden food hamper from the wagon while her husband saw to the horses. He led the cow over to a grassy part of the meadow and tied her to a fallen tree, leaving her to graze.

"Stay with mama, Wally-boy," Millie called out to her youngest son, who was tottering from one wildflower to another, collecting colorful blossoms with both hands. "Stay with mama," she called out again. Baby Walter was just over a year old, and unsteady on his feet, but that didn't stop him from being a daring adventurer. He looked over at his mother with a big smile, showing off four white teeth.

Little Matt and Roy were busy herding ground squirrels around the meadow when the dinner bell sounded. "Come and eat, before it's gone," was Millie's standard slogan to coax all three of her boys to the come running at mealtime.

"Come on, Roy," little Matt said as he took off running toward the picnic blanket. "Come on, boy." Roy followed closely, only taking one last detour along the way to push an overly-bold ground squirrel back down its hole.

"I think we can make pretty good time, if the weather don't turn against us," Matt said, munching on a boiled egg and looking up at the sky. "Probably get into Hannibal the day after tomorrow." It was more than a hundred miles, and towing the cow made it more difficult to cover ground quickly.

The Chisholms loaded their bedding back into the wagon just before dawn on the fourth day out of St. Louis. They decided not to spend any time building a morning fire or preparing breakfast. Apples and boiled eggs would do just fine. They were anxious to see their new home.

The wagon with the oddly-matched team pulled into Hannibal in mid-afternoon, and stopped in front of the Farmers Bank. Matt climbed down from the wagon, brushed himself off and walked into the bank to introduce himself and get directions to the old Simpson Farm. It only took a few minutes. Matt apologized to the banker for being in such a hurry. He wanted to get his family settled at the house before nightfall.

"Shouldn't take more than half an hour," Matt said to his wife as he took up the reins again.

Millie took his arm and smiled lovingly at her husband. "Aren't you excited, Matthew?"

"Yes, ma'am," Matt said, returning her smile. "Get up there, hosses. We're almost home."

Millie had her blue gingham curtains and Matt had acquired a few head of sheep and two more dairy cows by early spring. Matt worked tirelessly to prune all the apple trees, trimming back three or four every day between his other chores until he finally got them all. He planted a large garden for Millie, making sure to include every vegetable that would grow in their rich soil, and for good measure, he planted two acres of corn. When September came, they had stored all the food they could possibly need for the winter and sold the rest in town. Matt got a good harvest of corn, and apples were abundant. The big Red Delicious apples were a favorite among the townspeople and they were easy to sell when the riverboats came in.

Millicent was content in her new home. She had everything she had ever dreamed of, and time to spend with her boys. Her aunt's dining table sat near the wood stove, and her large oval hook rug lay in front of the stone fireplace, just as Millie had pictured it. The former owners had raised a large family, and over the years had added on two sleeping rooms to the original house. It was room enough for a growing family.

Matthew didn't mind the hard work that came with the farm, and was pleased that he could provide his family with everything they needed, but he wished that he could spend more time building his livestock herds. He knew that he made a better stockman than a farmer. His heart just wasn't in farming. Pulling weeds and scratching in the dirt to plant seeds wasn't how Matt wanted to put food on the table. He would rather grow meat. He loved to work Roy on the sheep, taking them from the corral near the barn each morning to drive them uphill to the pasture, then going up to fetch them back to the barn in the late afternoon. Roy was always keen to work. Sometimes the dog would lie next to the pasture gate and watch the sheep for hours, waiting for his master to arrive and bid him to bring them back to the barn.

"I think I'll buy a ram when I go into town this week, Millie," Matt announced to his wife at dinner. "If we grow the herd we can sell most of the lambs in the spring and shear enough wool to make a living."

"Who's going to help with the crops?" Millie asked. "You can't harvest corn and pick apples while you shear sheep. You're going to need help, and these two little boys keep me busy."

Matt didn't bring up the subject of the ram again, but he was determined to look for a wooly suitor for his ewes on his next trip into town. It was nowhere near as busy as St. Louis, but livestock was being loaded and unloaded at the dock in Hannibal with more and more frequency every day.

Matthew harnessed Chief to the wagon and loaded half a dozen bushels of apples, covering them to keep the road dust off. His oldest son had been pestering Matt to take him along for the past couple of weeks, and Millie could use a well-deserved break. Matt left Roy in charge of watching the livestock and set off for town right after breakfast. His son chattered like a magpie during the entire trip into town, assaulting Matt's consciousness with a relentless barrage of questions, comments, and observations.

They made the train depot their first stop. Matt was sure he could sell at least a bushel of apples to the departing passengers who were heading west on the Hannibal and St. Joseph Railroad. The new line had just been completed that year, and stretched the entire width of the state, from the Mississippi River to the Missouri. More travelers were taking advantage of the inexpensive transportation with every passing week. It was much faster, and far more comfortable than a stage coach ride.

Matthew walked through the depot with little Matt right on his heels and a basket of apples in his arms, allowing the waiting passengers to see his fresh produce. He walked out onto the platform where the waiting train was already being loaded with mail and baggage, and the customers began to line up to buy his fresh fruit. In less than an hour he sold all but a few of the apples he had carried into the station. He sat with his son on the platform bench and they munched on apples as they watched the big, black locomotive belch smoke and steam as it strained to pull away from the station, picked up speed and disappeared around a bend.

"We better get back to work, son," Matt said, patting his boy on the knee. "We still have a few more stops to make before we go home." Matt stopped by the ticket agent's window and gave the station employee the last two apples from his basket. A large notice posted on the wall caught Matt's eye. He paused long enough to read it, took off his hat to scratch his head and think, then carefully read it again.

"Let's go, son. We've got a lot to do." Matt climbed into the wagon and released the brake. "Get up, Chief." He steered the wagon into the center of town and drove absent-mindedly toward the mercantile. He was turning an idea over in his head.

Alvin Carlson had operated the mercantile store for over fifteen years, and did business with most of the people in town. He liked trading with Matthew Chisholm. The young man always brought fresh produce and eggs, and never argued or complained about the price he received. More importantly, he never failed to make a purchase in the store while he was in town. Today, he came without a list, but he needed a number of things, nonetheless.

"I guess I'll take enough fabric for a dress, and a dress pattern. Some thread, too." Matt's eyes moved across the shelves holding the bolts of cloth. He was uncertain which material to choose.

Mrs. Carlson came to his rescue, showing him some of the more popular colors and patterns. "Is Mrs. Chisholm having a birthday or an anniversary perhaps?" she asked.

"No, ma'am." Matt didn't look the storekeeper's wife in the eye. He was afraid the woman would ask more questions.

Little Matt took up where Mrs. Carlson left off. "Is that for Mama?"

"Yes."

"Is it for a tablecloth, Pa?"

"No."

"Is it for a dress?"

Matt walked to the counter, lifted the glass lid off one of the candy jars and extracted a peppermint stick, handing it to his son. "Put this in your mouth, and hush." Little Matt was happy to comply.

Matthew finished his shopping spree with the purchase of a large iron skillet, a big pot with a handle and a lid, and a selection of cooking spices that he picked out with Mrs. Carlson's help. He waited at the counter while Mr. Carlson packaged his goods in paper and tied them with string. Mrs. Carlson stood at the counter and smiled. Matt stood on the other side of the counter and blushed.

"Such a nice young man," Agnes Carlson said to her husband after Matt hurried out the door with packages under both arms and his little boy in tow. "I'm sure his wife appreciates everything he does for her."

"The man's got something on his mind, that's for sure," Carlson responded, watching through the window as Matt loaded his goods into the wagon. "But you shouldn't stare at him that way, Agnes. It makes a man uncomfortable."

Agnes Carlson quickly brushed off her husband's remarks. "I wasn't staring," she defended. "I was just making polite conversation."

"Being nosey, that's what," Carlson muttered to himself as he walked out of his wife's hearing range.

Matt stopped by the livery stable and asked the owner if he knew of any sheep for sale. He was particularly interested in a couple of rams, no more than two or three years old. The liveryman assured Matt that he would put the word out that he was in the market for some breeding stock, and told him to check back when he was in town the following week.

Matthew still had a couple of bushels of apples, but decided against going to the docks or the farmers market, and instead turned the wagon toward home. Shaking the reins, he urged the big draft horse to pick up his pace. Chief responded with a shake of his head and a rattle of the harness, and continued plodding along at his normal speed.

"You're back early," Millie commented with mild surprise. "Did you sell everything so soon?"

"No, it wasn't a very good day," Matt replied.

Little Matt offered up a more accurate explanation for the unsold merchandise. "We just went to the train station and the store, that's all," he blurted. "We watched the train leave until we couldn't see it anymore. It was big and loud—and smoky, too." He wondered why his Ma and Pa were just standing there looking at each other without talking.

"Well, you two better go and get washed up," Millie said. "We might as well eat early. I don't want to interfere with your holiday."

Chisholm and son rolled up their sleeves and jacked on the pump handle until it yielded a fresh supply of water. They cleaned up for dinner and drank a little water. Matt was stalling for time, reluctant to go back into the house right away. He drew in a deep breath, pursed his lips and blew it out.

"What's a holiday, Pa?" little Matt asked.

Matt carried the packages into the house and set them down on the floor near the rocking chair.

"Pa got a lot of nice things for you at Mr. Carlson's store, Ma," the little blabbermouth said. "And I got some candy so I'd hush up."

Millie didn't have time to prepare anything fancy, so she served mutton fried in grease, fried eggs, and some biscuits left over from breakfast. Setting the food on the table, she wiped her hands on her apron and pulled out a chair across from her husband. She was in a hurry to find out what was on Matt's mind, and the dinner table was the best place to do it. She looked directly at her husband, unblinking, until he surrendered.

Matt sat up straight in his wooden chair and squared his shoulders, then looked down and cleared his throat as he began to speak. "There was a notice from the Children's Aid Society of New York posted at the train depot," Matt said into his dinner plate, biscuit in one hand and a fork in the other. He looked up at his wife to see if she was waiting to hear more.

Millie waited for the rest of the news. Matthew waited a little longer, so Millie went first.

"What did it say?" she asked quietly. She could tell by his posture and demeanor that it was something her husband had been thinking about all day.

Matt was grateful for the invitation to explain further. "Well, there's a bunch of orphan kids with no folks or family and they're bringing 'em out west to find foster homes and people to adopt 'em," he said quickly. It seemed to be going well so far, so Matt kept talking, often repeating himself. "I guess there's boys and girls of all ages. They'll offer 'em up for adoption or try to put 'em in foster homes. The ones who aren't taken will stay on the train west to St. Joseph, and they'll stop at towns along the way to see if anyone's willin' to take 'em in."

Millie looked at her husband, waiting to see if there was more. Matt looked down at his plate again, then back to his wife, waiting for her response.

"I guess they'll be coming in around three weeks or so," he added.

"What are you thinking, Matthew?" his wife asked. "That we take in one of those children to live with us?"

That was exactly what Matt was thinking. "There's bound to be some older boys. Some big enough to help out with the chores. We've got plenty of room here in the house."

"Is that the only reason you're considering this?" Millie asked. "So you can have someone to help you with the farm work?"

"No, of course not," Matt defended, sitting back in his chair. "That's just the practical part of it that I thought might help convince you to at least go and see them. It just seems like the right thing to do—takin' a boy in who doesn't have any family. I had to spend most of my nights in Benson's Livery Stable after my Ma and Pa died, and I did jobs for anybody who'd give me work. I would've been grateful for a home."

Millie knew her husband was sincere in his motives for taking in a foster child, and having an extra pair of helping hands around the farm would be a bonus.

"Would we get to choose the child?" Millie asked. "Would we get a good look at them and talk with them before we decide?"

"Oh, sure!" Matthew responded enthusiastically, heartened at the prospect that his wife was giving the matter serious consideration. "All the children will be at the town hall, and we'll have to get recommendation letters before we'll be considered as foster parents."

"Mr. Ellis at the bank might write us a letter to show that we're responsible, and I'm sure the pastor will give us a letter," Millie offered. "Do you think that will do?"

Matt felt better, now that his wife seemed to be agreeable to the idea of going to see the children. "I'm sure it will, dear."

Millicent looked at her husband thoughtfully for a few moments. She had heard enough for now. "Eat your dinner, before it gets cold," she insisted.

Little Matt was already stuffing his mouth with biscuits and dropping pieces under the table for Roy. He was too preoccupied with food and with sneaking food to the dog to hear about the possibility of a new brother coming to live with them.

Richard Hooton

The Chisholms waited for more than two hours with other prospective foster parents at the train station. It was a windy day, and had been threatening to rain since early morning.

When the train finally arrived, a crowd of onlookers had gathered to see the children, eyeing the orphans with curiosity as they stepped off the train.

Roy spotted the little auburn-haired girl on the train platform right away. The child's appearance stirred a memory within him of the little girl who came down the lane to meet him when he arrived home from the pastures with his master at the end of the day. The dog watched from the wagon as the little moppet walked slowly along the platform, hand in hand with her older brother.

The boy displayed a somber demeanor. He knew there weren't going to be many chances for adoption at the stops along the line, not without being separated from his little sister. The only people who had looked at them so far had either wanted a boy strong enough for farm work or a little girl to raise in town, but not both.

A number of townspeople had come out to see the children—more than thirty homeless little street urchins from the seedy tenement districts of New York, who were now preparing to be marched out in front of prospective parents in the hope that some would be taken into foster homes. Those who were passed over would board the orphan train and continue the journey toward St. Joseph.

The children had all been scrubbed and dressed in decent clothing, made possible by the charitable donations given to the Children's Aid Society. Most of the townspeople who gathered at the train depot were simply curious, but a few were sincere about taking a child into their homes and had already presented their reference letters to the adoption agent.

The children in this particular group ranged in age from three to fourteen. They were mostly frightened and confused, and looked anxiously into the faces of the prospective foster parents who had come to look at them. When they were passed over in favor of other children, many felt the sting of rejection. It was difficult to maintain hope. They could only rely upon what the agents from the Society told them about a better life in the West.

The interviews by the adoption agent were fairly simple. The foster parents must provide a safe and caring home, and provide the children with a basic education and religious instruction. Most were from Christian backgrounds, but a few Jewish orphans had also been sent west for adoption, most of which were taken in by Christian families. The adoption agents tried to have the children taken into a home of their own faith, but more often than not, it was impossible.

Jared Tolliver refused to be taken without his little sister. His mother made him promise many times during her last days on earth that he would not let anything separate them.

"All you have is family, son," his mother had repeated over and again from her sick bed until she was very sure he understood. "Your father is gone, and I can't be here to take care of you, so it's up to you now. Don't let anything happen to your sister."

Several other brothers and sisters had been separated along the way since they left Albany. Many tears had been shed, and it took much soothing by the adoption agents who accompanied the children to calm a child when it was forced to board the train and continue on to the next stop, leaving a brother or sister behind. Most could not understand why they were not allowed to remain together.

The moment Millicent Chisholm set eyes on Betsy she fell in love with the little girl. The brown-eyed little beauty with cropped auburn hair reminded Millie of her younger sister when they were children.

"I can't let my sister go with you, ma'am. Not unless I stay with her. I promised my Ma," Jared said, with a determined frown on his young face. "I'm a hard worker, and I'm strong. We won't be any trouble, if you just let us stay together."

Matt liked the boy's sand. He stood his ground and refused to go with anyone who wouldn't take his little sister in the bargain, and the boy was prepared to put up a hard fight if anyone tried to take her from him. Millie approached the two children, bending to talk to the little girl.

"You won't be taken from your brother," she said, looking up at

Jared. "Will she, Matt?" she turned her gaze up at her husband, who was standing next to her, speechless. He shook his head, dumfounded by his wife's apparent willingness to take in as many orphans as they could load into the wagon.

Betsy clung to her big brother's coat sleeve and held up three fingers when Millie asked the girl how old she was. Millie knew these two children needed to stay together as much as they needed to find new parents. She kneeled down on the rough platform boards in front of Betsy and took her by her two little arms, looking straight into her deep brown eyes.

"Do you think you and your brother would like to come and live with us?"

The ride back to the Chisholm farm was a pleasant one for Jared. He had never seen such lush, green pastures or so many trees. It was so different from the dirty streets and run-down buildings he had become accustomed to in New York. He was relieved that a family was willing to take them in without trying to separate him from his sister. At an earlier stop in Illinois, one of the adoption agents had warned him not to be so obstinate when he balked at a farmer's request to take him and leave his sister. He put up an argument and the old farmer decided the boy would be too stubborn to be of any use on the farm. Jared remembered thinking that the old man would probably have worked him like a mule every day and then beat him every night for not working hard enough.

Betsy sat in the back of the wagon with her brother and her new friend, Roy. The dog reveled in the attention he was getting from the little girl. "Pretty dog. Good boy," she praised, alternately stroking Roy's fur and hugging him around the neck. Roy's tongue lolled contentedly as he sat quietly and submitted to the girl's attention.

A couple of afternoon showers had knocked down the dust in the road, and enhanced the fresh smell of late summer flowers and cornfields they passed on the way home. Matt Jr. kept turning around to kneel on the seat between his parents and stare at the little girl and her big brother. "Are you coming to stay with us?" little Matt asked.

Jared smiled and nodded. He had a good feeling about this family.

Things could have gone worse—a lot worse. He had kept his promise to his mother.

Matthew found life to be much easier with another pair of hands to help with the chores. Jared did half a day's work every morning before he hurried off to school, where he eagerly absorbed everything he was taught. He quickly learned how to take Roy to the upper pasture and bring the sheep back to the barn before nightfall, and he chopped and carried wood to the house every night before supper. After eating, he would immerse himself in the reader his teacher had given him and practice his numbers with some welcome help from his new foster father. Matt was more than willing to help the boy. He was a hard work-er. They were both lucky.

Millie enjoyed having a little girl around the house—someone she could pamper a little. Her boys had no problem adjusting to the new-comers. There was plenty of room in the big farm house. Little Matt the jabber-mouth was happy to have more people in the house to talk with until his mother would send him off to bed, and baby Walter was happy to see a bigger plate of biscuits at the supper table.

Jared soon began to stay up a little later than usual in the evening, just so he could talk for awhile with his new foster parents. He liked the Chisholms and wanted them to know that he was grateful for what they had done. Jared had been told before they left New York that he and his sister would have to be very lucky to be taken in by a good family and to be allowed to remain together. All too often, brothers and sisters were separated in the adoption process.

"I can bring in more firewood if you need it, Mrs. Chisholm," Jared offered.

"We have plenty, Jared," Millie answered. "Thank you."

"You've done a man's work today," Matthew said. "You rest now."

"I'll do whatever needs doin', Mr. Chisholm," Jared assured his fos-ter parent. I'll work hard for our keep every day. Me and Betsy ain't never had such comforts as we do here."

"We admire your willingness, Jared. You always do more than your share. Get yourself off to bed now."

Millicent smiled to herself. She would help the boy with his grammar later. For now, she would be content with his politeness.

"That boy's got gumption," Matt observed aloud.

The next day, Jared arrived home from school in the early afternoon, dropped his books off at the house and went to the barn to find Matthew. He found Matt busy at work, trimming Chief's hooves and fitting him with a new set of iron shoes. Jared took a seat next to a large blacksmith's anvil that was nailed to a big tree stump. He watched carefully as Matthew filed a hoof and drove the square nails on an angle up through the holes in the heavy horseshoe, then cut them flush with the hoof where the nails protruded. Jared wanted to learn everything about farming and ranching. He was eager to help with any chore.

"Should I turn some water down the ditch to the lower pasture, Mr. Chisholm?" Jared asked.

Matthew lowered the big horse's leg to the ground and wiped the sweat off his forehead with the back of his hand.

"No, I thought we would move the sheep down to the lower pasture," Matt answered. "They've grazed that upper hillside for three weeks or more, so I think it's time to let it recover. How would you like to try your hand at working Roy on the sheep?" Jared's face lit up. He never tired of watching Roy work. He admired the way Roy would respond so quickly to the whistles and commands from Mr. Chisholm. The dog knew exactly what to do.

"Do you think he would work for me?" Jared asked expectantly.

"There's only one way to find out," Matt said. "He's always eager to work, just like you. I don't think he'll mind if you're the one to send him after the sheep, since that's all he ever wants to do."

Roy arrived at the upper pasture gate ahead of Matt and Jared. He lay down patiently outside the gate and watched intently as the sheep grazed their way further up the hillside.

"Get around, Roy," Jared called to the dog.

Roy hesitated for a brief moment to listen for the sound of Matt's voice, just to be sure the command from the boy met his master's approval.

"Go on, boy," Matt commanded softly, reassuring the dog that it was all right to take its instructions from Jared.

Roy raced around behind the sheep and lifted them into a tight band. One or two ewes turned to stand off against the dog, and one in front stamped a hoof at the intruding dog.

Roy didn't tolerate defiant sheep. He crouched low to the ground and moved slowly, stealthily toward the small band of sheep, keeping his powerful eye locked on the stubborn ewe. The animal's resolve melted away in the face of the wolf-eyed herding dog, and the ewe turned quickly to join the others on the trot down the gentle slope toward the pasture gate.

Jared smiled, pleased that he could be a part of the herding experience with such a magnificent dog as Roy.

"He's bringing them a little too fast," Matt observed. "Tell him to steady."

"Steady, Roy," Jared called out to the dog. "Steady."

Roy heeded the boy's command and slowed his pace, allowing more distance between him and the sheep.

Jared couldn't help feeling proud of his own effort, even though the dog rarely made a mistake in reading the livestock and judging their movements.

Matt and Jared stood clear and allowed the dog to do its work. Jared opened the gate and stood aside as Roy moved the sheep through the opening and into the lower pasture. He could barely contain his pride at being allowed to work with Roy. Jared loved his new life on the Chisholm farm.

The next time Matt went into town, he took Matt, Jr. and Jared along so they could learn the routine of taking produce to market and trading at the store. Both of the boys would need to know how to buy and sell. Along with raising sheep and growing crops, it was the family's livelihood. Roy almost always went along for the ride, content to be close to his master in case any work was required of him. He usually stayed in the wagon and waited patiently for Matt to come out of the mercantile or bank. At any of their other stops, Roy could usually keep an eye on his master until he came back to the wagon.

During one trip into town, Roy disappeared when Matt and the boys were in the mercantile longer than Matt expected to be, and the dog didn't come when Matt and the boys called and whistled.

"I guess he got tired of waiting and started home on his own, boys," Matt said, although he was worried that someone may have taken his dog.

"Keep an eye out for him, boys. And keep calling," Matt instructed. "Maybe he's looking for us by the livery stable."

Matt stopped the wagon in front of the livery stable at the edge of town and asked if anyone had seen Roy, but no one had. They spoke to people at one or two houses along the road beyond the livery stable, but the people they approached simply shook their heads when asked about the black dog.

"I'm sure he's gone home, boys," Matt said, trying to be as positive as he could. It wasn't like Roy to leave the wagon when they were away from the farm unless he was invited.

"Keep calling, boys. He may still be somewhere close enough to hear us."

Matt drove the wagon at a slow pace as he and the boys kept up a chorus of calls and whistles, sometimes impatiently. They were nearly a half-mile out of town when Matt snapped the reins and urged the big draft horse to pick up its pace, hoping to find Roy waiting for them when they arrived at the farm.

The boys sat in silence in the back of the wagon, their legs hanging over the back as they stared sullenly down the road toward town.

"Do you think someone took him?" little Matt said to Jared.

"There he is!" Jared answered the younger boy with an excited yell.

"Whoa," Walt reined in the horse and turned in his seat to look back down the road.

The black dog was racing up the road from the direction of town, leaving a low plume of dust in the air behind him.

Roy caught up with the wagon and leaped into the back without ever slowing down. The dog was met with pats and hugs as it turned and found a spot to settle down between the boys. Roy's tongue hung out of one side of his mouth as he panted heavily.

"That's going to be the last time Roy rides into town with us for a while," Matt resolved. "We can't afford to lose him. I want you boys to watch him better from now on."

"Yes, sir," the boys answered in unison.

Summer passed in a blissful panorama of events for Jared and little Matt, and they became inseparable friends. Matt looked up to the older boy no differently than he would have if Jared had been his real brother, and Jared always let the younger boy tag along as he finished his daily chores. They carried in firewood together for the cooking stove and the fireplace every evening before supper.

Two or three times a week, Jared would take little Matt along when he went fishing at a pond down the road from the farm, and they nearly always came home with a string of perch for Millie's frying pan.

Matt helped with the two little children when he wasn't busy with the crops or the livestock, but most of the time Millie had to manage Betsy and little Walter on her own. There were days when she would swear there were ten of them instead of two, but she always managed to give them the time and attention they needed, and never complained about not having enough time to finish her own daily work around the house.

The summer temperatures that year were extremely favorable for crops, and by early September the apple orchard on the Chisholm farm yielded a rich harvest of crisp, juicy fruit. The boys helped Matt with the picking, and eventually learned how to fill a bushel basket without eating more of the delicious red apples than they picked, although they learned faster from the bellyaches than they did from Matt's frequent scolding.

Before long, the barn was packed with rows of apple-filled bushels to take into Hannibal. Matt and the boys loaded the wagon twice a week and made the round trip into town to sell them at the market and to the riverboat passengers and crew when they came in to the landing.

By the time most of the apple crop was sold, school was about to begin, and it would be little Matt's first year. Matt wanted to sit next to Jared on his first day in the tiny, one-room schoolhouse, but Miss Evans always insisted that the younger children all sit up front. It was easier for her to help them with their work, and to discipline them when they needed it. Besides, she couldn't see their little heads if they were seated behind the older, larger students. The boys both liked school, and they adored their teacher. She always seemed to have something new and exciting to teach them every day. Jared was becoming a very good reader, and rarely had much trouble with arithmetic.

Matt began to invent reasons to drive the wagon into town for one errand or another before the boys got out of school, and always waited to give them a ride home.

"Those boys both have strong legs," Millie would tell him. Matt's defense was that by giving them a ride back to the farm, it would permit the boys to spend more time on chores and homework. Millie allowed her husband to think he had aptly justified his frequent transportation service.

"Millie, I think I'll take a load of squash and pumpkins into town today," Matt announced to his wife. "Mr. Carlson said he could use some fresh produce for his customers, and I'm sure I can sell the rest at the riverboat landing."

Millie smiled. "We're almost out of salt," she said. "And bring me some thread if you think about it."

Matt loaded the fall produce into the wagon and called Roy to join him for the ride into town, then decided it would be a good idea to give Millie a break from the little ones.

"Why don't I take Betsy and Wally with me today," Matt offered. "Give you a chance to get some things done without having them under foot all day." Millie was grateful.

The two smaller children were always excited about a trip into town, and hurried to put on their coats so they could join Roy in the wagon.

"You be a good boy and stay put today," Matt said to Roy. The dog sat in the back and watched alertly for any signs of birds that might be startled by the wagon along the road into town. He sniffed the air for the scent of rabbits, squirrels, and raccoons, and nudged Matt's hand whenever he suspected there was something in the trees worth stopping to investigate.

"Just wait, boy," Matt soothed, trying to calm the excited dog. Roy was always a bundle of energy.

Little Matt was the first child to bolt out the door of the school-house and down the steps toward the waiting wagon. He climbed up into the back of the wagon and kneeled up behind his father, out of breath from running and excited about sharing his new-found knowledge from the classroom.

"Pa, do you know who the President of America is?" little Matt asked, genuinely convinced that there was no way his father could possibly know the answer, since he was not in the classroom that day. "It's Abraham Lincoln," the boy exclaimed proudly, certain that he was helping to educate his father.

"You don't say," Matt replied in mock surprise.

"Yep, and the first President was George Washington," the boy followed up, with an air of bold confidence. "He was a General."

Jared came down the steps with the older students, carrying his primer and a Charles Dickens novel loaned to him by Miss Evans, both strapped together with an old leather belt. Matt noticed that Jared's trouser legs were about six inches above his ankles, and wondered why he hadn't seen it sooner. The boy was growing fast.

Betsy spotted her older brother among the other children and called to him even before he was within hearing range.

"Jared!" The little girl waited for her brother to acknowledge her greeting. "Jared, we brought Roy with us today. He's being good and staying put."

"Thanks for waiting," Jared said as he climbed up onto the seat beside Matt and handed his books to his little sister. It made Betsy feel immensely important to hold her big brother's schoolbooks.

"I think we'll stop by Carlson's store and get you some new trousers next week, Jared," Matt said. "I think you're runnin' out of leg room."

Jared didn't want to tell Matt that he was beginning to feel a little embarrassed with the way he looked, but some of the other boys at school had the same problem, so he wasn't alone.

"That would be fine, Mr. Chisholm," Jared said, trying to hold back a smile at the prospect of getting new trousers with legs that went all the way to his shoes.

"We have to make a stop at the livery stable on the way out of town," Matt advised the children. "I need a sack of oats for the horses." Matt reined in the big draft horse outside the open doors of the livery barn and climbed down off the wagon.

"You wait here until I get back," Matt instructed the children. "And you boys keep an eye on Roy so that he don't run off again."

Roy's eyes were fastened on the road up ahead, and no sooner had Matt walked inside the livery stable than the dog jumped out of the wagon and ran up the road to a small house surrounded by a low wrought iron fence. He let out a bark of greeting, then another, and stuck his muzzle through the fence to wait for a reply.

"Roy, come back here!" Jared called out to the dog. "You kids stay here," he instructed as he jumped down from the wagon and ran after the black dog.

"You kids stay here," little Matt parroted, and he jumped down to race after the older boy.

The two boys arrived at the wrought iron gate just as a middle-aged woman, wearing a flour-dusted apron and with hands coated in bread dough, came through the front door and stepped onto the porch. She scowled at Roy before looking up to address the boys.

"Is that your dog?" she asked, in a tone that clearly revealed her disapproval.

"Yes ma'am," Jared answered politely, kneeling down to constrain the dog. "We're sorry if he bothered you."

"Oh, it's no bother," the woman said, with a slight air of exasperation. "You want to see his pups?"

Little Matt sat in silence next to Jared on the wagon seat and waited for his father.

"Your pa isn't going to like this," Jared worried.

"Nope," the younger boy agreed.

"What if he makes us take them back?" Jared asked.

"Betsy and Wally will start cryin' and makin' a big fuss," little Matt assured the older boy. He had it planned fairly well for a six-year-old. "It's our only chance, Jared."

Matt came out of the livery stable with a big sack of oats on his shoulder and dropped it into the back of the wagon. He climbed up onto the wooden seat and took the reins without noticing the two tiny balls of fur that Betsy and Wally held on their laps.

"Git up, Chief," he called to the big Belgian draft horse. Chief leaned into his harness and started the wagon rolling toward home. A muffled whine came from the back of the wagon, followed by a pair of high-pitched yips.

"Whoa, Chief," Matt rescinded, pulling back on the reins. "What the devil was that?"

Four otherwise talkative children all kept their mouths buttoned shut. Matt turned and looked into the back of the wagon, at the two little children who cradled the puppies like a pair of doting nannies. Wally was the first to look up at his father.

"Puppy, papa," the two-year-old explained to his father, with an enormous smile on his little face.

Matt looked at Jared first, then at little Matt, and read the expressions on their faces.

"Matthew Fielding Chisholm, you had a hand in this—I *know* it," Matt said sternly. "I can see it on your face. The dogs are going right back to where you found them."

"What on earth are you doing with those dogs?" Millie asked when the wagon pulled up in front of the farm house. She held a broom that served the dual purpose of sweeping the house and chasing chickens off the porch, and now she considered swatting her husband with it.

Matt decided that a brief explanation would be the best option.

"Millie, you remember that time a while back when I took the boys into town and we couldn't find Roy?" Matt reminded his wife. "Well, it seems he went a-courtin' and now we got these pups."

He looked to his wife for understanding, raised his eyebrows and shrugged. He hoped there would not be another confrontation over the pups like the one he experienced at the livery stables. His first attempt to separate the two little ones from the puppies was not entirely successful. Besides, the pups were already beginning to grow on him, and it couldn't hurt to start training another generation of working dogs. Children and dogs all scrambled out of the wagon at once and squeezed through the front door of the farm house for sanctuary.

"They better not mess my floor," Millie warned, following behind her children.

Matt put an arm around his wife as they walked into the house, and looked on as the pups became acquainted with their new home. The tiny black-and-white pup nestled comfortably in Betsy's lap, while the black pup with one pricked ear and a white tail tip frolicked around little Wally's feet, trying to grab at a shoelace. Matt listened as the older boys cautioned the little ones to be careful not to hurt the pups. Roy had already settled onto his favorite rug next to the fireplace, and eyed the pups with mild interest.

"Who's going to take care of them?" Millie inquired sensibly of her husband.

Jared and little Matt waited and listened for their patriarch to come up with a wisely-worded answer that would satisfy the final decision maker in the home.

"Everybody, I suppose."

CHAPTER FIVE

THE SHEEPMEN

Wood River Valley, Idaho—1896

Walt Stewart dug up a wild sego lily from the hillside with his knife, cut off the stem and leaves, then peeled the white bulb just enough to remove the dirt, and savored its moist flavor. Its look and texture was similar to an onion, but with a much milder taste, and a pleasant departure from the jerked beef he always carried in his saddlebags. Walt munched on the sego bulb snack for a minute, and dug up another to fill the void in his belly. He looked up and down the heavily-wooded river bank a hundred yards below him for signs of livestock movement along the grassy banks, but failed to see anything. He had spotted hoof prints and trails dotted with sheep droppings a mile or more upriver, so he knew they were close by. He folded his buck knife and slid it back into his hip pocket.

"C'mon Snip, let's go find some sheep." One hand grasped the reins and the saddle horn together as Walt slid his boot into the stirrup and swung his lanky, six-foot frame up into the saddle. The old Paint stallion lifted its head from the sweet grass it had been grazing and turned its ears forward, alert and ready. With a little prodding from Walt's spurs, the horse began to make its way down a deer trail toward the river below. The banks of the Wood River were thick with green grass, willows and cottonwood trees. It had become the perfect place for sheep to wander and graze, although out of sight of their human stewards, and undisturbed except for an occasional mountain lion or coyote that would come down from a mountain canyon during the night to take a lamb or an old ewe.

A few wolf packs had already moved out of the region in search of less hostile hunting grounds. Ranchers and sheepmen killed them on sight, and guardian dogs harassed the wolves if they tried to come close to the sheep. The Great Pyrenees guardian dog was a fierce protector, bred over a span of several millennia specifically for the job of guarding sheep. It blended in with the herd easily, its white fur camouflaging it perfectly among the ewes and lambs. First brought by the Basque shepherds into North America in the seventeenth century, they had gradually made their way to the Far West as the land was settled by immigrants and more shepherds found them useful.

Walt carried a Winchester lever-action repeater rifle in his saddle scabbard for just such an occasion as crossing paths with a predator. He didn't hesitate to fire on a wolf or coyote whenever he caught sight of one. Wolves meant nothing to him except devastation to his livestock herds. He didn't care how long they had existed in the region, or whether they kept deer and elk herds thinned, taking the old, sick and injured animals first. His only concern was for his livestock. It never occurred to him that the wolf had to make a living, too.

The water level in the Wood River dropped in the early fall, particularly due to the sparse October rainfall. Snowmelt had already made its last contribution to the river in early summer. The sheep were able to graze along the receding river banks, in and out of the thick willow stands, and they could cross along the wide gravel bars where the water ran shallow. It would take some time to locate nearly a thousand of the woolies.

Walt gave a shrill whistle. Two border collies abandoned their pastime of chasing jackrabbits and came racing over a nearby ridge and through the sagebrush, each dog testing the other to see which of them would be first to reach the horse and rider.

"Come, dogs," Walt commanded. "Go find sheep."

Ring and Jill were two of the best sheepdogs Walt had ever worked. Born into the same litter three years earlier, the brother-sister duo had begun working stock around the pens when they were only six months old, and had ventured out with the trail herds soon afterward. They worked well together, balancing off each other to turn the sheep and move them in the direction they needed to go. Both dogs had a strong eye, and never backed down from a stubborn or strong-willed ewe that felt the urge to challenge their authority with the stamp of a hoof or a feinted head-butt. Ring greeted such behavior by moving in a little closer, crouched and ready, eyes locked intently on the sheep to rebuff their challenge. The woolies nearly always lost their resolve, and quickly turned to join the rest of the herd.

Jill used a little more finesse with the sheep, but it was no less effective. She blocked their path and gently urged them to change direction and to give up any thoughts of escape. She was very persuasive. It sometimes took her a little longer to accomplish her task, but she rarely failed. If her efforts fell short, she would try again until she succeeded. What she lacked in size and strength, she made up for in style and patience. Like their parents before them, both dogs were extremely intelligent and highly instinctive.

Walt rode down into a thick stand of trees and willows near the river bank and found an opening where he could cross out onto a gravel bar to get a better view along the river bed. From the middle of the river bed, Walt was able to spot the first small band of black-faced sheep downriver as they moved out of the willows and crossed the open expanse of gravel river bed toward the opposite side. More sheep burst through the barrier of willows and rushed out onto the river bed, eager to join the others on the opposite bank. It was obvious the dogs were not far behind them, rousting each small flock out of the willows as they pushed them into the open. Walt caught a glimpse of black and white fur at the edge of the willow stand just before it turned and disappeared back into the thick growth. Ring and Jill loved their work.

Walt urged his mount up from the river bed onto the bank and moved through the willows into a clearing. An anxious congregation of sheep was gathering, and a rough count convinced Walt that more than three hundred had been flushed out so far. As he pushed the wooly band south along the river bank, more sheep rushed out of the thicket, eager to join the larger herd. The dogs performed flawlessly. Each in turn brought a small band of black-faced woolies across the river bed, then made a wide arc back upriver and around the willow stands to go in search of more sheep.

This was the second year the brother and sister team of border collies had moved the herd over the Galena Summit into the summer pastures high in the Stanley Basin and brought them back again in the fall, moving them to their winter grazing fields in the lower elevations to the south. It was becoming routine for the pair, and they knew the trail well that led over the Sawtooth Mountain Range into the Wood River Valley. It was their home. When they weren't busy herding sheep, they took the time to sniff every brush and badger hole along the way.

Walt took another rough count and figured he had nearly seven hundred sheep, all moving along together down the valley. He had most of the herd, and he expected the remaining sheep were being brought up by Ring and Jill, or they had already meandered further south, following along in the safe company of the big Pyrenees Mountain Dog that led the herd by day and protected them by night. Walt rode south toward the pasture where his hired shepherd had set up camp earlier in the day. He saw the smoke from the wood stove in the sheep camp and let it guide him in. It appeared that a fairly large number of livestock had followed the big mountain dog and were already grazing near the sheep camp.

Walt smelled Vasco's biscuits as he rode up to the old canvas-covered, wooden-wheeled sheep wagon that was the shepherd's home away from home during the long summer months.

Vasco Beraza was a proud Basque shepherd whose family tree bore generations of shepherds before him. He immigrated to North America when he was nearly thirty years old, hoping for the opportunity to work for other ranchers until he could save enough to buy some land and start his own herd. In the meantime, he performed his job well for his employer and he was a good camp cook, which kept him in the good graces of his boss.

"Hallo, Patron," Vasco called out to his boss from the door of the wagon. "I tink you find most of them sheeps, si?"

"I think so, Vasco," Stewart answered, stepping down out of his saddle with a mildly painful groan. "I'm getting too old for this," he complained.

"Are you going to share any of those biscuits, or did you just make enough for you and your dog?"

"Si, Patron," Vasco answered cheerfully. He had come to know his employer's wry sense of humor after working for him nearly five years.

"I fix patatas, too. It be ready soon," he added. He continued to scrub potatoes in the all-purpose tin washpan. The indispensable pan hung in a metal rack on the front of every sheep wagon when it wasn't in use, and was used for mixing bread dough, scrubbing potatoes, washing up before supper, shaving in the morning, and sometimes as a dog's water bowl.

"But no butter, no strawberry jams, no bacon, no café," Vasco apologized, with raised eyebrows and a shrug of his shoulders.

"Aw, that's all right, Vasco," Walt said. "It's my fault. I shoulda brought ya provisions sooner. I'll ride into Hailey first thing in the morning."

"It's good, boss," Vasco consoled. "We got lots patatas. We eat good today."

Vasco never complained. He was happy to have human company after so many weeks alone with the herd. That kind of solitude wears on a man, and causes him to yearn for human companionship. He longed for some conversation. He would often talk to his big Pyrenees guardian dog, telling it how much he missed his wife and son, and how he was going to have his own place someday. Goliath always listened patiently, as long as he got a few biscuits for his trouble. Vasco never tried to talk to the sheep. No one can talk to sheep, no matter how lonely they think they are. They don't listen. A man might just as well talk to a tree stump.

Walt filled his belly with as many biscuits and potatoes as he could stomach and rode back out to get his dogs and whatever livestock they had found. Less than a mile out on the trail he saw the low dust cloud from a large band of sheep coming his way, followed by two black and white dogs, each one flanking a side of the herd to keep the sheep moving in a straight line. Walt was pleased with his dogs. They always brought him sheep, even across the most difficult terrain or in the foulest weather. He turned his horse and led the way back toward camp with more than a hundred woolies in tow, pushed along by Ring and Jill.

Vasco began talking as soon as Walt rode into camp. "Them smart dogs find the rest of the sheeps, huh, boss?" Vasco observed, with a big smile.

"Yeah, they found them. Always do," Walt answered.

"I build a good fire, boss. Gonna be cold tonight, I tink."

Walt looked up toward the western sky over the ridge of mountains. Some dark clouds were moving in, and it felt cold enough for snow. He might stay inside the camp wagon for the night. The sheep camp wagon was built to house one shepherd, but it could hold as many as three or four in a pinch. There was room for his bedroll on the narrow floor next to the wood stove, or on the bench seat opposite the stove. It was a cramped space, but it beat waking up with six inches of snow on top of him.

The two men sat around a big campfire and traded well-worn stories while they watched a cottontail rabbit roast on a spit. Small game was plentiful in the valley. Sage hens and pheasant were plentiful, and there never seemed to be a shortage of rabbits, even with all the coyotes around. Trout fishing was good in the Wood River and in Silver Creek during the summer and fall. The small valley was a good meat locker. Vasco had baked more of his tasty biscuits, and cooked more potatoes and beans. It was going to be a feast. Ring and Jill lay near the fire so they could keep a close eye on the rabbit, their ears pricked up and eyes fastened on the roasting meat. The aroma was almost overwhelming to their powerful sense of smell, and both dogs were certain the rabbit had cooked long enough. It was time to eat.

Vasco inspected the rabbit and turned the spit one last time. Ring and Jill licked their lips and drooled. They didn't have to wait. Vasco dished up a hefty portion of food for Walt and himself, then pulled the roasted rabbit off the spit and piled it on the tin plates. The men gave their leftover meat and bones to the grateful dogs, along with a biscuit or two.

"How long your papa herd sheep, boss?" Vasco asked, sipping on a cup of gritty campfire coffee.

"Long time, Vasco," Walt answered. He stared into the fire and absentmindedly poked at the embers with a long stick. The two men had the same conversation several times before, but Vasco didn't care. He just wanted to talk.

Walt didn't mind. He knew the feeling that came from spending too much time alone. It took a special breed to endure days on end with no human contact, not to mention the lack of home comforts. Besides, Walt liked talking about his father and telling of how he had been such a knowledgeable and hard-working shepherd in Scotland.

"Nobody understood livestock better than my father," Walt said, with genuine pride in his voice. "He hardly ever lost a spring lamb to the cold. And he always found the best grazing for them. It was always fat lambs that he delivered to market in the fall."

It had been many years since Walt left his homeland with his Uncle James and sailed to America. He could barely remember the journey. It seemed like such a long time ago. What he did remember clearly was that his mother had died of tuberculosis and his little sister died six months later of a rare childhood disease. The inexperienced country doctor from the village of Dun couldn't tell Walt's father exactly what the malady was that claimed his little girl's life, but it sapped the rosy color from her cheeks and caused her frail little body to weaken and waste away in a few short months. His father aged before his time from the ordeal of losing a wife and daughter. His hair turned gray and he lost the spring in his step.

When Walter Stewart had learned that his brother James was preparing to immigrate to America with his small family, he insisted that young Walt go with them. Walter promised to join them someday to settle in the Utah Territory, where there was plenty of land for anyone willing to work it.

"My father came to America not long after I arrived with my uncle and his family," Walt explained to Vasco. We got a letter from him, telling us he had arrived in St. Louis and that he was working in the stockyards with his dog. He was saving money so he could make the trip to Utah."

Walt poked at the glowing coals with his stick, and lost himself in thought.

"We never heard from him again after that."

"You never know what happen to him?" Vasco asked quietly.

"We did get a letter with some money in it from the wife of a man he worked with at the stockyards. She said he died of pneumonia. He was scarcely fifty years old, and I used to believe he would never die. My Uncle James used the money to buy our first sheep—he said it's what my father would have wanted for us."

"You know what happen to his dog?"

"I never thought much about it, Vasco," Walt said. "I reckon the man he worked with took care of it. It was a good herding dog." He nodded, for emphasis. "My father always trained good herding dogs."

The sun had been down for a few hours, and the cold followed quickly. A chill wind blew down from the mountains, and the men decided to turn in before they both froze stiff. Walt built a good fire in the wood stove and settled into the cramped wagon for the night. Ring and Jill curled up together under the wagon to keep warm, satisfied with their day's work and content with their full bellies. The dogs had everything they needed.

Walt always heard sounds in his sleep. When he woke, he could never be sure if they were real or imagined. This time he was sure.

"You hear that, boss?" Vasco spoke in a loud whisper, as he scrambled in the dark confines of the camp wagon, feeling for his boots and coat.

Walt heard it. He jumped up and swung the camp wagon door open. It was a cloudless night and the full moon cast its pale glow across the valley to give a clear view of the open range. The unmistakable caterwaul of a mountain lion came from off in the distance, followed instantly by the sound of barking dogs.

Walt pulled on his boots, grabbed his coat and rifle, and was out of the wagon in a hurry, but without his shirt or trousers. Vasco was right on his heels. The men ran toward the sound of the barking dogs and arrived in time to see the big Pyrenees guardian dog lunging at the angry mountain lion, alternately snapping and snarling in a deep, threatening tone. The lion's ears were pinned back in a defensive posture as it crouched and turned, trying to back away, but being frustrated in its escape attempt by the two border collies.

Ring and Jill flanked the desperate lion, and each in turn rushed in to plant a nip on the lion's lowered haunches as it whirled angrily, first toward one and then the other, swiping a big paw at the irritating dogs. Ring escaped a near miss of the powerful predator's extended claws as it whirled back in his direction after forcing the smaller female dog to back away. Hissing and snarling, with fangs and claws bared, the lion swept a paw toward Ring's head and retrieved a souvenir of black fur from the dog's neck.

Goliath took advantage of the lion's momentary distraction and charged in to grip the beast by its neck. The brave guardian dog had never encountered the ferocity and speed of a cornered mountain lion. The tawny predator lashed out with a well-aimed paw and brought down a powerful swipe across Goliath's shoulder. The big cat's long claws penetrated the thick, white fur and tore through flesh, but failed to knock the dog to the ground. Goliath did not feel the pain. He was focused only on the lion, and intent upon doing his job to protect the sheep. The two animals squared off against each other again.

The crack of a rifle shot resounded in the night air and a single bullet whistled past the lion's ear, kicking up rock and dirt a few feet beyond and causing the startled mountain lion to leap into the air and spin half way around. The dogs crouched and waited. They were well familiar with the sound of their master's rifle, and they knew he was nearby.

Vasco rushed toward them frantically, picked up a rock the size of his fist and hurled it nearly sixty feet at the threatening cougar. It struck the wild animal on the hip hard enough to send the big cat dashing off into the night. The two men rushed up to the dogs, searching in the pale light for signs of the big cat.

The mountain lion had already disappeared into the brush and ran toward a nearby canyon without looking back. Its keen hearing told it that no dogs were in pursuit. The big cat slowed its pace as it gained distance and elevation up the canyon toward its secluded den, where two young cubs waited quietly for their mother to bring home a meal. The mother lion would not forget her unpleasant encounter with dogs and men, and her cubs would have to go hungry for another day.

Goliath had never been so close to a mountain lion before his joint encounter with the help of the border collies. Usually, the big guard dog chased off lone coyotes or urged a pack of hunting wolves to change their minds and look for a vulnerable elk calf or a sick mule deer instead of expecting an easy meal from a large band of slow-moving sheep. He lost an occasional lamb or ewe to the marauding predators, but discouraged most of their attempts. He did his job well, and taught his distant cousins that it would be more profitable for them to hunt wild game.

"I think your dog was mauled pretty bad, Vasco. You better look him over real good," Walt said.

The worried shepherd kneeled beside his big dog as it lay panting in the dirt. Goliath rolled onto his side when he heard the soothing voice of his master and felt Vasco's comforting hands. He let a low whine escape his throat when his master's hands touched his gashed shoulder, feeling for the wound.

"I feel blood, I think," Vasco said, as he gently prodded with his fingers around Goliath's neck, head and shoulder. The red color was not visible in the moonlight, and might easily have been mistaken for dirt until Vasco's fingers came in touch with the oozing wetness of the dog's blood. "I can't tell how bad it is, though. Maybe we better try to carry him back to camp, boss."

The men gently lifted the dog onto Walt's coat and used the makeshift stretcher to carry the heavy dog back to the sheep camp. Walt fetched an oil lamp out of the wagon and gave Vasco some light, then shoveled a few hot coals out of the wood stove and took them outside to start a campfire. He piled on brush wood until the warm fire lit up the night with its blaze and kept the chill air away.

"I'll make some coffee, Vasco," Walt offered. "It could be a long night."

Walt woke up, shivering in the cold of the early dawn and his back sore from leaning against his saddle and the wooden-spoke wheel of the camp wagon. A woolen blanket was wrapped around his shoulders and his Winchester lay across his lap. The fire had nearly died out, so he piled on a few pieces of dried brush and dead tree branches. Vasco was awake and kneeling over his dog, and Ring and Jill were lying next to him, watching.

"How's he doin', Vasco?" Walt asked quietly.

"I think he be all right, boss," Vasco answered, without looking up. I put ointment on the scratches, so the blood stop. Goliath drink some water, and he sleeping now. He no eat nothing, though."

"He's lucky that big cat didn't do more damage. I've never seen a dog would tangle with a lion like that," Walt praised. "You know, before you came with Goliath, we always had to protect the herd with a rifle."

"Golly is fierce protector, boss," Vasco said proudly, emotion sounding in his voice. "Pyrenees dog guard sheeps for tousands years. Not afraid of nothing."

Walt nodded. "I wouldn't argue with that. You're a pretty fair shot with a rock, Vasco. Lucky you didn't hit Goliath instead of the cougar."

Vasco grinned. "I would never hurt Golly."

Walt tossed off his woolen blanket and hauled himself up from his uncomfortable bed in the dirt.

Vasco looked at his employer and grinned. "You gonna wear something besides your boots and those long-handled underwears today, boss?" Vasco asked, cheerfully. "Maybe you scare the sheeps."

Walt looked down at his wardrobe and realized it was lacking. "I sure ain't dressed for a dance, am I?"

Walt hoisted himself into the sheep wagon and finished dressing, then set out to check on the herd. He hoped they had not scattered during the night when the commotion erupted between the dogs and the lion. If he was lucky, they hadn't gone far. He saddled Snip and called the dogs, then rode south to find the herd, leaving Vasco to tend to his dog and stir up some hot breakfast while he was gone. He appreciated Vasco's cooking talents. The resourceful Basque could make a meal out of flour and beans and bacon grease. Walt didn't have the ability to make anything except burned biscuits and bad coffee. He couldn't wait to get home to his wife's cooking.

"Get up, Snip," Walt grumbled, prodding the horse with his boot heels. "We don't have all day."

The sheep had moved down along the river during the night, and were strung out for nearly a mile. Most were grazing peacefully when Walt rode up with Ring and Jill in the lead. Seeing the dogs, the sheep immediately began bunching together and moving up toward the higher ground above the river bed. Walt spent the next hour pushing the livestock together and getting them all pointed southward, with help from his dogs. Once he was satisfied the wooly beasts were grazing in the right direction, he turned his horse and rode back toward the sheep camp, and hopefully, a hot breakfast.

"I'll ride into town and pick up some provisions today," Walt said, through a mouthful of fried potatoes. "Just give me a list of what you need."

Walt decided he needed a hot bath and a change of clothes, so he made ready to leave as soon as Vasco finished his list. Goliath was up on his feet, though walking a little slower with his bruised and gashed shoulder. He was devouring a stack of hotcakes when Walt mounted his horse for the ride into Hailey.

"You dogs stay here," Walt called to Ring and Jill, just as they rose to their feet to follow him. "Stay here," he reinforced, in a stern voice. The dogs instinctively wanted to follow him, thinking there was herding to be done, but they did their master's bidding, and lay down again to watch Goliath consume another plate of hotcakes.

Walt made straight for the Prairie Hotel and a hot bath after leaving his horse in care of the livery. It wouldn't hurt to be clean and free of stink when he stopped by the mercantile to stock up on food and dry goods. The townspeople who shopped in the store would be appreciative that he had taken the time for a bath and change of clothes.

The hotel manager and part-time desk clerk greeted Walt as he strode through the door to the lobby and approached the front desk.

"Hello, Stewart," he said, loud enough for everyone in the lobby to hear. "You look the same as you did last year, right down to the trail dirt. Smell the same, too."

"Are you still alive, Jenkins?" Walt grumbled, only half in jest.

"I think you brought enough dirt off the range to cause erosion," Jenkins jabbed back. "Maybe you should have left some on the mountain."

"I can remedy that if you'll set me up with a room and a bath," Walt responded sourly. He was annoyed that the overweight man entertained himself by poking fun at trail hands, but treated the railroad men like visiting celebrities. The railroaders came into the hotel more often, and the company paid for their stay. They ate well, and used all the hotel's services, bought newspapers and souvenirs to take home for their families.

He had known Carl Jenkins for more than thirty years, and even though he only saw the man once or twice a year, he always wondered why the man was content to remain at the same job year after year. Jenkins had been at the hotel through five owners and two name changes, and seemed to be indispensable. Apparently, the man knew how to take care of the guests and keep them coming back.

"You know where the baths are," Jenkins said cheerfully, turning the guest book toward Walt and handing him an ink-dipped pen to sign his name.

"Just leave your clothes with Mr. Sheng and he'll have you spruced up in no time. Extra if he cleans the boots, you know. You staying the night?"

"Maybe tomorrow. I have to take provisions out to my shepherd. He's run out of almost everything."

Walt always felt more human after a hot bath and a shave, and he always enjoyed looking around the stores in Hailey to see what was new. Maybe he could find something for his wife and grandson before he made the ride home, he thought. For now, his mind was on getting his livestock moved into the holding pens so they could be loaded on the train to Salt Lake and Denver. He could usually find a buyer or two at the hotels in Hailey and Bellevue, awaiting the fall drives into the valley.

It seemed that it was harder every year to sell the entire crop of lambs for a fair price in Salt Lake, so he usually had to continue on to

Denver with whatever was left of them, particularly if there were more than two or three hundred that failed to sell in Utah.

Sheep outnumbered the people in Idaho by a wide margin. The vast range lands of southern Idaho were ideal for grazing sheep, and it had grown into the largest sheep ranching region in North America. It meant that lamb buyers from all over the United States looked to the area ranchers as a main source of lamb, but it also had its drawbacks— if demand was low, the market was flooded with livestock that would be hard to sell.

Most of the lambs were sold in the fall of the year to make way for the new crop of lambs in the spring. The markets for lamb and wool lay to the south and east, and Utah always saw a flood of lambs arriving at the railroad stockyards in Ogden and Salt Lake in the fall. Walt Stewart resolved himself to getting the best price possible for his lambs every year, even if it required staying with the train until he reached a rail hub where could get a good price. One year he had to stay with the train all the way to Omaha. It meant the difference between staying in the sheep ranching business and failing. At the age of sixty-three, he didn't have many options. Besides, he didn't know anything else.

Walt sat down for a hot meal in the hotel restaurant and caught up on news and gossip from the waitress and some of her other customers. He learned who had died since last year, who had a new baby or grandchild, whose crops had been ruined by hail, and what new families had moved into town. Thirty minutes or so of news was all he could stand. He walked back to the livery stable for his horse.

Walt stopped by the post office first, then made straight for Adamson's Mercantile and gathered up as many provisions as he could carry, including some that weren't on Vasco's list. Vasco always appreciated a couple of jars of currant jelly and blackberry jam for his biscuits and hotcakes. Plenty of beans and flour, a large rasher of bacon, and some new potatoes and fresh coffee would be welcome, too. His shepherd only got one or two deliveries to the sheep camp during the long summer months in the high pastures.

It was late afternoon when Walt rode back into camp, loaded down with everything from soap to sugar. Ring and Jill must be gone with

Vasco, he thought. Goliath was tied up to a wagon wheel so that he couldn't follow. The big dog probably needed another day to rest before going back on patrol. He greeted Walt with a big, baritone "woof" as he rode up.

"Hello, Golly. How ya feelin', fella?" Walt said to the big, white gladiator. Goliath answered with a wagging tail. He could smell bacon.

Walt sat down on the wagon step and cleaned his Winchester while he waited for Vasco to come back. It wasn't long before two border collies came running up to greet him, and they seemed unusually happy to see him. They could smell the bacon, too. Vasco would be close behind.

"Any mail, boss?" Vasco asked. Walt didn't see or hear the man walk up.

"You're a stealthy one, Vasco," Walt observed. "Sure. Couple of letters from your wife over there in my coat pocket."

Vasco grinned as he hurried to retrieve the general delivery letters from Walt's coat. He saw the postmarks were about a month apart, one in August and one in late September. The letters were thick with lots of news and I-miss-yous. Vasco was pleased. He sat down to open the letter with the earliest postmark and began to read.

"My boy is learning to read English good, boss," Vasco announced, looking up from the letter with a broad smile on his face. "Rosa says he has been reading books and newspapers all summer."

Walt looked up from his rifle cleaning chore and smiled. "You can be proud of him," Walt said nodding for emphasis.

Vasco beamed. "I am. He reads everything for his mother when they go to the store or the post office."

Walt thought of his own grandson and how fast he was learning. He hoped the boy would grow up to be something else besides a sheepherder like his grandfather. Maybe he would become a merchant, or perhaps a teacher. Idaho had just achieved its statehood, so the future was bright for young people—anything was possible.

Vasco finished reading the first letter, then folded it neatly and returned it to its envelope. Still beaming with joy and pride from the loving and encouraging words from his wife, Vasco looked up at Walt as he opened his second letter, smiling like at kid on Christmas morning.

"I can see why you work so hard, Vasco," Walt observed. "I'm sure you spend all summer thinking about the day when you can go home to your family."

"I like my work, boss," Vasco assured his employer. "I don't worry about going home until my work is done."

"Oh, I know that Vasco. I never had such a hard workin' fella as you. Still, it will be good for you to see Rosa and your son real soon. Another three or four days and you'll both be headed for home."

Walt empathized with the Basque shepherd and the lonely life he had chosen. Walt missed Marjorie and his grandson already, and it had only been a week since he left them to ride out to meet Vasco and the herd.

"I read this again later," Vasco said happily, tucking the letters into his pocket as he got up to prepare their evening meal. He stirred up a skillet full of bacon, potatoes, carrots and onions in a kind of goulash, along with a big iron Dutch oven full of biscuits, and they ate like kings.

Dark clouds blew in from the west over the mountain tops. The men sat inside the camp wagon and ate, looking out through the open door at the sudden downpour, while three dogs lay under the wagon out of the rain, their bellies full of biscuits. Neither man would ever let a dog go hungry—especially a useful herding dog.

"Maybe I'll do a little fishin' in the morning if this rain lets up," Walt said.

"You catch and I cook," Vasco replied. "I fry them up good with butter and sage. You'll see—I cook fish real good."

Walt had to admit there was something about eating campfire cooking that he had always liked, ever since he was a boy. He was always hungry around the sheep camp. Food always seemed to taste good when it was cooked over the open fire, even if it was just a slightly charred rabbit on a spit, or burnt potatoes and a small trout full of bones.

The next morning dawned cool and soggy, but most of the rain had been wrung out of the clouds during the night. It was perfect weather for fishing. Walt always kept fish hooks and line in his saddle bags. It was more than catching a meal for him. Fishing was one of the most relaxing things he did in his life, even from the time of his youth. He would cut a willow and tie the line to one end. During the spring and early summer he would dig for worms by the stream bank. Later in the summer and early fall his favorite bait was grasshopper. The trout liked both.

Walt walked the stream, dangling his line in the water and letting the current carry the baited hook into a deep pool a few yards down-stream. He waited patiently while the current swirled his bait, tempting the trout to snatch it from him so that he could put them on a plate. He didn't have to wait long. The Wood River always yielded plenty of tasty brook trout. It wasn't fished much, except by a few kids from Hailey and Bellevue, or the occasional shepherd passing through.

His makeshift willow pole dipped and bent toward the water, then began a lively dance as a large trout struggled to free itself from the barbed hook. Walt hoisted the pole and line quickly up onto the river bank and dropped the wriggling trout onto the grass.

"One or two more," Stewart said aloud. "And we'll have just enough for a good meal."

What he was really fishing for was relaxation and enjoyment, and he had found it. He walked and fished for more than an hour before he turned back toward camp, carrying his day's catch on a willow stick inserted through the gills and mouths of the fish.

Vasco greased the iron skillet when he saw Stewart approaching with his catch of the day. There was nothing like fresh trout for breakfast.

Walt took the time to savor his morning meal of trout and fried potatoes before getting ready for the ride back into town. He needed to arrange for the sale of more than six hundred lambs, and that might take a few days.

"S'long, Vasco," Walt called from the back of his horse. "I'll be back tomorrow—or maybe the next day." Ring and Jill started to follow along.

"You dogs stay here," Walt commanded. The dogs paused, looking at him as though he might soon realize he made a mistake leaving them behind, and would call them to follow him after all. They watched him until he disappeared in the distance, and then turned their attention to Vasco and the tempting food smells coming from the direction of the campfire.

Walt made the hour-long ride south to the town of Bellevue and checked in at the International Hotel. Anything worth knowing could be learned in the lobby of the International. Every sheepman in the territory hung out there at least once during the year.

"Hello, Stewart," hotel owner Donald Campbell greeted, as the sheep rancher walked into the busy lobby. "Gonna sell some lambs to the city buyers?"

"Thought I might," Stewart responded affably, accepting Campbell's handshake. "It's good to see you again."

"Three or four in town this year," Campbell offered. "Came up from Utah. I heard a buyer was here from Denver, too."

"I won't bring my herd in for a couple of days yet," Walt said. "Need to let them graze a little more."

"You've got plenty of time. Trains are comin' in every day. A bunch of Laidlaw's sheep are being brought in and loaded right now," Campbell added. "Maybe you ought to look up some of those buyers that are in town."

Stewart heeded the hotel keeper's advice. He rode to the outskirts of town, down by the livestock pens along the spur track, and asked around for the lamb buyers. He noticed a man dressed in a wrinkled brown suit, his scuffed shoes coated with dirt and manure dust.

"Howdy," Walt nodded toward the man. "I don't think I know you, but you don't look dressed to work in the loading pens, so I'm guessing you're one of the buyers that came up from Salt Lake to meet the drive."

"The name's Ben Thompson," the man said, extending his outstretched hand in greeting toward Walt. "I represent the Utah Lamb Co-op."

"I've got nearly a thousand head of Hampshire sheep to bring in tomorrow or the next day. Probably six hundred lambs or more," Walt explained. "Maybe you'll be interested in some of them."

"We have just about all we need, but I'm happy to take at look at them. Maybe we can offer you a good price for a few, but we nearly have our quota. I'll only be here for two more days, though," Thompson said. "Can you have them here before I leave?"

They'll be here," Walt assured. "We'll start moving them in tomorrow."

"My name's Stewart. I'll look you up tomorrow afternoon."

Walt enjoyed a shave and another hot bath before he got a steak in the hotel restaurant. It was his second hot bath and restaurant meal in less than a week. He was living well. So well, in fact, that he slept through the night and only woke himself with his own snoring just before the sunrise. He had been snoring so loudly, he was surprised that no one was banging on the wall from one of the rooms next to him. He decided that it would be a good time to dress and ride back out to the herd.

Vasco would be pleased to hear that they would be moving the sheep into town. It would put him one day closer to being reunited with his wife and son.

Walt arrived back at the sheep camp in time for breakfast and gave Vasco the news.

"They'll be ready for us first thing in the morning, Vasco," Walt informed his shepherd. "We can go in as soon as they finish loading Laidlaw's sheep on the train."

"That's great, boss." Vasco was genuinely excited.

He calculated that it would only take him two or three days on his own to move the remaining band of ewes the last twenty miles from Bellevue to the Stewart Ranch. Then he could spend some much-deserved time with his family. He hastily threw water and kicked dirt on the campfire, then rushed to pack up the sheep camp wagon for the drive toward town. Walt was already riding out to round up the herd and point them in the right direction. Ring and Jill sensed that work was at hand, and were already on the move.

"Get around there, Ring," Walt called loudly to his dog. "Bring 'em."

"Walk up, Jill," he urged the little female border collie, calling her to tighten up the distance between herself and the dawdling sheep in the rear of the herd. He trusted that Ring would pick up any stragglers.

Walt rode up alongside the herd to keep the sheep moving in the direction of town, prepared to turn them if they began to stray. Goliath was already at the lead, calmly walking ahead of the woolies and setting a steady pace for them to follow.

Walt was always amazed at the rapport the big guardian dog had with the sheep. It was a trust that came as a result of the dog being raised among the herd, lying down with the lambs and ewes at night and walking among them during the day. Some of Goliath's behavior was trained, but most of his protective nature was instinctive. It had been bred into his bloodline for thousands of years. Walt relaxed and settled back in his saddle for the ride into Bellevue.

It was late afternoon when the herd arrived at the outskirts of Bellevue. They set up camp just outside of town, and the two men sat around the campfire and swapped stories of their reckless youth until the fire burned itself out and the dogs were thoroughly bored with all the unnecessary human chatter. It became cold as soon as the sun went down, so Walt banked a good fire in the sheep camp wagon's wood stove and the men settled in for the night.

At first light Walt saddled his horse and rode into town. He noticed a familiar wagon at the livery stable, one that spent most of its time sitting idle next to his horse barn. It was flattering to think that his wife missed him so much that she couldn't wait for him to finish his business and come home. Walt found her with his grandson at the mercantile, along with Vasco's wife, Rosa and their son. The ladies had dressed in bright gingham dresses with white lace collars for the trip to town. Walt thought that his wife looked as pretty as the day they first met whenever she dressed up in her crisp, freshly washed and ironed Sunday best.

"This is a nice surprise," Walt smiled as he approached his wife of nearly forty years. He reached for his grandson and gave him a one-armed hug around his shoulders. Marjorie was pleased to see the attention Walt gave to his grandson. The boy looked up to his grandfather with genuine admiration and respect.

"Hello, Rosa," Walt greeted Vasco's wife. "So you decided to make the trip with Marjorie?" Walt was never good at small talk with the ladies.

"Hello, Mr. Walt," Rosa answered, with a big smile.

"Vasco will be right pleased to see you," Walt said, with a friendly nod of his head.

"I'll be happy to see him, too," Rosa beamed.

"Well, I have to go talk with a stock buyer for a bit. After that, we can all ride out to the camp. It's not far," Walt said.

Walt walked back to the International Hotel and found Ben Thompson sitting in the hotel lobby with his wife. He removed his hat as he approached the couple, and they both stood to greet him. "Good morning, Stewart," Thompson said. "This is my wife, Sarah. She has a good eye for judging the weight and condition of lambs, so I bring her along on all my buying trips."

"I'm pleased to meet you, Mr. Stewart," Sarah Thompson said. "My husband told me you were bringing in a herd of Hampshires."

"Yes, ma'am," Stewart acknowledged. "Around six hundred lambs in the herd and they all look pretty good."

"They're a fine breed," Sarah agreed. "My father raised Hampshires in England, and imported some of the first of them to the west. They always showed an ability to put on good weight from grazing. We'll be anxious to take a look at them whenever you're ready."

Walt was only able to sell about half of his crop of lambs to the Thompsons, but that was more than he expected. He would have to ride with the train to Salt Lake and negotiate a sale for the rest when he arrived. His lambs had been well-grazed during the summer, but were not too fat. He was sure they would fetch a good price.

He walked briskly on his way back to the livery stable and found Marjorie and the others waiting with the wagon and team, ready to travel.

"Climb up here with me, Jake boy," Walt said to his grandson, as he mounted Snip for the ride back to camp. Jacob eagerly jumped down from the wagon and reached for his grandfather's hand to be lifted up onto the back of the saddle.

Vasco heard Goliath bark a greeting at the approaching wagon from his sentry post near the herd, and took off running in the direction of the visitors the moment he recognized his wife and son in the wagon. His son jumped down from the wagon the second Marjorie reined in the team and brought them to a halt. Vasco swept the boy up into his arms and kissed him on both cheeks. Vasco was a devoted father.

"Petri, how are you, my son?" Vasco hugged him tightly and patted the boy on his back. "You are getting so big!"

He turned to help his smiling wife down from her seat next to Mrs. Stewart and was rewarded with hugs and kisses, as Rosa demonstrated her affection with unabashed enthusiasm.

Walt and Marjorie looked on approvingly, even though they themselves would never have shown such an outward display of affection in public. The Basque people, however, were not so reserved, and didn't hesitate to let their feelings be known. Marjorie thought her husband could learn something from the Basque people.

Jake and Petri called to Ring and Jill, and the boys entertained themselves by throwing sticks for the dogs to fetch while the grownups sat inside the camp wagon, warmed by the fire in the wood stove as they engaged in grownup conversation.

"We've got a good crop of lambs this year," Walt said. "Thanks to Vasco and Golly, we haven't lost too many on the trail. If I can get a good price for them, I think we'll be all right for another year."

"We've never gone without eating, thank the Lord," Marjorie said. "We always seem to have everything we need."

Ranchers seldom held a conversation that didn't include talk of crops, livestock, and the weather. It was the axis their world turned upon. Their livelihood depended upon those things, and they were constantly mindful of any changes that affected them in any way, no matter how minor.

Vasco and Rosa sat on the bench seat next to the wood stove, holding hands like newlyweds and listening politely as the older couple talked. Rosa was an unusually shy woman, and rarely spoke up unless a question was directed at her. She preferred to sit quietly and listen while her husband spoke with Mr. Stewart. It made her proud to hear him speak with such confidence to his employer, and to be treated with such respect. Rosa loved her life in America, and was especially proud that her son would grow up in the American West with a chance to make something of himself.

"We'll get an early start in the morning, Vasco," Walt said. "I expect you and Rosa have a lot to catch up on, so we'll leave you two alone. I need to get back to the hotel anyway."

Walt called to his grandson, then turned to tie Snip's reins to the back of the wagon for the drive back into town.

"Can I ride Snip, Grandpa?" Jake asked.

"Sure, why not," Walt said to the ten-year-old boy. He let Jake untie the horse himself, and watched for a moment or two while the boy struggled to get a foot up into the stirrup. There was a time when he might have stepped in and hoisted the boy up into the saddle, but the lad was becoming more independent every year, so Walt watched and waited while Jake led his mount over to a wooden chopping block and used it as a stair step to help him climb aboard.

They bid a brief farewell to the Beraza family, and Jake led the way back to town, sitting tall and proud in the saddle.

Early the next morning, Jake Stewart rode behind his grandfather on the way back to the herd, and Vasco was ready when they arrived, with the team of horses already hitched to the wagon. Breakfast was finished at the sheep camp by the time the sun came up. It didn't take long to move the herd into town and down to the loading pens.

It took a few hours to sort and separate the lambs from the rest of the herd, but once it was done, the loading began immediately. The trains tried to stay on schedule, so even the brakemen helped with the loading.

Walt explained to his wife that he would have to go with the train to Salt Lake, and maybe as far as Cheyenne and Denver. It was never a certainty that ready buyers would be waiting at the railhead every year, but more buyers would be available as the sheep were transported farther east.

"I'm sure I'll be home in a week or two," Walt assured. "Jake, you help Vasco move the herd back to the ranch. And be sure to help your dad, and mind your mother and grandmother."

"Vasco, you bring your family up to the ranch for Thanksgiving, and we'll start the holidays out right."

"Si, Patron. Gracias." Vasco and Rosa smiled and nodded, grateful for the invitation.

Walt kissed his wife goodbye and boarded the train. The boys sat on the top rail of the loading pen fence, and watched as the locomotive belched smoke and the wheels squeaked and groaned until the train gained traction on the steel rails. They watched until the train was nearly out of sight, then climbed down and helped Petri's dad round up the sheep.

"I'm going to drive a train like that someday," Jake said to his younger friend.

"I don't think they'll let you," Petri said, unable to picture Jake in his mind as a grown man.

Jake tied Snip to the back of the wagon and pulled himself up onto the seat next to his grandmother, and Petri joined his parents in the sheep camp wagon. Goliath led the band of sheep down a well-used trail that marked the way south, while Ring and Jill brought up the rear, and the small caravan rolled south toward home.

CHAPTER SIX

THE GAMBLERS

Hereford, Texas—1936

Texas was a harsh environment in which to squeeze out a living in 1936, especially in the panhandle, where much of the land had been devastated by several years of severe drought. Texans weren't alone in their misfortune during the Great Depression. The entire country was affected by the drought in one way or another, as the nation reeled from economic loss, food shortages and climatic changes of catastrophic proportions. It was impossible to grow crops and raise livestock without water, and a lot of Midwestern farmers and ranchers had given up trying. More than a few Texas ranchers had lost their land in foreclosure sales to bankers from Chicago.

That didn't discourage Bob and Harold Chisholm. In spite of the objections from their wives, the two brothers risked everything to buy a small ranch in the Texas panhandle. Small by Texas standards, that is. They bought three full sections of land southwest of Amarillo—nearly two thousand acres of what used to be fertile soil. Water was sometimes plentiful if the weather cooperated, and the men had already laid plans to collect rainfall in tanks and store it for the dry times in between the scarce rainfall.

"Is this the reason we left St. Joseph?" Bob's wife asked, staring incredulously at the sight before her.

"We'll fix it up as quick as we can," Bob assured his wife. "It won't take long with both me and Hal workin' on it."

The main ranch house wasn't much to look at. In fact, it was a sorry sight. The entire spread was just a haphazard collection of dilapidated barns, corrals and bunkhouses laid out in a reckless array that lacked any semblance of planning. The once-thriving ranch had become a dusty remnant of its earlier existence, at a time before Mother Nature had dealt her harsh blow to the landscape and driven its inhabitants away in despair. At the time the Chisholms made the purchase, all the stock ponds were dried up and there was no rain in sight. Bob trusted that normal rainfall would return to the parched land in time, if they could hold on for a while. Until then, they were determined to scratch out a living any way they could.

The brothers began to unload their furniture and belongings from the old Ford truck with the help of their two oldest boys. Their wives had already walked to the old house to determine whether it was habitable. Mary Chisholm was the first to push through the rickety old door, and it hung on one hinge as it swung open. Mary turned and called out to her husband.

"You better bring your screwdriver, Bob!" she instructed. "And maybe a can of gas," she muttered quietly to herself as she turned and stepped onto the worn linoleum floor of the kitchen.

Old wooden shelves sagged on broken wall brackets, and a heavy wooden table that had obviously doubled as a chopping block sat in the middle of the floor. A kerosene lamp rested on a window sill next to the wood stove, which had apparently been used for both cooking and heating the house. The only positive thing that Mary noticed was that none of the windows were broken out.

There was no electricity on the ranch. Power lines had never been installed from the main highway to the ranch house.

"Well, Beth," Mary said to her sister-in-law, "I suppose we better dig out the broom and mop if we're going to get this place clean enough to sleep in tonight."

Bob and Hal rummaged in the back of the truck for their tool box and went to work on the water well. According to the banker in Hereford, the windmill-driven well was still pumping water when the last owners were evicted after the foreclosure, so it shouldn't take much time to get it up and running again.

Hal oiled the pipe fittings and wrenched the rusted pipes apart to clean and refit the pump apparatus while Bob and his oldest boy climbed the tower ladder to replace two missing windmill blades. They finished the repairs by mid-afternoon and took a break to join the rest of their family in the picnic lunch the ladies had prepared.

They went back to the windmill and pump to test their work, and when they released the catch on the windmill, the blades began to spin freely in the breeze. Before long, they had a small but steady flow of water coming from the rusty pipe. Hal rigged a pipe into a stock watering trough and they let it run until the water cleared up and the trough overflowed.

"Well, little brother, we have water," Bob said.

"It looks like there's plenty of dry firewood around," Hal observed, pointing with his wrench in the direction of some fallen-down outbuildings and wood fences.

"Yep," Bob agreed. "It'll help us clean up the place to burn the wood off those old buildings."

The Chisholm boys were undaunted by obstacles and challenges. They came from hardy stock, and had grown up facing more hardship than most. Their great grandfather had come from eastern Missouri to settle in St. Joseph after soldiers from both the North and the South had looted their farm of livestock and produce until he could no longer make a living.

Most of their family had lived in St. Joseph for nearly seventy years, but never had much success with farming. They raised enough livestock on their tiny farm to keep the family fed, but had to work jobs in town to make any money.

Their oldest brother stayed behind in St. Joseph, Missouri, where he ran a small feed store, but he was barely able to survive and feed his own family. There was no work at the store for Bob or Hal.

The whole country had been plunged into a terrible economic depression. Men were out of work everywhere, and the stories of long bread lines in the big cities of the east were especially discouraging to the Chisholm boys. They decided to pool together what money they had saved and go in search of a place where they could grow their own food and create their own jobs, without relying on part-time work and pittance wages.

The middle of the dust bowl seemed the right place to gamble the last of their savings. At least they would have a chance to come out of the Great Depression with something instead of nothing. All that it would require was hard work and a little luck. Bob and Hal could handle the hard work—the luck would be left to providence.

"Well," Bob began, in his patented Missouri drawl, "I guess we better figure out where everybody is going to sleep tonight, hadn't we?"

"Beth and I already figured it out, Bob," Mary said. It was her way of demonstrating to her husband of fifteen years that she would be in charge of the house. "There's two sleeping rooms for the grownups, and the kids can sleep out here on the cots and the extra mattress. We'll string a clothesline and hang sheets to give the girls some privacy."

"Well, then," Bob said with a shrug, both hands extended and palms held upward as a sign that he ceded control of the domicile to his wife. "What's for supper?"

"Whatever I find to fix for ya," Mary answered. "Meanwhile, you boys can finish bringin' in the rest of those beds, and find the box of pots and pans."

"Yes, ma'am," Bob acknowledged the instructions good-naturedly. His wife rarely interfered in men's business, but she always had the last word around the house. To Bob's way of thinking, it was a fair trade.

The children were all kept busy with chores. Mary's two girls helped their mother sweep out the house and clean the windows, while the two older boys brought firewood and carried belongings from the truck to the house. Mark and Hal, Jr. were not only cousins, they were best friends. Five-year-old Cassie closely followed Beth around the house, trying to help her mother with every task, but mostly just getting in the way.

Bob and Hal walked down to survey the condition of the barn and corrals so they could decide what could be repaired and which

Richard Hooton

structures weren't worth saving. They decided there was enough salvage-able wood on some of the outbuildings to fix up the barn and main cor-ral. Whatever wasn't usable would be firewood. They could pick up new hardware for the doors and some rolls of barbed wire the next time they drove into Hereford.

"I dunno, Bob," Hal said to his older brother as they walked the field beyond the barn. "This dirt don't look like you could grow much of anything in it."

"We can start with a few head of cows," Bob responded. "If we water that pasture area real good and seed it again they'll have grass to eat. Then we can dig some manure into the ground over there behind the house and plant potatoes and beets and carrots—whatever we can grow underground to keep the sun and dust off of it until the rain comes back to Texas."

Hal looked out over the parched land and nodded.

"You always were an optimist, Bob," he complimented.

"We'll start first thing in the morning," Bob encouraged, as he looked over at his younger brother with a smile of encouragement and clapped him on the shoulder. "Let's go get some supper."

Spirits were high when the family sat down for supper. All the kids treated their first meal in their new home as a sort of picnic. Mary and Beth had done their best to make a meal out of vegetables and flour, the only food the family had brought with them. There was no meat, and no milk or eggs or cheese. Pan-fried bread, fried potatoes, and a kind of vegetable soup made from carrots and onions was their banquet.

"This isn't half bad, Mary," Bob said to his wife, as praise for their first meal at the ranch.

"You always know just what to say, Bob," Mary responded with a wry smile. "Finish your soup, Ellen," she said to her youngest daughter.

"Bob said we should plant a vegetable garden behind the house," Hal contributed to the supper table conversation. "Potatoes and turnips, and maybe some carrots and onions. Stuff like that. Stuff that'll grow underground and not be eaten by bugs and birds, or burned up by the sun."

"It'd be nice to have some fresh tomatoes," Mary said in response.

"Well, we'll see, Mary," Bob said. "We'll grow what we can." Bob decided quickly that it would be best not to call attention to the fact that due to the long drought, most of the land in the central plains that had come to be known as the Dust Bowl was nearly depleted of any of the rich nutrients required to grow crops. Some things wouldn't grow very well, or at all. At least not until the soil could be rejuvenated. Bob thought that consistent irrigation, along with mixing in manure and straw or hay, would be a good beginning. Something had to grow; he was sure of it.

The next morning, the men gave Mark and Hal, Jr. the task of tearing down one of the old outbuildings that was beyond repair, pulling out the nails and sawing it up into lengths short enough to use in the wood stove.

"You boys make sure you stack up a good supply of wood on the porch right next to the door," Bob instructed. "We don't want to hear from your mothers that they've run out of wood for the cook stove. It'll be a lot more peaceful around here if you always keep plenty of wood on that pile."

Bob and Hal set about the task of repairing the fences, first around the barn and corral, and then the larger pasture. The sooner it was done, the sooner they could go into Hereford and pick up a few cattle. Maybe even a dairy cow or two.

"We better make a list of the things we'll need from town," Hal said to his older brother. "A few rolls of barbed wire for starters. And some staples."

"I reckon we should drive into Hereford tomorrow, first thing," Bob replied. The sooner we bring some livestock out here, the sooner the gals can have fertilizer for their garden," Bob laughed, without looking up from his task of nailing a lower rail back onto a fence post.

The brothers had worked together on their father's farm near St. Joseph from the time they were old enough to use a shovel until the day they left the small farm when they were in their early twenties. They had long ago established a rhythm in the way they shared their chores and worked on projects, so they learned how to finish a task without wasting time—and without stumbling over each other. Once the Chisholm boys began a task, they rarely took a break or stopped to eat until it was completed. The corral fence was repaired by mid-afternoon and the large rectangular enclosure ready to hold its next occupants. It could easily hold forty cattle without overcrowding. The larger pasture would require barbed wire to finish the job, but Bob was determined to begin setting and replacing old or damaged fence posts around the pasture that very afternoon.

No one had taken notice of the few dark cumulus clouds that drifted in from the southwest. A stray cloud dropped its moisture in a steady downfall directly over the Chisholm Ranch. Bob and Hal stood with the boys in the open door of the barn and watched until it blew over them, leaving a fresh smell in the air and the unmistakable aroma of wet soil. Rainfall was the gift that watered the seeds lying dormant in the earth—seeds that waited for the life-giving moisture to unlock the next cycle of growth.

"There'll be more," Bob assured. "There'll be a lot more. It's time for the rain to come back to the panhandle."

"Bob, I think your optimism is what makes it happen," his little brother said, only half in jest. "You won't have it any other way."

Bob grinned. "There ain't no percentages to be gained by frettin' over it," he said. "You just gotta believe things are gonna get better."

Mark and Hal, Jr. listened respectfully as their fathers conversed, gaining hope from Mark's dad and his positive outlook. The boys viewed the move to Texas as one big adventure, and it never occurred to them to question their fathers' judgment or their reasons for moving their families to this dusty brown prairie.

Hal, Jr. felt a paw on his leg, and looked down to see that his border collie had sought temporary refuge in the barn when the rain began to come down.

"Whatcha been up to, Pete?" Hal the younger asked his dog. "Out chasin' rabbits, I'll bet. Did ya' find any?" Pete squirmed and whined a little, and offered a raised paw again to his young master.

"Did you feed that dog today?" Hal, Sr. asked his son.

"Course I did, pa," the boy answered, with a slight air of indignation. "You *know* I always feed him."

"I know you do, son," Hal acknowledged. "I just wanted to be sure you didn't forget, what with the excitement of the move and all."

"I'd never forget to feed Pete," his son insisted. "Besides, he'd remind me if I ever did."

Hal, Jr. kneeled beside his dog and wrapped an arm around its neck. Pete raised his head and panted contentedly, gratefully accepting the attention he was getting from his young master.

The occupants of the barn were unanimous in their approval of the new surroundings. The ranch provided everyone with plenty of wide open space and opportunity. Anything was possible.

"C'mon, Red, get a move on," Bob called to his freckle-faced nephew from the open window of the old Ford truck. "You comin' with us or not?" he said with a grin.

Hal, Jr. ran toward the truck, grinning back at his uncle as he hurried to climb in the back with Mark. The boy's red hair and bright red freckles had earned him the nickname when he was around six years old. He didn't mind being called Red—it made him feel special. It wasn't long before the moniker caught on with the rest of the family. All except his mother, who would always call him Harold. By the time Hal, Jr. started going to school, all his friends were calling him by his new nickname, too. It stuck.

The men had decided at the last minute to take the boys with them on the thirty-minute drive into Hereford. The two young Chisholms didn't have very many chores to do yet, at least not until some animals could be brought to the ranch, but they might prove useful in town if some bags of feed and seed needed to be loaded.

Mary hurried out to the truck from the house, waving a piece of paper at her husband to keep him from driving away until he had further instructions.

"Take this list with you, and don't forget the gingham for the curtains. Any color will have to do if they don't have blue," she said. "And don't lose that list."

Richard Hooton

Bob assured his wife that he wouldn't come back without the items on her list. It was mostly food, a few kitchen wares, and the gingham material.

"Let's get out of here before she thinks of something else," Bob said as he ground the gearshift into low gear and rolled the truck out toward the highway.

It didn't take long at the feed store to learn who had livestock for sale. It was the place every farmer or rancher in the county posted their sale notices. They bought thirty bales of hay and a few sacks of feed for a start, then filled up the truck with gas at the crossroads station before they stopped to pick up all the items on Mary's shopping list. Bob didn't feel comfortable buying gingham fabric, but shopping for his wife was one of the compromises he had to make to keep his marriage running smoothly.

With the packages and grocery sacks loaded into the cab, Bob steered the truck onto the highway and they headed back out to the ranch, snacking on chocolate bars as they drove down the narrow blacktop road toward home.

Hal looked over the list of names of the ranchers who had cattle for sale.

"We shouldn't have any trouble finding the starter stock we need," he said, as he perused the list of names and directions to the ranches where the Chisholms would negotiate for their first cattle. "We should be able to afford forty head or so, and maybe a couple of dairy cows. Hopefully, we can find a good bull at a fair price."

Bob agreed. "It won't be long before we'll be growing our own beef and putting our own fresh milk in the icebox every day," he laughed. "Once we have an icebox, that is. Mary said she wouldn't come to Texas unless I promised to get us one within a week after we got here. I expect she'll remind me if I don't find her one in the next three or four days."

Three girls came running from the house when they saw the truck roll up to the barn doors. They waited until Bob turned off the motor and pulled the hand brake before they rushed to the cab to see what treats were in the shopping bags. They helped the boys carry everything into the house as the men began to unload the bales of hay.

"You boys come right back to help with the hay," Hal said. "We still have a load of heifers to pick up today."

"We will, Pa," Red Chisholm assured his dad.

Pete followed the youngsters to the house, staying close on Red's heels. The dog attached itself to the boy when it was still a pup, selecting its own master in the way that only dogs will do with their uncanny sense of connection. Hal Chisholm told his son that the dog was his responsibility and that he must learn to care for it and help it to become a useful herding dog. He worked with Red and his dog every day to assure that they would gain the skills needed to work with livestock.

The Chisholm men held a generations-long tradition of working with herding dogs—a tradition that led all the way back to Hal's great-great-grandfather in Hannibal, Missouri before the Civil War. Over the years, their family had preserved the bloodline of the dogs that possessed superior intelligence and remarkable herding instincts, and they bred the offspring to similar dogs so that those instincts might be perpetuated.

It was a discipline that rewarded the Chisholms with generation after generation of quality herding dogs which were widely regarded as some of the finest sheep and cattle dogs anyone had ever seen.

"We better get going if we want to pick those heifers up before the sun goes down," Bob said, as they finished stacking the last hay bales in the barn.

"Let's go boys," Hal said, as the men walked toward the truck. "Bring your dog, Son," he added. "We'll probably need some help getting those heifers up a loading chute."

"Here, Pete!" Red called to his dog, as he climbed into the back of the truck with his cousin. Pete came running from the porch, where he had been waiting by the door to see if something good to eat might come out of the kitchen. Pete always welcomed the tasty handouts the girls offered him on occasion. For him, it was just a matter of being in the right place at the right time. He was an opportunist.

Pete lowered his haunches as he reached the truck and sprang effortlessly into the back with the boys, settling in for the ride next to his young master. The dog sensed that work was coming. He loved herding livestock, and could keep it up all day if he were asked. His stamina and concentration were extraordinary.

They arrived at the Swensen Cattle Ranch in less than an hour, and the boys waited in the truck while their fathers got out and spoke with the rancher for a few minutes. Red's father waved at the boys and gestured for them to go with him. Pete followed them around the side of the barn to a corral in the back and dropped to the ground next to the fence. A loading chute was built into the fence next to a back corner of the corral.

Forty white-faced heifers stared back at the approaching group of men and their dog, quickly shifting their attention to the black-and-white dog that lay motionless, waiting for a command from its master. Bob and Hal climbed up and sat on the top fence rail with Mr. Swensen, where the men got a good look at the heifers before they negotiated for a fair price.

"There may be a struggle when we try to get these heifers to go up the chute," Mr. Swensen warned. "They've never been loaded before, so they probably won't want to cooperate."

"My boy's dog can get them started for us," Hal replied confidently. "He's pretty good at moving livestock."

"You don't say," Swensen remarked. He seemed genuinely impressed. "You're sure you don't want me to saddle a horse?"

"Pete can do it, mister," the ten-year-old boy insisted, respectfully. "He can herd most anything with legs."

Swensen laughed. "Well, I'm sure you know your own dog, son. Let him give it a try, then."

Bob brought the truck around, backed it up to the loading chute and snugged it in tight so there would be no gap between the truck bed and the chute that might cause the heifers to balk. It only took a few inches of open space to cause the livestock to stop and retreat, for the same reason they wouldn't attempt to cross a cattle guard in a road. The animals feared trapping a hoof. Even the chute looked like a trap to the heifers. It would take some persuasive action on Pete's part to get them loaded.

Three men and two boys climbed into the corral and walked slowly toward the heifers to push the animals in the direction of the loading chute. Pete stayed close to Red's side, inching forward until the young cows became so agitated that it appeared as though they would bolt. Pete dropped to the ground and lay still, allowing the livestock to calm. Like all herd animals, the heifers felt the safety in numbers. They bunched up on one side of the corral, as far from the men and dog as they could get. It was time for Pete to go to work.

"Here," Red commanded. "Walk up." Pete moved in a stealthy crouch, moving himself into position to cut the first few heifers away from the rest of the small herd and push them into the corner. It was quick work for Pete, who had already learned before he was two years old how to separate a calf from its mother. He had no trouble cutting the reluctant heifers out of the herd, two or three at a time, until he had fifteen of the young white-faced heifers pushed into the corner of the corral next to the loading chute. He allowed the others to slip by him and escape to the other side of the corral, safely away from the intimidating dog.

"Walk up," he commanded again, and Pete gently closed the distance between himself and the livestock, focusing his attention on the heifers nearest to the loading chute ramp. The young cows backed away and made an attempt to escape from the corner, turning first in one direction and then the other, but always finding their escape route blocked by the incredibly fast dog. After two or three unsuccessful tries to get past the dog, the first two heifers turned and started up the ramp. The men moved in quickly to turn the rest of the heifers toward the chute and urge them to follow.

"That'll do, Pete," Red called. Pete instantly backed off and returned to his young master's side. "Good boy, Pete."

Walking abreast, the men and boys pressured the young heifers to enter the chute and climb up into the truck. If a heifer failed to cooperate, and attempted to avoid the opening to the chute, Pete was there immediately to turn it back.

Fifteen heifers were loaded into the truck in less than ten minutes, and the rear panel was locked into place. Swensen was truly impressed.

"Do you want to sell that dog, son?" Swensen asked.

Red looked up at his father, who was standing next to him with a hand on his shoulder to show his approval for the job well done. Red smiled up at his dad.

"No sir," he said politely. "We hardly ever sell one of our dogs once they've been trained to work."

"Sure could use a dog like that," Swensen said. "Well, if you ever change your mind, you know where to find me."

"Yes sir," the boy answered, looking up once more to see the look of pride on his father's face.

Bob Chisholm paid Mr. Swensen, and they all climbed into the old Ford truck for the drive home.

Red and his cousin Mark were squeezed into the middle of the cab between their dads. Pete sat on the floorboard with his muzzle pushed up alongside Red's leg and howled as his noisy human companions sang *"Oh, Susanna"* off key for the first few miles of the drive back to the Chisholm Ranch.

"I think we've got a good start, Hal," Bob said to his little brother. "We can come back for fifteen more in the morning, and maybe pick up a few from the Sadler Ranch later in the week. We'll be in business before you know it."

Bob was already thinking about putting some tomato plants in the ground for Mary. Bob was a planner. If Mary wasn't happy, nobody was happy. Planting a good garden was not just a considerate thing to do for his wife—it was prudent, and a little bit selfish. It meant better meals, even when tomatoes were out of season.

"I think we can turn one of those old bunk houses into a chicken coop," Hal said.

Bob took his eyes off the road for a brief moment to look at his brother.

"Now you're thinkin', little brother," Bob praised. "Now you're thinkin'. We'll turn that ol' place into a ranch yet, won't we, boys?"

Mark and Red grinned at each other. They liked helping their dads with the ranch work, and they liked being part of the conversations that decided their future. It made them feel grown up and important. Growing up generally happened faster for rural kids than it did for children in the city. Out of necessity, children who grew up on a ranch learned early in life about work and responsibility. It became a natural part of their daily lives.

Bob slowed the truck as he drove past the house where Mary and Beth and the girls were gathering outside the kitchen door to see the new arrivals. He rolled the window down and casually hung an elbow out as he drove by the house toward the barn and corral.

"Hello, Mary," he greeted his wife. "I brought you some cows."

Mary Chisholm stood on the porch, hands on her hips, and shook her head in mock disapproval as her good-humored husband rolled by with the first of their herd. Her face lit up with a warm smile, never taking her eyes off him as he leaned out of the truck window and looked back at her with a big ape grin on his face.

Mark and Red started out their Saturday by collecting more firewood for the wood pile. It was a weekend, but they weren't going anywhere, and their dads didn't want them to get bored, so they were assigned a chore that would keep them occupied for most of the day. The boys decided it would be much simpler to get the wood all in one place, rather than scavenging around the barn and corrals for old boards, wooden barrels and fence posts.

It was agreed. They would tear down one of the old bunk houses—the one farthest from the house, just in case their folks decided to convert one closer to the house into another chicken coop. It would be easy to cut it into small pieces and wheelbarrow them to the house.

The boys went to the barn and rummaged through the tool box for a hammer, saw and crowbar. Red opted for a heavy sledgehammer he spied leaning against the partition wall of a horse stall. Their dads used it to pound fence posts, but the boys thought it would work nicely to speed the demolition process. They were in business.

The wood shingles came off the roof first—they were ideal for kindling. Mark pulled the cross slats off the rafters with the crowbar, and Red whacked at the rafters with the sledgehammer until the nails loosened and the old lumber separated from the rest of the structure and dropped to the floor.

It was going exactly according to plan. In another hour or so they would have the rest of the small building knocked to the ground, and they could begin sawing and stacking the first load from their new cache of firewood into the wheelbarrow.

Mark pried the old board siding off with the crowbar and threw it into a pile, while Red wielded his heavy sledgehammer and assaulted one of the bunks until it surrendered its lumber for the pile. The door frame and casing also appeared to be an easy source of good firewood, so Red lifted the giant hammer over his shoulder and took a mighty swing. The door frame cracked and the walls groaned as they listed to one side, then collapsed in a dusty heap on top of the young, red-haired demolition expert.

Mark stood frozen in place, unable to believe his eyes. He dropped the crowbar to the ground and took a step forward.

"Red! Red, are you all right?" he called. He heard coughing—then a couple of cuss words.

"Go get my dad. I can't move."

"Are you hurt?" Mark asked, walking around the collapsed structure to see if he could find an opening to the inside.

"I can't move," Red repeated. "Get my dad."

"We're gonna get in trouble," Mark warned. "Are you sure you can't get out?"

"Just get my dad, will you?"

Hal dropped the oil filter he was changing and climbed out from under the old truck when he heard his nephew running and frantically calling his name.

"Uncle Hal!" Mark screamed at the top of his lungs. "Red's trapped under a bunkhouse."

"Uncle Hal," he called again.

"Where is he? Show me," Hal demanded, taking his nephew by the shoulders and turning him around to face the boy back in the same direction he had just come from. Mark took off at a dead run, leading his uncle out past the barn to what was left of the farthest bunkhouse.

"Red," Mark yelled as he neared the demolished structure. "Red, your dad's coming."

Hal raced after his nephew and reached the collapsed structure with heart pounding. He began looking for a way inside, then spotted the back half of his son's dog sticking out through what was left of a doorway. Pete's tail was wagging—it was a very good sign. Hal took a deep breath, and let out a sigh of relief.

"Son, are you all right?" he asked, as he tried to see past Pete into the dusty dark interior of the structure. "Are you hurt?"

"No, dad. I just can't move," Red replied, rather calmly, given his situation. "Can you get me out of here?"

Hal grasped Pete by his haunches, gripped a handful of fur and hip in each hand, and pulled the dog back. "Come on Pete, get out of there." Pete struggled to go back inside, but Hal pulled him back again. "Come on Pete, let me in there."

Hal lay down and pushed his head into the dark, dusty confines of the demolished bunkhouse and was barely able to make out the shape of his son's body under the wreckage. He squinted, allowing his eyes to adjust to the dim light, then relaxed a little as he saw that the boy was trapped under a lower bunk. It kept the wall from falling in on top of him.

"Hang on, Son," Hal comforted. "I'll get you out of there." He looked around for something he could use to lift the weight of the wall off the bunk and saw the crowbar lying on the ground where Mark had dropped it. Suddenly, there was a change of plans. Hal began prying the siding off the exterior wall that had collapsed directly over the bunk, splintering the old wood as he broke the siding loose. Two boards came loose, then three, as the crowbar lifted the siding away from the framing and exposed what was beneath it. He saw his son's denim pant leg, and reached through the opening in the wall to give the boy a reassuring pat.

"I'll have you out of there in a minute, son."

"Hurry, dad." Red was less frightened once his father arrived, but he was beginning to feel a little claustrophobic and didn't want to spend any more time under the wood pile.

"Let's not tell your mother about this, all right?" Hal was certain that Beth would not be pleased to hear the details of her son's workday, and it would probably be best to keep the day's adventure a secret.

"The boys collected a sizeable pile of firewood today," Hal told the family at the supper table. "Should be enough to last a month."

"We still have to cut some of it up," Mark added. "And bring it to the house."

Red chewed on his food and looked at Mark, then at his dad, as they outlined the progress they made gathering firewood that day. He deliberately kept his mouth full of food so that he wouldn't have to talk.

Summer arrived with sweltering heat and very little rainfall. Bob and Hal rigged a series of storage tanks along the upper fence line of their pasture so they could let the windmill pump continuously to fill the tanks with water. They rotated irrigation of the fenced pastures for three consecutive days and gave the grass a chance to grow, then watered the adjacent pasture for three days. They were able to move the cattle into a green pasture every three or four days, and were always able to provide grazing for the livestock. It wasn't rain, but it was the next best thing.

Their ingenuity not only kept them in business, it kept them alive. They always had chicken and eggs to eat, thanks to Hal and his cleverly converted bunk house chicken coop; and Bob managed to maintain a garden that would provide root vegetables and squash from June to October. They even grew a few garden plants that Bob didn't expect would survive the dusty, arid heat.

For the most part, the men enjoyed working the ranch and repairing the old buildings. It kept them busy and helped pass the time when there wasn't much else to do. While replacing the rusty, broken hinges on the barn door, they laid plans to clear and till a hundred acre field in the spring. They would plant it with alfalfa and trust there would be a good rainfall to help it along.

"Hal, whatta ya say we pick up some paint next time we're in town so we can watch while the boys paint the house and barn?" Bob asked his younger brother. "I think they need something productive to do."

Hal chuckled. "I think we better get four brushes if we want to see the job finished before Christmas," Hal replied.

"I suppose you're right," Bob mused. "I just thought it would be a good idea to get it done before Mary pointed out the cracked and peeled paint on the house."

Bob asked for a quick vote while all four of the Chisholm boys unloaded the paint from the truck into the barn. He entertained himself by testing the others to see who had any good sense.

"So, where do you think we should start first—the house or the barn?" Bob asked. "Red, how do you vote?"

Red grinned sheepishly at his uncle's query. "I vote we paint the house, or Aunt Mary will be sore at all of us."

"Bob, I want supper tonight," Hal said. "So I'm takin' my bucket and brush to the house first, no matter how the rest of you vote."

"I think we should paint the barn first," Mark said with a smirk. "It'll make the cows happy." Mark and Red giggled and elbowed each other.

"Smart-aleck kid," Bob said, pulling his son's hat off and swatting him on the back of the head with it. "You paint this barn first, and you'll probably get to sleep in it."

The four would-be Rembrandts all got busy scraping and painting, while little Cassie sat on a chopping block and watched them work. Pete lay patiently at the girl's side and watched the men for awhile, then lost interest in the project and flopped onto his side to take a nap.

"The King of England don't eat better than this, does he dad?" Mark said to his father at the supper table. He took a drumstick off the serving plate, passed the plate down the table, then dished up a hearty helping of mashed potatoes.

"No, he surely doesn't son," Bob said, injecting certainty into his tone as he agreed. "He *surely* doesn't."

"This is a real nice meal, ladies," Hal said to Beth and Mary. "You girls, too. Thank you," he said, nodding toward his nieces. Beth smiled warmly at her husband.

"That's the truth, Mary," Bob said to his wife. "This chicken is delicious."

"That was a good idea you had to paint the house first, son," Hal said with a smile.

"Why? Were you planning to paint something else first?" Mary asked, looking across the table at her husband.

"Nope," Bob answered, looking into his pile of mashed potatoes as he forked a mouthful. "Pass that plate of sliced tomatoes down here, will you, Red?"

The heifers put on a lot of weight grazing on green grass through the summer, and the addition of a proven Hereford bull and thirty older breeding cows to their herd meant they were on their way to becoming genuine cattle ranchers.

In October, they began buying hay to keep their herd fed through the winter, and their savings account was dwindling. If their luck held out, they might make it through the winter and sell off some of their fattened livestock in the spring. With another year or so to build their herd, they could begin selling some steers and make enough to keep the ranch going until times got better.

"A letter came from your brother today," Mary said to Bob and Hal at the supper table. "He said they're thinking about coming for a visit in the late spring. He said they have a little female border collie about eight months old that's showing some promise and good instincts. They'll bring her along, just in case you want her."

Christmas Eve arrived with a coating of hoarfrost on the ground—a sure sign of moisture in the air. The men got the feeding and other chores out the way early in the morning with the help of their boys.

"Why don't we drive out to that dry creek bed where it's thick with sage and wheat grass?" Bob suggested. "Let's see if we can't scare us up a turkey."

"Yeah," the boys chimed in enthusiastically. "Let's have a turkey for dinner tomorrow, dad," Mark said.

"Yeah," Red seconded his cousin's motion. He cupped his gloved hands around his mouth and exhaled deeply, watching his breath as it disappeared in the cold winter air.

"Let's see if Pete can help us find a bird, shall we, Red?" Hal said to his son. "He's not a hunting dog, but he should be able to sniff them out and then go around to drive them toward us. It's worth a try."

"Mark, go and fetch that four-ten shotgun from under my bed and let's go find us a turkey," Bob said. "There's shells in the glove box, I think."

Bob parked the truck a quarter of a mile from their intended hunting grounds, and the four hunters walked in silence to the spot where the dry creek bed was thick with brush and dry grass along the banks. It provided good cover for the birds, and seemed a likely place for turkeys to gather and feed.

"You boys go stand in the creek bed and block their easy way out," Hal said. "Red, why don't you go ahead and send Pete around to the other side, and we'll see if our dinner is in this brush."

Bob and Hal spread out about ten yards apart and walked along the thicket, keeping back a fair distance from the brush to give the big birds room to come out into the open.

"I don't think you're gonna get more than one shot, Bob," Hal advised, in a loud whisper. "If Pete and the boys flush birds out of the brush, there probably won't be any more behind them. It's not a very big thicket."

"I think you're right, Hal," Bob agreed. "I'll take careful aim. But if one flies right at you, just grab it and hold it down so I can shoot it."

Hal grinned, and chuckled quietly. His big brother was a clown.

Bob sobered and pushed a shotgun shell into the chamber, snapping the barrel closed as he raised it into the air.

"Can you see those boys?" Bob asked.

"I can hear them whispering," Hal answered.

"Pete, go around," Red commanded in a voice just above a whisper.

The dog started to go, and then hesitated, looking back to his young master for assurance and more direction. There was no livestock here, and Pete wasn't sure what he was being asked to do.

"Go, Pete," Red commanded, more emphatically, and the dog circled around behind the thicket on the opposite stream bank from where the men stood waiting for signs of a turkey. Pete trusted his master, and he knew there must be something that needed fetching on the other side of the brush or he wouldn't have been sent.

The dog's heightened sense of smell detected something in the brush, and its keen hearing tipped it off to the presence of something moving away from the spot where it lay crouched and listening. Instantly, Pete followed his senses into the thicket and crept quietly toward the sounds of frightened birds. Step by silent step, he inched ahead through the thicket, pausing to listen for the rustling sounds that gave away the birds' location. A few more cautious steps and Pete emerged into the open area of the creek bed, where the boys could see him. The sounds in the brush kept Pete focused.

Mark and Red saw the turkeys cross the creek bed up wind of where they stood silent and unmoving. Moments later, Pete emerged from the thicket and stepped out onto the dry silt. The dog paused, sensing his master's presence, but without turning his head to look in Red's direction. His strong eye was locked on the brush ahead of him.

"Walk up," Red called in a raised whisper. "Walk up, Pete."

The dog crouched lower to the ground and slipped quietly into the thicket.

"Something's coming," Hal rasped.

"I've got it," Bob responded, lowering the shotgun with his thumb on the hammer.

The men watched carefully, scanning back and forth along the length of the thicket for any signs of movement.

It seemed like a long wait. The two men stood still, listening for any tell-tale sounds of movement in the brush. Suddenly, and without warning, three turkeys burst out of the brush and took flight. The instant they saw the men, their flight direction changed, but they were already within ten yards of the shotgun barrel. In one fluid movement Bob cocked the hammer and took aim, paused for less than a second, then discharged his casing full of steel pellets at the big bird.

The shot struck a wing and brought the bird down, but it tried to fly away again in a desperate bid for survival. Hal raced toward the bird and caught it by the neck before it could make good on its attempt to lift off the ground. The Chisholms had their Christmas turkey.

"C'mon out boys, we got one," Bob called out to their sons. Mark and Red came running around the end of the thick brush and up from the creek bed where they had stood frozen in place, awaiting the outcome of the hunt.

"Where's Pete?" Red asked, looking around for his dog. Everyone looked toward the brush and began whistling and calling for Red's dog.

"Here, Pete. C'mon boy." Red called and whistled as he ran toward the thicket.

"Here, boy," he called quietly as he approached the edge of the brush. A black-and-white head lifted cautiously off the ground and Pete's dark brown eyes fastened on his young master as the boy approached.

"Come on, boy," Red soothed, as he spotted Pete lying in the thicket, partly camouflaged by the brush. "It's all right."

Pete got to his feet and followed Red back to where the others were gathered to admire their big turkey.

"He was just scared, that's all," Red explained in a loud voice as he and his dog hurried back toward the rest of the hunting party. "He doesn't like gunshot sounds."

"We'll make sure Pete gets plenty of turkey meat for his trouble, Red," his Uncle Bob promised. "He brought that bird straight to us, so he can help us eat it. Besides, it's a *big* one."

"Must be twenty-five pounds or more," Hal guessed.

"Yep," Bob agreed. "We're gonna have us the biggest turkey dinner in Deaf Smith County."

Five-year-old Cassie squealed with delight when she spied the

Raggedy Ann doll under the decorated Redberry Juniper Christmas tree. It was the only thing she asked her mother to get her for Christmas. Cassie clutched the soft, floppy doll to her chest with both hands for more than an hour, and refused to part with it until her mother insisted she put it down long enough to eat a little breakfast.

It wasn't a year for a lot of presents, but everyone got something they wanted, or at least something that was useful. The men and boys all got gloves and overalls, and the two boys got new mackinaws to replace the worn-out winter coats they had outgrown. The women and girls were pampered with a few fanciful gifts, in addition to the fabric and dress patterns that Mary and Beth were always grateful to receive.

Bob said grace at the family table that afternoon. He was mindful of the times they were living in, and gave thanks for the abundance they enjoyed while so many others had nothing.

"Merry Christmas, everyone," Bob said cheerfully, after everyone around the table had a chance to say amen."

"Merry Christmas," everyone returned, with special enthusiasm coming from the youngsters.

Bob and Hal stood on the porch after dinner and talked as a light, steady rain came down. Pete lay stretched out on his side next to the pile of firewood, his belly full of turkey. Hal loved the rain and the smell of wet soil. It was a precursor to green grass and abundant crops.

"I hope this becomes a regular event between now and springtime," Hal commented on the welcome rainfall.

"We'll be all right, Hal," his older brother assured.

"Merry Christmas, Bob", Hal said, basking in the light of his brother's optimism.

"Merry Christmas, Hal."

CHAPTER SEVEN

WOOLGATHERING

Heber Valley, Utah—1956

"Mom, I'm leaving now", Sarah called up the stairs from the back hallway next to the kitchen pantry. The screen door banged as she hurried out through the back porch of the old two-story farmhouse. She munched on a day-old cinnamon roll as she crossed the gravel drive to her dad's old Chevy pickup truck.

"Rex, Maggie! C'mon dogs. Hurry, load up!" Two sleek, black and white border collies raced from the barn and jumped into the back of the pickup, ready for a ride to anywhere. Sarah fired up the engine and revved the motor a couple of times before slipping it into gear and pulling out onto the highway toward Heber City. Her destination was the local feed store, a frequent stop-off and gossip corner for farmers and ranchers in the valley.

Sarah Bradley Thompson worked her family farm like a man. She got up in the morning with the chickens and went to bed long after the night owls had begun to hunt for mice in the fields behind the barn. She chopped firewood and she drove tractors. She planted in the spring, irrigated in the summer, and harvested in the fall. She milked cows and she sheared sheep; and every year, when the annual ram sale was held at the fairgrounds in Salt Lake City, it was Sarah who selected the best Columbia rams and loaded them into the stock truck for the drive down Parley's Canyon into Salt Lake Valley.

She held the reputation of being one of the best sheep ranchers in the Intermountain West, and her negotiation skills were second to none. The fine breeding stock from the Thompson Farm always fetched top dollar at the sales. It was the one thing that helped to keep the farm operating in the black year after year.

The year appeared to have a prosperous beginning. The ewes had wintered well and the spring lamb crop was good. There were a couple of stillborns, but those were more than offset by a fair number of twin births. The lambs were all doing well, getting fatter every day on mothers' milk and pasture grass. It seemed as though it would be a good year for the livestock.

Sarah had inherited her job by default when her older brother was killed in the days that followed the D-Day invasion in Normandy during World War II. Like many young men of his time, Dan Thompson heeded the call to enlist in the army a few months after the attack on Pearl Harbor, and a couple of years later he scrambled ashore with his comrades-in-arms on the Normandy coast at a place called Omaha Beach. Most of his platoon made it up over the sea cliffs, only to get tangled in the thick hedge rows that lined the fields and irrigation ditches around the farms and countryside. He was nineteen when a bullet from a German infantryman's rifle ended his life. It was a difficult time for everyone, but Sarah's father took it especially hard. He had a bad stroke a few weeks after Dan was killed, and six months later he had another, even more severe than the first. He didn't make it through the winter. Sarah believed he just gave up living. She and her mother were left alone to manage the farm.

Sarah had come from a very long line of farmers and ranchers, a line that extended all the way back to her sheep farmer ancestors in England and Wales more than a hundred years earlier. Her great, great grandmother, Sarah Bradley, had come across the Atlantic when she was eight years old and traveled by wagon train from Iowa to Utah. Sarah had farming and ranching in her blood, and would never be happy doing anything else.

The pickup truck pulled into the gravel parking area next to the loading platform at the feed store, with its familiar red and white checkerboard Purina logo. Sarah pulled the hand brake and jumped out of the truck to mount the stairs, as two black and white dogs hung halfway out of the back of her truck, waiting for their invitation to join their owner.

"Wait there, dogs," Sarah called back to them over her shoulder. "I'll be back." Her dogs were some of the best trained sheepdogs in northern Utah. They were well-trained and very biddable. Always ready to work and eager to please, they did just as Sarah asked. Her livelihood depended on it. She needed them to help her move the livestock from pasture to pen and back again almost every day, and getting those dumb woolies up a loading chute into a stock truck was near impossible without the help of her dogs.

"Mornin', Hank," Sarah greeted the feed store owner at the counter. "Got any feed without mice or weevil in it today?"

Hank Sorenson returned a friendly grin. "Now, Sarah, you know those mice come free with the hay," he responded good-naturedly. "I never charge extra for them."

"I know," Sarah responded in an understanding tone, as though they were having a serious conversation. "And don't think I don't appreciate it. Just wish my horses liked meat, that's all."

"Listen, can you get this order together for me while I take my dogs out to lunch?" Sarah asked, handing Hank a slip of paper with her list of dog food, oats, and chicken feed.

Hank nodded and took the list. "Most people in town would love to be one of your dogs," he said. "They eat real good."

Sarah just smiled and ambled out the door and down the street toward the Rocking Horse Café. She loved the big, juicy burgers and homemade fries at the Rocking Horse. So did Rex and Maggie. "C'mon dogs, let's go have a treat," Sarah called toward the pickup. The two border collies vaulted out of the truck bed and raced to catch up. Hank was right. Nobody else in Wasatch County ever bought hamburgers for their dogs—nobody.

Sarah picked up the café copy of the Salt Lake paper and slid into a booth by the front window so she could keep an eye on her dogs while they kept an eye on her. She thumbed through the local news and turned to the classifieds to see what farm equipment and livestock was for sale. A small announcement caught her attention.

Stockdog Competition—4th of July Weekend
Competitors contact Harold or Emily Watson
Watson Ranch, Ogden, Utah
Sheep and Cattle
Fun, Food and Prizes—Bring the Family

Sarah read the announcement a couple of times, thinking it might be interesting to test Rex and Maggie against other dogs from around northern Utah. They had never competed before, so she wasn't exactly sure what to do to get them ready, but it was still more that a month before the event.

"Oh, well, it might be fun," she mused. She tore the ad out of the paper and stuffed it down into her shirt pocket.

Rex and Maggie sat next to the newspaper rack by the front door and watched through the window, drooling as Sarah hurried through her early lunch, then collected the grease-spotted paper bag from the waitress and headed for the door. Her dogs were at the door to greet her, tongues dripping saliva.

"What's this, hungry dogs?" Sarah teased, kneeling down on the sidewalk to open the paper bag. It was all the two dogs could do to contain themselves, squirming for position in front of Sarah, eyes and noses fixed on the bag.

"Easy now, don't gulp your food," Sarah cautioned as Rex and Maggie both gulped their food. She did her best to break it into smaller bites for them to prevent them from choking. Their rule was: Chew dry dog food, swallow burgers whole.

Sarah helped Hank load up her order of feed and asked her dogs to get into the pickup for the drive back to the farm. During the drive home, she thought about the upcoming sheepdog competition in Davis County. It was only a two hour drive to Ogden. Maybe her mom would like to get out for a day and try to enjoy herself doing something other than exchanging gossip at a quilting bee.

A few dark clouds blew over the Wasatch ridge from the west and began to drop rain over the Heber Valley. Sarah pulled the pickup over to the side of the road before it started to pour, opened the passenger door and whistled for Rex and Maggie to get into the cab with her. The dogs happily complied, although they didn't mind the rain. They worked in rain and wind and snow and freezing temperatures all the time, but Sarah wanted them to be inside with her anyway, to keep her company for the rest of the drive home. Sometimes she just liked to talk to them. Other than the occasional conversations she had with her dogs, Sarah was completely sane.

Sarah told her dogs about the competition coming up on the Fourth of July and explained to them how they would have to work hard to prepare for the trials and beat out the other dogs for the best prizes, whatever they might be.

"You'll have to concentrate, Maggie, and don't let those big sheep bully you. Rexie, don't you get crazy on me and try to grip one of those woolies, or we'll probably have to buy it." Rex watched out the passenger window, counting the cows in the pastures along the way, while Maggie kept a close eye on the windshield wipers. Both dogs waited for Sarah to say something they actually understood.

The old Chevy pickup pulled up to the barn and Sarah jumped out to push open the big rolling door so that she could back the truck inside. She left the feed in the truck and walked across the barnyard toward the back door of the house, shooing a rooster and a few chickens out of her path along the way. Maggie got the idea and helped disperse them. Rex ignored the birds, mostly. They couldn't be herded very well and they weren't big enough to present a real challenge.

Sarah's mom was sitting at the kitchen table, listening to the news and weather on the radio and watching her rhubarb pie cool. Fresh baked bread was on the counter, and the aroma of lamb stew drifted across the kitchen from a big kettle simmering on the stove. Sarah's mom lived to cook. Cook and sew and clean house. Her mom had always been domestic that way, and Sarah was grateful.

"Radio says it's going to rain today," Martha Thompson said.

"It's raining now, Mom," Sarah reported.

"Oh, you know what I mean—all day," her mother said, as she

slapped at her daughter with a dish towel. "Do you want some pie?"

"No thanks, mom," Sarah declined. "I grabbed one of your rolls this morning before I left to go into town."

"That won't keep you until supper."

"I'm okay, Mom—really." It would hurt her mother's feelings to know that her daughter would prefer to grab a greasy burger at the cafe rather than come home for a proper meal.

Sarah pulled the scrap of newspaper out of her shirt pocket and pushed it across to table to her mother.

"There's a sheepdog trial near Ogden over the Fourth of July weekend, Mom. I thought we could drive up, just to get away for the day and have some fun. Maybe take Rex and Maggie to see how they do."

Her mother read the ad, then looked at her daughter, and raised her eyebrows.

"Sure. It sounds like it would be a nice time," her mom said. She got up from the table and pushed a thumbtack through the newspaper announcement, securing it to the small corkboard on the wall next to the Frigidaire. It was where she kept all her birthday, wedding and baby shower announcements, along with photos, greeting cards, doctor appointments and other reminders.

Sarah watched her mother secure the newspaper ad to the wall with a thumbtack. She didn't understand why her stay-at-home mom was suddenly so agreeable to a trip out of town. Her mom rarely traveled further than the church, the market, or the grange hall, where she and her friends would meet to construct a patchwork quilt and gossip about people they didn't know very well.

Sarah decided that if it was going to be so easy, she wouldn't press her luck. She didn't ask any questions. The last time she asked her mom to go with her to the National Ram Sale in Salt Lake, her mother declined with a brief explanation.

"I just don't know any of the people there anymore, not since your father passed away. Besides, you don't need me tagging along. I wouldn't be any help at the sale, and you might meet a nice young man at the fairgrounds," Sarah's mom spoke wishfully.

"I meet sheep at the fairgrounds, Mom."

Sarah lifted her oilskin mackinaw off the hook next to the back door and sat down in a chair on the sun porch to pull her rubber boots on. She stomped a woolen-socked heel down snugly into her boot and bounced down the stairs and out into the rain.

"C'mon dogs, let's go find sheep." All she really had to say was "C'mon." Even the smartest dogs have a fairly limited vocabulary, but Rex and Maggie understood some words perfectly, and they knew their boss lady was dressed for herding in the rain. The three happy companions crossed through the gate into the lower pasture and began their rainy day walk up the slopes toward the higher pastures to look for sheep.

Rex was a large collie with strong instincts and a powerful eye. His presence made the grass eaters feel like they were being stared down by a predator, but he kept a comfortable distance from the sheep so they wouldn't panic and bolt. Livestock always seemed quite willing to move in a direction away from him and his wolf-eyes, and he was rarely challenged. Rex never lost a stand-off with a sheep.

Maggie, on the other hand, possessed speed and finesse. She was quick as a cat, but was prepared to wait patiently while the woolies made up their minds to move in the direction she wanted them to go. Whenever the sheep moved the wrong way, Maggie was there to meet them and turn them around. She would sometimes stare at sheep in the pasture for hours, watching them graze and drift, thinking through her game plan for her next confrontation.

The soggy trio reached the top of the hill just in time to see about sixty ewes disappear into the trees. Another smaller flock was still grazing on the grassy slopes of the upper pasture. Sarah sent Rex into the trees to fetch the wandering sheep.

"Rex, go!" He raced up the slope in a wide arc, then slowed just before crossing into the dense woods, listening for the sounds of the flock as he moved higher to get above and behind the sheep. Sarah whistled, signaling the dog to keep moving and go deeper into the trees. She stopped abruptly and waited. Both the livestock and her dog were out of sight. It was time to trust Rex's instincts and experience. Sarah couldn't help him now. It was best to leave him to his job.

Maggie waited by Sarah's side, quivering with anticipation, softly whining for permission to go to work. Sarah turned her attention toward the remaining livestock in the upper pasture. It was beginning to rain hard, and she needed to move the livestock down into the small pasture next to the barn, away from the high ground and the trees. She had worked hard to build her herd, and she didn't want to lose them to coyotes or mountain lions or lightning strikes.

The flock was not more than a hundred yards up the hill, but it was beginning to drift higher in the direction of the trees.

"Maggie, away." Sarah sent the clever little female dog off to the right in a wide bend, and watched as Maggie quickly covered the distance around and behind the sheep, rapidly moving in a steady, half-crouching posture to turn the less-than-brilliant animals around and start them back down the hill. A few tried to change direction, but Maggie quickly moved to block their escape and helped them to change their minds. The livestock moved reluctantly at first, stiff-legged and stubborn, not trusting the dog's intentions. After a few moments, they gave in to Maggie's more powerful will and allowed the dog to drive them down the slope toward the safety of the fenced pasture next to the barn, where a number of small pole barns with shed roofs offered shelter for any that were smart enough to get out of the rain.

A bright flash and a loud clap of thunder from the lightning strike lit up a large formation of granite boulders high up on the mountainside. Sarah began to worry that the livestock Rex was sent to round up would panic in the storm and scatter deeper into the trees. She scanned the tree line, her eyes searching back and forth in the general area where the sheep had vanished, hoping to catch a glimpse of Rex or any of the sheep he was sent to fetch. She turned and followed Maggie and her flock of thirty or so down the slope to the lower pasture. She had to see them safely put away before the storm got any worse.

Maggie already had the sheep moving on a straight course toward the open gate to the fenced lower pasture. Sarah followed them down the slope to close the gate and gather some hay from the barn to scatter under the shed-roofed pole barns, hoping to entice the woolly numbskulls to get in out of the rain. Maggie kept the sheep cloistered under the pole barns until Sarah could bring an armload of hay and scatter a few small piles under the dry enclosure.

Every minute or so Sarah would turn her gaze up the hill in the direction of the trees, hoping to catch a glimpse of Rex and the remainder of the herd. Another lightning flash and another loud thunderclap left Sarah feeling uneasy. Her best herding dog shouldn't have so much trouble bringing sheep out of the trees, unless they were too panicked to cross out of the trees and into the clearing.

Sarah thought about saddling a horse and starting up the hill with Maggie, but a horse wouldn't be much help to Rex in the trees, and especially not in a storm. It was useless to think of driving the truck up the hill. The ground was saturated with water, and so rain-soaked that the truck would be mired in the mud before it traveled a hundred feet up the hill. They would just have to watch and wait.

Sarah brought another dry bale of hay out of the barn in a wheelbarrow and next to the pen. The sheep already had enough hay for awhile, so Sarah sat down on the bale of hay and coaxed Maggie up to sit next to her. Sarah put her arm around the border collie for comfort.

"What do you think, girl? Is he coming?" Maggie whined and leaned forward a little, never taking her eyes off the hillside. It was impossible to make out any shapes in the darkness, but Maggie seemed to be fixed on something high on the hillside.

A loud crack accompanied the next bright flash of lightning, so close that it lit up the hillside momentarily. Sarah thought she saw white shapes on the upper slope near the tree line. Maggie must have seen them, too. She let out an excited yip and jumped down from the hay bale. Sarah called her back before the dog could reach the pasture gate.

"Maggie, here! Just wait."

The last thing Rex needed was any help or interference. If he had found all the livestock and was bringing them down the hill, it would be no problem for him to control a small band of sixty sheep. He could keep them moving in the right direction, and they would stay together without much encouragement. That's what sheep did.

Maggie was staring out into the darkness beyond the fence, pacing and whining, then rushing a few steps toward the fence and back to Sarah again, being careful not to disobey her boss lady's command to stay close by her. Sarah knew that Rex had to be somewhere nearby, and that Maggie's keen senses were aimed in his direction. She waited and listened. Sometimes, being a good handler simply meant having patience and trust in the dog's skill and instincts. Human instincts were also an important part of the partnership between handler and dog, and those instincts told her it wasn't the time to overreact and interfere.

Under the pole barn, a few sheep raised their heads and looked out into the darkness beyond the fence. Maggie was on her feet, whining.

"Good boy," Sarah whispered, sensing that Rex was close by. She pulled the hood of her mackinaw up over her head and walked out into the rain. She reached the pasture gate just as the first few rain-soaked sheep reached the fence line and began to bunch up against the gate. Sarah couldn't see through the rain more than a few feet beyond the gate, but she knew her wolf-eyed dog was just behind them, keeping the livestock bunched together. She unlatched the gate and swung it inward to allow her soggy flock inside. They quickly crowded through the open gate and hurried over to join the others by the small piles of hay.

"Hi, Rexie. Where ya been?" Sarah's tone was relaxed and confident and it conveyed a sense of ease and well-being to her dogs. She knew Rex could keep his head about him in a storm, and never give up or lose his focus. He was bred for the task, and he was always up to it.

"Nothing wrong here, huh Maggie? It's all in a day's work." Both dogs followed Sarah through the barn and across the open ground to the back door of the house. She rewarded them with a little leftover pot roast mixed into their dry dog food and let them settle in on the porch to keep out of the rain.

"I was beginning to worry about you, Sarah. Did you get all the sheep down the hill?" Sarah's mother asked. "Terrible storm," she added. No farmer or rancher can resist making a comment about the weather. She washed her hands at the kitchen sink and dried them on a dish towel as she peered out the window into the rainy night.

"Everything's fine, Mom. Rex brought the stock down by himself.

Maggie and I barely got wet. What's for dinner?"

Sarah usually ate her meals without much talking, always in a hurry to move onto her next chore. It wasn't so much that she minded a little pleasant dialogue over dinner, but it always seemed that her mother made enough dinner table conversation for both of them. All she had to do was listen and nod occasionally.

"It will be real nice to see Emily and Harold again."

Sarah stopped chewing her meatloaf and looked up at her mother. "Who?"

"The Watsons, dear," her mother explained. Sarah just looked at her. "Where we're going for your dog competition on the Fourth of July, don't you remember? I haven't seen them since just after high school. We went to school together, you know."

"So that's why you were so agreeable to coming with me. And I thought you wanted to watch Rex and Maggie when they compete with the other dogs."

"I do, but it will give me a chance to catch up on old times with some high school chums, too."

"Gossip, you mean," Sarah grinned.

Sarah had already selected twenty-five young rams to take to the Salt Lake Fairgrounds for the National Ram Sale late in the summer. Her Columbia rams were always in demand at the annual sale. She normally bought five or six new rams at the sale every year, too. Introducing fresh blood into her herd helped to keep the gene pool from getting shallow.

Once the first cutting of alfalfa had been baled and put up for the coming winter, Sarah had more time to work her dogs. The Fourth of July dog trials in Ogden were only a couple of weeks away, and it was important to work Rex and Maggie every day to keep their skills tuned up for the task ahead. Sarah had never competed in any organized trial before, but she had a lot of practical experience. More importantly, she had confidence in her dogs.

She worked both dogs every day after she took care of her morning chores. It seemed as though sheep always had to be moved somewhere, or back again, so there was plenty for them to do.

Twice a week, Sarah would take Rex and Maggie into town for a juicy burger at the Rocking Horse Cafe. The dogs always sensed when she was going into town, and didn't wait for an invitation. They were already in the back of the pickup before she could open the cab door and climb inside. It was a tradition the dogs had come to expect.

She decided to make the trip into town a regular reward for a job well done with the sheep. She worked the dogs alternately for fifteen minutes each until she was certain that their focus was unwavering and their instincts were becoming more fine-tuned every day. If they didn't do their best, there was no ride in the truck, and no hamburger.

"You've been making a lot of trips into town lately, Sarah," her mom said at dinner. "Did you find something you like more than taking care of the farm?"

"Nah, I just thought it would be good to take the dogs out for a ride a little more often. It relaxes them, and they look forward to it."

"They must look forward to those relaxing visits to the Rocking Horse Cafe, too," her mother chided, setting a plate of Yankee pot roast on the table and pushing a bowl of baking soda biscuits in front of her daughter. "Eat up."

Sarah ate in silence, filling herself with more potatoes and carrots than her appetite required. Her mother's reputation as a cook was at stake.

The Fourth of July holiday dawned clear and warm. It was a perfect day for the drive to Ogden. Sarah fed the livestock early, while her mom packed a picnic basket. Two apple pies for the Watsons were wrapped in aluminum foil, then carefully placed inside a cardboard box and set on the floorboards of the old Chevy pickup. Her mom never paid a visit to anyone without taking a food offering. It just wouldn't be polite.

Mrs. Thompson was packed and seated in the cab of the pickup, ready for the drive to Ogden before Sarah could brush her dogs and load them into the back.

"Did you forget anything, Mom?" Sarah asked. "After the first ten miles, it'll be too late to turn back."

"I have everything I need, smarty," her mom retorted.

"Are your dogs ready for the competition?"

"We're as ready as we're gonna be," Sarah said. "I've worked them every day for the past month. I don't know what else to do to help them be any better."

The drive down the canyon into the Salt Lake Valley was a pleasant one. Sarah and her mom reminisced during the hour long ride, recalling their summer vacation in Idaho when she and her brother were not yet teenagers. She remembered catching fish in the Salmon River and watching in disgust as her dad and brother cleaned them. The experience turned enjoyable once her mom began frying the trout in an iron skillet over the open campfire. Sarah's dad always said food tasted better cooked over an open fire.

The time passed quickly and the conversation was light for the remainder of the drive north to Ogden. Sarah didn't have any trouble finding the Watson Ranch. She followed the directions she had been given, and only had to stop and ask for help once when she missed a turnoff while she was talking.

Harold Watson had posted himself near the parking area set aside next to the barn, and greeted all the new arrivals with a friendly smile and a handshake. His wife Emily was seated with another woman at a table which was used to sign up the competitors and check them in for the trials.

Sarah and her mom were among the last to arrive. While her mother said hello and got reacquainted with the Watsons, Sarah leashed her dogs and took them to the signup area. She counted at least ten other dogs and their handlers waiting near the table or by the pasture gate. With the help of some of the other trial organizers, Harold had set up the trial course with a large square pen and a gate which extended the full length of one side of the enclosure, along with two sets of fence panels with twelve-foot openings to simulate gates in a fence line, spaced about fifty yards apart on opposite sides of the pen.

"Piece of cake," Sarah said aloud to her dogs. "Easy as pie." The meadow grass was short and the course was devoid of natural obstacles. No trees or boulders or ravines—nothing but a gently sloping pasture.

Rex and Maggie could handle this in a walk. She took Maggie back to the truck and waited by the pasture fence with Rex so she could watch the first competitors and wait for her turn on the trial course.

Sarah watched carefully as the first handler sent his dog on the two-hundred-yard outrun to the end of the pasture, where a small band of five large Suffolk sheep had been set out and were being discouraged from wandering away by two men and their sheepdogs. A small pile of hay kept the sheep occupied until the trial dog could complete its wide outrun and come in behind the sheep to start them down the fetch line on the first leg of the trial course.

A sleek, black-and-white dog fetched the band of two-hundred-fifty-pound ewes effortlessly toward its handler, moved them counter-clockwise around the handler's post and began the drive away toward the first of the cross-drive panels. Sarah was impressed. The man did not whistle or give a single voice command—at least none that she could hear. It appeared that the dog knew the course and the routine, and did not need any assistance from its handler. The big, black-faced sheep walked calmly ahead of the dog, and when they began to drift off line, the dog quickly flanked the sheep on their wandering side to correct their direction and send them straight through the opening between the two panels.

The skillful dog completed the course flawlessly and brought its band of sheep to the pen in less than six minutes, leaving the dog and handler an additional six minutes to finish penning the sheep before their time ran out. The ewes began to exhibit some stubbornness when the handler swung the pen gate wide open and asked his dog to move the wooly animals through the opening. The reluctant sheep were hesitant to walk into a twelve-foot square trap, and kept turning and backing away from the dog, then moving from one side to another in search of a way out. Patiently, the dog moved back and forth with them to block any exit, until finally the sheep turned and walked into the safety of the pen to get away from the unyielding sheepdog. The handler swung the gate closed behind them, and his task was complete. He made it look easy.

Sarah watched four more handlers work the course with their dogs, and was somewhat relieved to see they weren't all superior competitors.

One young female border collie failed to finish the course in the allotted time. Another dog got frustrated with the obstinate sheep and rushed in to grip one of the large ewes on its hind leg as the sheep made continuous attempts to evade the opening to the pen. The result was immediate disqualification.

Sarah made a mental note to take extra care to keep her dogs calm. Twelve minutes appeared to be plenty of time to finish the course, even if it took a few tries to complete the pen.

"Come on, Rex, let's go find Mom," Sarah said. Rex kept his eyes on the sheep in the open field for a second or two before heeding Sarah's command to follow her. He had watched the other dogs work and sensed he had a turn coming. He was eager to begin.

Sarah saw that her mother was engaged in animated conversation with Emily Watson and decided not to interrupt them. They had to be reminiscing about their high school days. She walked over to where some of the handlers were congregated with their dogs, talking about the trial course and how best to help their dogs work with the big Suffolk ewes. The dogs were always at a slight disadvantage when they worked with unfamiliar sheep.

Sarah listened for a few minute, then left the little discussion group without contributing to the conversation. She looked around for Harold Watson, and spotted him standing next to a holding pen and talking with the man who had been the first competitor on the field.

"Hi, Mr. Watson—I'm Sarah Thompson." She extended her hand and was greeted warmly by the rancher.

"Well, Sarah, it's good to know you. I saw you when you came in with your mother. Did she tell you we went to high school together?"

"Yes, sir—she did," Sarah nodded.

"Yeah, she's over there with Emily, and they've been gabbin' up a storm all morning," he laughed. "I don't know how they find so much to talk about. All I remember about school was that I barely made it out of there with a diploma." Harold remembered his manners and introduced Sarah to the man who had been standing next to him.

"Sarah, do you know Jack Stewart? Jack, say hello to Sarah

Thompson. She's here to compete with her dogs and see how they'll do with these big Suffolk ewes."

"Hello, Sarah. It's nice to meet you," Jack said, smiling as he took her hand. Sarah gazed up into his piercing gray-blue eyes a bit longer than she should have.

"Hi," was all she could say. She hadn't noticed how handsome he was from a distance while he was working his dog through the trial course—she had been more intent on watching the dog work the sheep and wasn't paying attention to the handler. She forgot what she meant to ask Harold Watson.

"Well, I think I'll go see what my mom's up to," Sarah said, looking for an escape. She nodded to Mr. Watson and left the men to their conversation. Her face felt warm. The otherwise confident young woman was flustered. She was certain Jack had seen her face flush.

"*Hi?*" she mocked herself in a raspy whisper as she walked away. "That's all you could think of to say? *Hi?* Ooh!" Sarah detoured to the parking area and put Rex in the truck with Maggie, then stood next to the truck for a moment, recalling her very brief conversation with Jack Stewart—a conversation that she had ended before it could begin.

"*Hi?*" Sarah chided herself again, then stomped her foot and huffed off to find her mom.

She composed herself by switching her thoughts to the problem of handling her dogs well enough so they could navigate the course without any serious errors. She went to the sign-in table to see when her dogs would be called up for their runs. Ten and twelve—near the end. She had a little more time to study the course and watch the other competitors.

"You didn't even eat anything, Sarah," her mom complained as the pickup rolled out onto the highway and turned south toward Salt Lake. Mrs. Thompson was easily distraught by anyone who failed to get enough to eat. Missing a meal when food was available was unnecessary.

"I was busy, Mom," Sarah replied flatly.

"The other handlers had time to eat," her mother fussed.

"I wasn't hungry," Sarah defended, trying another excuse that her mother might find more acceptable.

"Fourth place wasn't a bad finish for Maggie, you know," her mom consoled, changing the subject. "And Rex was doing fine until he missed that gate panel and then gripped that sheep when it wouldn't go in the pen."

"He was terrible," Sarah said with disgust. "I was terrible. I should have given him more direction to keep the sheep from drifting to the outside of the gate panels—Rex has never had to move sheep through an imitation gate before. He didn't understand that they couldn't just walk around it instead of going straight through the middle."

"Why do you think he grabbed that ewe?" her mom asked. "He's usually more disciplined than that, isn't he?"

"It wasn't his fault. He just got frustrated when it wouldn't go where he tried to put it—I should have backed him off a little more," Sarah explained, holding her dog blameless.

She gripped the steering wheel more tightly with both hands and leaned forward in her seat to make the truck go faster.

"That young Stewart fellow from Idaho was a nice man, wasn't he?" Sarah's mom observed.

"Who?"

"Jack Stewart—I think that was his name, wasn't it?" her mom said.

"I wouldn't know," her daughter fibbed.

"He was right there with you when you were talking to Harold, dear. Don't you remember?"

"No."

"He sure was a handsome devil," her mom continued.

"I didn't notice," Sarah lied.

"Well, he noticed you. I saw him watching you while you worked the dogs. He noticed you a lot," her mom emphasized.

"He did?" Sarah said, lifting her voice and sitting back in her seat.

Her mom laughed. "I thought you said you didn't notice him, or even remember his name."

Sarah blushed for the second time that day.

"Sarah Thompson, I think you're twitterpated," her mother teased.

"I *am* not!"

"It's just my opinion, dear."

"I'm *not*," the twitterpated young woman insisted for a second time. She remained silent for a minute, until she was overcome by curiosity. "Where from in Idaho?"

Sarah used the remainder of the drive to Salt Lake to daydream about what might have been if she had gotten better acquainted with Jack Stewart. She regretted that so much time on the farm had left her social skills lacking. It probably wouldn't have turned out any different- ly, she decided. If she had been more talkative, she might have bored the man with a lot of senseless drivel. Who could think of anything sensi- ble to say while being held hostage by those riveting blue eyes, she thought. Sarah almost missed the turnoff to Parley's Canyon.

"Would you like me to drive, Sarah?" her mom offered.

"No, I'm fine, Mom—thanks." Sarah was quietly grateful to her mother for not engaging in a lot of conversation about her reunion with her old high school chums. Sarah could hear all about it at dinner, and vowed to herself that she would do her best to appear interested.

Sarah stayed up for a while after her mother had gone to bed. She walked out to the barn and pens to check on the sheep and horses, then gave Rex and Maggie a little extra treat from the fridge when she came back inside. She picked up an old copy of Life magazine, settled back into the old easy chair that had been her father's favorite chair, and thumbed through the pages without actually reading anything. She was thinking about steel-blue eyes and trying to re-create the vision in her memory.

Sarah got up and walked to the fireplace, picking up the old and cracked wooden carving of the sheepdog that rested on the mantle. Her grandfather had given it to her when she was ten years old. It had been in her family for a very long time.

"My grandmother gave this to me when I was about your age," Sarah remembered her grandpa telling her. "She came across the country to Utah in a wagon train," he had told her, as he presented her with the carving and urged her to take special care of the family keepsake. "You were named after her."

Sarah turned the carving over in her hands, feeling the small curve of the whittle marks that created such an uncanny likeness of a sheepdog's rough coat. She admired her most prized possession for a moment, then returned it to its place of honor on the mantle before climbing the stairs to her bedroom.

The old, one-ton hay truck was equipped with side panels so that the rams could be loaded for the ride into Salt Lake. Sarah knew she could buy hay and feed at the Utah Fairgrounds for the two-day sale, so it wouldn't be necessary to bring another truck.

The rams looked exceptional this year, and she was certain they would fetch a good price at the sale. It took less than fifteen minutes to coax the sheep up the loading chute into the truck, with Rex and Maggie pushing from behind.

Sarah retrieved the sack lunch that her mom had prepared for her and left in the refrigerator with her name written on it. Writing names on the lunch sacks was a habit her mom had gotten into when Sarah and her brother were in elementary school. She wondered who would open the refrigerator now and take her lunch if her name hadn't been written on the sack. She asked her mother one final time if she wanted to come along, but her mom insisted that she should stay behind to watch the dogs and feed the animals.

"So long, mom," Sarah said, going out through the kitchen door to climb into the idling truck. "I'll be back Saturday night—not too late, I hope."

There were always other sellers and exhibitors on hand at the fairgrounds to help with the sheep. It would be rude not to help, since most of the farmers and sheep ranchers showed up short-handed. Sarah had already arranged in advance for two side-by-side exhibitor pens to hold her rams. It didn't take long to locate the pens with the help of a livestock tent layout sheet given to her at the exhibitors' gate.

"*Thompson Farm—Columbia*" was printed in bold lettering on numbered white card stock and stapled to the wooden fence panel to identify the exhibitor and the livestock breed. Thompson Farm had been assigned a good exhibit pen location near the entry door and a short distance through the aisles to the arena and sale ring. It was one of the benefits of registering early and attending year after year.

Sarah pulled a bale of straw off the small stack between the pens, snipped the twine and scattered the loosened straw around the floor.

"Can I give you a hand with that?" a man's voice offered. Sarah stood up and stared into a familiar pair of gray-blue eyes.

"I'm Jack Stewart. Remember? We met at the dog trials at the Watson place." Jack thought she needed help remembering their brief introduction a few weeks earlier.

"Hi," Sarah said, lost for words again.

"Can I help you with that?" Jack offered again.

"Oh, no, I'm almost finished," Sarah declined, finding her voice. Realizing what she had just done, she quickly reversed her direction. "I mean yes. Yes, I *would* like some help. I swear, these bales of straw seem to get heavier every year," she complained feebly, trying to appear helpless.

"Here, let me do that," Jack said, lifting another bale off the stack. He suspected that the tall, athletically-built young woman didn't encounter much trouble with tossing a thirty-pound bale of straw around the pen. He smiled up at her as he clipped the baling twine and scattered the straw. "I was about to walk across to the diner for a cup of coffee. I'd love to have some company."

Sarah beamed. "I'd love to," she said.

"I don't remember ever seeing you at the ram sale before," Sarah said, as she settled into the booth at the diner.

"I've only come down twice before," Jack replied. "I think seven or eight years ago was the last time. My father usually brings one or two of my older brothers along. I get left behind to feed livestock and take care of the ranch," he lamented, with mock self-pity.

"How is it that you got to come this year," Sarah asked. "Did everyone draw straws and you lost?"

"I volunteered," Jack answered, looking deeply into Sarah's big brown eyes. "If you want to know the truth, I called the Watsons the week after the sheepdog trials to thank them for their hospitality, and Mrs. Watson told me that you came to the National Ram Sale every year. I couldn't think of any other way to see you again. You weren't very talkative the first time we met."

Sarah couldn't believe it. Jack had actually come to see her. She couldn't remember any time in her adult life when she had felt like this about a man. She had a couple of boyfriends during high school, and almost got engaged to Roger Swenson when she was twenty-one. She didn't care much that he had two left feet on the dance floor, but he never talked about anything more interesting than pulling a calf. None of the men she dated had ever ignited a spark in her.

Jack Stewart ignited sparks—lots of them. Sarah Thompson made an important decision about her future as she sat with Jack in the diner that morning.

During the next two days, Sarah and Jack helped each other feed livestock and move the sheep back and forth from the pens to the arena and sale ring. They worked as a team to help load the sold rams into the buyers' waiting trucks and trailers, and ate every meal together. They sat in the exhibit tent when the sale ended each day and talked late into the evening. Sarah even bought a few of the Ramboulet rams from the Stewart Ranch to breed with her Columbia ewes.

Before the sale ended on the last day, Sarah asked Jack if he would like to come to dinner at the Thompson Farm.

"I know it's out of your way, but I was hoping you could give me a couple of tips on training my dogs for trialing. And you can stay in the guest room, so you'll have all day tomorrow for the drive back to Idaho."

Jack didn't hesitate to accept. He would have gone out of his way if she had lived in Oklahoma.

Sarah's mom was on the back porch of the old farm house to greet her daughter and their visitor when the trucks pulled around the side of the house and stopped next to the barn. She immediately recognized the young man who stepped out of the pickup. She smiled as she watched him walk over to help Sarah unload the new additions to their herd, then turned and went inside to start dinner.

"Mom, you remember Jack Stewart don't you?" Sarah said, as she led Jack through the kitchen door, followed by Rex and Maggie. She was a little concerned that she hadn't called her mother to let her know she would be coming home with a dinner guest.

"Of course I remember Jack," her mom said with a welcoming smile. "It's nice to see you again. Come in and make yourself to home."

Sarah guided Jack into the living room and deposited him into her father's favorite easy chair, then hurried to the kitchen to help her mother with dinner.

"What's for dinner tonight, Mom?" she whispered.

"Lamb roast," her mom responded. "Nothing fancy."

"Did you bake any pies today?" Sarah asked, momentarily worried that Jack might not want to see her again if he didn't get dessert.

"Don't I always? You didn't give me much notice, you know," her mother lightly scolded.

"I know, and I'm sorry. But I didn't want to let him get away." Sarah turned and watched Jack get up and walk to the fireplace mantle. He lifted the carving of the sheepdog from its display shelf and held it carefully with both hands, turning it to inspect the fine craftsmanship.

"I'm going to marry that man," she announced in a low voice, leaning close to her mom's ear.

Her mom dropped some potatoes into a pot, set them in the sink and handed a scrubber to her daughter, then slid the roasting pan into the oven and set the timer.

"Does he know?" her mother asked.

CHAPTER EIGHT

THE GOOD TEACHER

Hereford, Texas—1985

Red Chisholm's rough exterior did little to conceal the soft spot in his heart. He treated his dogs with a special affection and care, always making certain that they were well fed and well groomed. They were given regular visits to the vet for checkups and vaccinations, and most importantly, they received constant training to hone their skills and shape them into the extraordinary herding dogs they were bred to be.

Red had tried to pass on his love of the breed to his children, although none had shown the interest that he had felt as a child. As long as he could remember, he had wanted to work with the remarkable dogs and direct them as they moved livestock from pasture to pen. Watching his grandfather work with sheepdogs on the family farm in St. Joseph, Missouri, he learned that patience and persistence were the keys to becoming a skillful sheepdog handler.

He was disappointed that his own children regarded the dogs as little more than pets, even though the border collies were vital to their livelihood on the ranch. None of his kids had developed a keen interest in working with the dogs, and Red knew that it was something that could not be forced upon a child. In a way, they were like the dogs themselves. Some of the pups had the instinct, while others were content to retrieve a ball or chase a rabbit down a hole. It had never occurred to Red that not even one of his kids would inherit the same desire that he felt for working with dogs and livestock.

Red Chisholm learned a great deal from his dogs. They taught him the meaning of words like loyalty and devotion. The dependable dogs were quick to forgive mistakes and bad tempers, and were always grateful for their evening meal. Their stamina was incredible, and their infallible instincts and keen eye were unmatched in the canine world. Red knew there were many fine dogs among the various herding breeds, but none that came close to the border collie.

Although he loved all of his dogs, Red's current favorites among his pack were Zephyr and Sky, two talented herding dogs that came from the same bloodline as his grandfather's border collies. He made certain that he bred any new dogs he might acquire with a dog from the Chisholm line, insuring the preservation of the strong herding instincts. He could usually determine within the first year of its life whether a pup was destined to become a good working dog.

Two-year-old Zephyr had proven to be just such a dog. Red called to him as he left his small office in the barn and walked back toward the feedlots. It was time to lend a hand to the men preparing to load the first of four semis with fattened steers that were destined for the packing house.

"Come on, Zep," Red invited in an encouraging tone. Sensing that it was time to go to work, Zephyr took off like a streak of lightning in the direction of the feedlots, showing the way to his good master.

"Zep, stay with me!" Red called out to the overzealous dog, halting the high-strung herder in its tracks and bringing him back at a more reluctant pace.

"You stay with me," Red urged in a calm and soothing voice. "It's not time yet."

Red Chisholm usually allowed his dogs to choose their own names. Sky was given her name when she first opened her brilliant blue eyes to take her first glimpse of the world, and Zephyr earned his moniker when he displayed his exuberance for running like the wind wherever he went, only slowing when he was called back to do his master's bidding. It took a few weeks of disciplined training to calm Zep when he first began to work with livestock. It didn't take long for him to learn that the cattle were easier to herd if his movements were slow and

Richard Hooton

deliberate, only resorting to his amazing speed when it was necessary.

Red reached the loading pens adjacent to the feedlots and drew in the heady aroma of cattle feed and steer manure. He had become so accustomed to the odor over the years, that it was no more offensive to his senses than the sweet smell that emanated from a field of newly-mown alfalfa.

Some of his men and a couple of the truck drivers were already hard at work, trying to push the first lot of steers into a loading pen. Red climbed into the large corral and beckoned Zep, who slipped in under the lower fence rail and hugged the ground next to his master.

"Why don't you fellas stand back and let the experts work?" Red jabbed with a friendly slap on the shoulder of one of the drivers.

"Take a break, why don't you?"

The cattle were all too familiar with the black-and-white streak of fur that moved stealthily, wearing them from behind until they viewed the constricted pen as a welcome sanctuary away from the pressure of the persistent dog. They knew the dog would not go away until they went willingly into the small enclosure.

Red knew how to read livestock as well as any cattleman, and used his years of experience to his distinct advantage. He looked the steers over to find one that eyed his dog with fear and distrust—one that couldn't wait to find an escape.

"Leave off that prod," he called out to one of the drivers he noticed standing just outside the loading chute. The man brandished a three-foot long, two-pronged cattle prod, ready to jolt the first steer with the battery-powered voltage and push it up the chute into the waiting trailer. "You're liable to cause a train wreck," he added with a surly voice.

Red never liked using the battery-charged devices except as a last resort, like when a stubborn steer balked halfway up a chute and refused to move. If too many steers were crammed into the narrow space, the use of a prod would do nothing but create a tangle of legs and hooves. He preferred to select one of the more skittish animals and let Zep urge it into the chute opening first, where it was likely to escape up the ramp of its own accord.

He chose a particularly frantic animal, and knew that Zep had also spotted the most agitated steer among the lot. The dog knew his job well, and waited for his master's command.

"Walk up, Zep," Red asked his dog in a calm voice, careful not to excite Zep into moving too quickly.

Zep crouched in his trademark herding posture and inched his way around the milling livestock until he could find the opening that would permit him to separate the first steer from the others and send it on its way. He backed it toward the chute opening, blocking its way when it attempted to rejoin the others. After a couple of unsuccessful attempts to get past the tenacious dog, it turned and sought an alternative.

"Zep, that'll do," Red called out quickly as the steer found the opening to the chute and rushed up the ramp to find refuge in the long stock trailer. It was important for a good handler to know when to back his dog away once the cattle began to move in the right direction. Zep broke off and rushed back to his master's side.

"Walk up," Red commanded again, and Zep pushed the remaining cattle toward to chute and allowed them to follow their leader into the waiting truck.

"Good boy," Red praised, as he reached down and patted Zep on the shoulder. "That'll do." The work was reward enough for the valuable dog, but its master's praise was welcome reinforcement for a job well done.

"Let's get the rest of these trucks loaded so these men can get on the road," Red called out to his workers, although he wasn't really in as much of a hurry as he appeared. Red loved this part of his work as much as any chore on the ranch—probably more. It made him feel like his work was more of a lifestyle than a business, and he enjoyed showing off Zep's prowess as a herder.

Red walked back to the confines of his small office in the barn, accompanied by his trusty, four-legged sidekick. He sat down at the old oak desk next to the refrigerator that held the livestock vaccine and a drawer full of carrots that he kept on hand for the horses. He rifled through the card index until he found the phone number for the packing house.

It was the teamster's responsibility to call and let the packing house know they were on their way and to provide a head count of their load, but Red preferred to make the first call to advise the beef packers of the pending shipment. Talking to other people in the cattle business, even the last ones in line, was more to his liking than doing paperwork at the behest of his accountant.

Most of the yearling steers had been shipped, and more would be coming in to his feed lot from ranchers in central Texas, ready to be fattened up on corn silage before being shipped off to the packing houses.

Red was ready to turn his attention to getting Zep and Sky tuned up for the first sheep and cattle trials of the summer. He kept a small flock of twenty sheep in a pasture apart from the cattle for the sole purpose of training his dogs. The sheep industry had never thrived in the Texas panhandle, but Red liked to enter his dogs in as many events as possible, so he trained them on both sheep and cattle.

"Come bye," Red instructed calmly, sending Sky in a wide arc to the left around a small band of ewes. He helped his dogs work every morning and again in the late afternoon, and gave them every opportunity to gain more experience.

He took advantage of nearly every invitation to a herding trial that took place within a twelve hour drive of the ranch. Sometimes, he would drive for two days if he believed the event was worthwhile and the experience could benefit his dogs.

Lodging accommodations could often present a challenge, especially for a traveler with two dogs, so Red modified a travel trailer large enough to house dog crates and still leave room for his rangy, six foot three inch frame to rattle around inside. A used Airstream proved to be the perfect home away from home for the vagabond rancher, and the convenience of parking close to where the trials would be held eliminated the need to travel back and forth from the closest dog-friendly motel.

Red's wife never really took to life on the road with the dogs, so she usually stayed behind to spend time with her grandkids and play bridge with her friends or join in a ladies' bowling league at the Ten Pin Alley in Hereford. She went with her husband to a few trials that were within a reasonable driving distance, but she usually lost interest after the first few dogs competed, and eventually stopped accompanying her husband to the events. Like many rural wives, Dora Chisholm didn't get much time away from the ranch until there was a lull in the annual cycle of events. Once the alfalfa seed was in the ground and the steers shipped, all activity subsided except for the day-to-day chores at the feed lots, and those could easily be managed by the foreman and some hired hands.

Dora talked her husband into a cruise one winter, just to get away from the dreary cold of the windy Texas plains, but Red was the kind of man who was happier with a weekend in Amarillo than a week on a Caribbean luxury liner. She decided that the next week-long vacation would be a trip to Disney World with her daughter and grandchildren.

Red preferred to spend time with his family at home, especially around the holidays. It meant more to him than any mind-broadening travel experience. Generally speaking, he hated to travel. The one exception Red made was the travel time required to get to the dog trials.

If a twelve-hour drive was necessary to make the eight hundred mile trip from Hereford, Texas to St. Louis, Missouri for a sheepdog trial, then he could grin and bear it. Stopping along the way to let the dogs explore the open prairie land and to watch as they sniffed out new smells in the brush was his idea of relaxation.

A truck stop café or a greasy-spoon diner was always his restaurant of choice while he was on the road. He salivated over the aroma of a pan-fried flat iron steak served hot with mashed potatoes and gravy, and his dogs were always waiting anxiously for him to come back to the pickup with a white Styrofoam box in hand. He vowed to spend as many retirement days as he could taking his dogs to the trials when he finally got ready to give up his life on the ranch and sell out to one of the big corporate feed lot operations. Red listened to his favorite country music as he rolled down the highway toward Santa Anna for the cattle trials.

Zep was usually one of the top finishers at the trials, mainly because of his good training and the experience gained from his full-time job on the cattle ranch. His natural instinct for working sheep was all the extra advantage he needed to compete in the sheepdog trials. It was an easy, five-hour drive from the ranch to Santa Anna, and it gave Red plenty of time to set up his trailer before nightfall and to look over the ranch arena where his dogs would compete. He liked to run through the course in his mind before he actually stepped into the arena with one of the dogs—it helped to eliminate surprises and to familiarize him with the various obstacles.

Red saw an old friend when he pulled his shiny caravan into the area designated for campers and trailers.

"Herbert, how the heck are you?" Red laughed as he climbed out of the cab and put out a hand for his fellow cattleman. "It looks like you ate most of your livestock yourself this year. Did you have any left to send to the packing house?"

"I don't need any diet advice from *you*, longshanks," his thick-middled friend replied with a big grin wrapped around the stump of a cigar. "I've seen scarecrows with more weight on them," he laughed, poking a finger at Red's big western belt buckle.

"Are your dogs ready for the trial? I know *you're* not," Red continued to jab at his witty friend.

"I think my female is going to do pretty good this year," Herbert Randall answered, suddenly changing to more serious conversation. "She's been performing really well. How are yours doing?"

"Zep's always ready," Red affirmed. "Not so sure about Sky. She sometimes gets a little rattled working cattle, but she's showing really well at the sheepdog trials. It took her a couple of years, but she's finally found her pace and rhythm and she isn't intimidated by the sheep."

The two men agreed to meet up later for dinner so they could jawbone about the cattle business. Red always enjoyed the company of a fellow cattleman—it gave him the opportunity to get another rancher's slant on the state of the beef industry and hear whether he was optimistic about its future. So much beef was coming into the country from foreign markets that he wondered if government subsidies would be enough to help him to compete and stay in business.

Trial day was always one of excitement mixed with an equal measure of nervousness for most of the handlers. Red was no exception. He wanted his dogs to do well, but sometimes they became more nervous than their handlers in an unfamiliar environment and from being around so many other dogs. It's the kind of thing that could cause a dog to lose concentration and make costly mistakes—and possibly a disqualification.

Predictable errors happened in stockdog trials all the time, and Red was determined that a lack of training would not be the cause of those errors. It was difficult enough when unforeseen occurrences spooked the livestock or broke a dog's concentration.

Red believed first and foremost in responsible breeding to guarantee the strength, agility, and physical well-being of his dogs, as well as to preserve their keen herding instincts. He refused to breed for conformation—he never cared for the practice of breeding dogs to obtain cookie-cutter images of the parents. What he did believe in was hard training to hone a dog's skill and instincts, the very qualities which combined to give a stockdog its extraordinary ability to herd livestock.

He didn't simply train a dog until it always got every move just right. He trained so well that the dog couldn't get it wrong. It was with that dedication to training and good breeding that Red Chisholm approached his favorite thing in the entire world—the stockdog competitions.

Red stepped into the ranch arena with Sky and unhooked her lead, ready to send her when the judge signaled that it was okay to begin. Sky moved quickly but cautiously around to the right of the five wary range cattle, leaving the horned, slightly bony cattle enough room to turn away and move in the opposite direction. There was something about Sky's demeanor that didn't seem very threatening to the cattle, so they lowered their heads and aimed their horns at her. Perhaps it was her small size combined with her hesitation that emboldened the livestock—whatever it was, they simply turned away and began to trot back toward the gate that led to the holding pen. Sky had to correct and dash around to block their retreat, losing a point or two on the judge's scoring sheet in the process.

At her master's urging, Sky held fast until she completed the course and successfully penned the cattle in the allotted time, but not without

Richard Hooton

a few bungled attempts to push the obstinate beasts around the designated course obstacles. Still, Red was satisfied that she remained persistent and finished the job. It was good for the little female's confidence and self-esteem—characteristics that were as important to a dog as they were to a human. Without them, an otherwise useful stockdog could simply lose the will and the desire to herd.

"We did all right," Red said, as he turned the pickup and trailer onto the blacktop. He reached across to stroke Zep's head, then dropped his arm around Sky to pull her in close and give her a rewarding hug. The dogs gazed down the highway and kept watch with their master as they picked up speed on the road back to Hereford. Red was content with the second place ribbon Zep won for his excellent work. It was blue ribbon quality herding for sure, but Herbert Randall's dog turned in an incontestable performance and walked away with first place. If he had to surrender the top spot to anyone, he was glad that it was to a man who worked hard to give a good showing at the trials. Herbert deserved the win.

"Every day's a new day," the tall rancher observed, philosophically. Zep and Sky turned to look at their master, and wondered what he was saying.

"Good dogs," he praised, using words and a tone that Zep and Sky understood very well.

It was a week before the next sheepdog trial, so Red motored back up the highway toward home and a night in his own king-sized bed. He could use the extra time to prepare his dogs for the upcoming Mutton Buster Trials in Oklahoma.

Red Chisholm knew it didn't pay to dwell on past mistakes. He always utilized them as a good learning experience and continued to forge ahead.

He learned much of what he knew about herding sheep from Zep. After so many years of working with livestock and acquiring every useful skill his father could teach him, he thought he knew just about everything there was to know about herding, but Zep always seemed to show him more. The big border collie showed Red that sometimes speed was necessary rather than caution, and that occasionally it took more patience than Red believed was necessary to coax wary sheep into the confines of a small pen. Zep possessed every valuable trait that was important to becoming a fine herding dog—instinct, intelligence, patience, and stamina.

Red mulled over an idea that had been percolating in his head for some time, and decided that it was time to attempt to register one of his dogs on merit with the American Border Collie Association. He had never owned a registered dog before, and he had come to believe that he could improve the bloodline of his own dogs if he could breed one of them with a papered dog. No responsible breeder would allow their bloodlines to be mixed with an unregistered dog, so the only option for Red was to get one of his own dogs qualified.

He was somewhat acquainted with the procedure from reading the rules and requirements in one of the newsletters that were sent out periodically by the association. The first condition would be easy—providing the association's register-on-merit committee with the most complete pedigree available. Red could trace the lineage of his dogs all the way back to his great-grandfather's dog in Missouri, but none of them had ever been registered. The Chisholms never thought it was necessary to prove a dog's working ability by having its name listed in the stud books.

The remainder of the conditions had to do with minimum age of the dog, vet checkups and certifications, and evidence of finishing in the top ten percent at three or more of the United States Border Collie Handlers Association sanctioned national events. After that, it was just a matter of sending a video of the dog working livestock for review and predetermination by the committee of the dog's skill at herding. If he was accepted, Red would have to travel with the dog to a place designated by the committee so that he could demonstrate his dog's skill and abilities to at least three of the association directors. Zep was the perfect candidate. He had a presence on the field that could not be ignored by sheep or men. It was time to infuse new blood into the line.

Red pulled off the blacktop and parked the pickup and trailer next to the barn, setting the brake and leaving the driver's side door open behind him to let his dogs out. Determined not to procrastinate any longer, he began to rifle through the desk drawers in his tiny cluttered office, looking for one of the last newsletters he had received in the mail from the American Border Collie Association headquarters in Mississippi.

He gave up after a couple of minutes of searching through his piles of old junk mail, magazines and livestock sale circulars. He unlocked the bottom cabinet door to his old roll-top desk and took out the fireproof strongbox that contained the journals and letters his family had maintained for over a hundred and twenty years to document the bloodline of more than forty generations of herding dogs.

He picked up the phone and dialed zero for the operator. "Can you help me with directory assistance for Perkinston, Mississippi, please?"

CHAPTER NINE

SHEEP TALES

Heber Valley, Utah—2001

"You can't actually *die* of boredom, Jack," Sarah said, as she walked ahead of her husband from the Wal-Mart store to the parking lot.

"I think you're wrong, Sarah. I'm pretty sure it could happen—I just don't want to find out first hand. I'd rather read about it in a medical journal." He set the new folding camp chairs in the back of the pickup and turned to face his wife.

"A supermarket tabloid, you mean," Sarah said, with genuine disgust. "You're not funny, Jack," she said, scowling at her husband as she poked a finger at his chest. "And you promised me a weekend in Sun Valley, so we're going."

Sarah didn't often put her foot down that hard, but when she did, Jack knew the conversation was over. It would be a cold ride home if she didn't get her way.

There is a powerful force that pulls on a man's heart to beckon him home. Jack was excited at first to accept the invitation to a family reunion, but his enthusiasm quickly faded when he thought about how boring it might be after the first hour or so of hugs and handshakes. Any last minute reluctance Jack may have felt about taking the weekend trip had been overcome by his wife's insistence. He tried to remember how many years it had been since he last visited with his family in Idaho. He couldn't recall exactly, but decided it had been far too many.

Jack glanced at the speedometer to be sure he wasn't going too fast through the half-mile long stretch of highway that passed through the little town of Shoshone, Idaho, then looked over at his wife and interrupted her reading.

"Sarah, how many years has it been since the last time we came up here for Thanksgiving or a family reunion, do you know?"

Sarah lowered her magazine into her lap and looked up at her husband. "I don't know, sweetheart, but it's been a long time."

"Eight, I think. Maybe ten," Jack guessed.

Sarah patted her husband on his leg, and picked up her book again. "You let me know if I can help you with any other important problems," she offered.

Jack smiled over at his lovely wife, turned to check the road ahead to make sure he was driving between the lines, then looked back at Sarah. He loved to banter with his wife—she always surprised him with her clever remarks, and it made their marriage more interesting.

"I didn't marry you for your subtle wit, you know," he said.

"You were quick to accept it as a bonus though, along with my dowry of sheep, weren't you big fella?" Sarah nudged, just to see if her hubby had a comeback. He was unprepared.

Jack looked over at his wife again, his big smile broadening. "If I have to stop this truck, you'll be sorry," he said, delivering his hollow threat with a good-natured chuckle.

"Is that all you've got?" Sarah questioned in her sweetest voice, not looking up from her magazine. Jack stared down the highway, trying to think of something smart to say. He stalled for a moment, just in case something might come to mind.

"I got nuthin'," he muttered finally, surrendering to his wife's superior wit.

It would be good to see family again. Jack's oldest brother had called a few months earlier and suggested a reunion for the family at the old Easley Hot Springs, a small summer retreat near Sun Valley that they had frequented when they were kids. He had fond memories of the picnics and of splashing around in the small, spring-fed pool that was the perfect size for ranch kids who didn't know how to swim very well. It was never more than an arm's reach for the novice swimmers to the edge of the pool or an inflated inner tube.

Sarah put her book down and reached into a brown paper grocery bag on the floor. "How about a picnic, cowboy?" she offered. "I have tuna sandwiches on wheat, or tuna sandwiches on wheat with Fritos and an apple."

Jack smiled. "I'll have that second choice," he opted. "It sounds like a better value. Did you bring anything to drink?"

"That'll be extra," Sarah said. She was at it again.

Jack sighed, exhaling deeply for the added effect. "I should have made you ride in the back seat."

Nothing prepared Jack for the changes that had swept over the Wood River Valley since he had moved away. The string of little towns from Bellevue through Hailey, and on into Ketchum and Sun Valley, had changed so much that it was hard for Jack to pick out a recognizable building. Ketchum resembled Vail, Colorado more than it did the sleepy town he remembered from his childhood. Sun Valley always enjoyed a good number of summer visitors, and came alive again during the ski season, but now it was a haven for affluent seasonal residents and their million-dollar condos. The big, stylish custom homes set on an acre or more were reserved for the very wealthy.

"Who's that old sack of spuds you brought with you, Sarah?" Jack's older brother Dan asked, as he approached them from the picnic tables lined up in a shady little grove of trees.

"A hitchhiker," she answered quickly. "I needed someone to drive so I could read. I paid him with sandwiches and a lesson or two in satire. Hope you don't mind if he hangs around for awhile—he eats a lot, though."

"Did he learn anything from the lessons?" Dan asked.

"He hasn't learned to surrender yet," Sarah said. "How's everyone doing?" she asked, as she hugged Dan's wife and turned to greet the rest of Jack's family.

Jack spent some time getting reacquainted with nephews, nieces, and in-laws before sitting down with his oldest brother for more serious conversation.

"The wool market's been poor for the last few years," Dan said. "Lately, the shearing crews all come in from Australia. Allan Wilde Shearing Company uses a bunch of young Aussie guys in their twenties—they can shear over two hundred head apiece every day and go out and ride their dirt bikes when they're finished. All the wool is shipped over to China for processing now—even Burlington doesn't process wool in the States anymore."

It took less than an hour to get completely caught up on what was going on with his family, before learning everything there was to know about the state of affairs in Blaine County. It could have been summed up in a two-page Christmas letter. He suddenly realized why he hadn't been home in twelve years. He was already getting bored.

"Remember when we used to go camping up Cherry Creek?" Dan asked. "We sat around and told campfire stories until it got too cold and we had to climb into our sleeping bags to stay warm."

"Yeah," Jack reminisced. "I think some of those stories got told and re-told so many times, it was hard to tell truth from fiction." There was something about re-hashing old times that always seemed to spark fond memories. Jack was suddenly enjoying himself again.

"You ought to think about coming up again in October for the *Trailing of the Sheep* fall festival," Dan invited. "It's been going on for a few years now, and it draws visitors from all over the country. Nancy took the grandkids to it last year, and they had a *great* time."

"I don't know," Jack answered. "Two trips in one year after so many years away from home might be more than I can handle."

"What else do you have to do?" Dan asked. "Count cows?"

Jack picked up the room key at the front desk of the Best Western Inn and went back to the parking lot to help his wife with their suitcases.

"Might be fun to poke around town a little bit," Jack said, exchanging the room key with Sarah for her carry-bag. "We're on the second floor."

"That's the spirit, Romeo," Sarah praised, leading the way through the lobby to the elevator. "We might even find a romantic little coffee shop."

"There's a Starbucks on the next corner," Jack said.

"This isn't the Ketchum, Idaho I remember," Jack marveled, walking along Main Street and pausing with his wife to admire the window displays at clothing stores and art galleries.

"I never saw so many art galleries in a town this size," Jack remarked.

"Didn't they have art when you were a kid, Jack?" Sarah asked, as she grabbed a handful of shirt at his elbow and steered him through the open doorway to an art gallery.

"Sure, on the calendars they gave away at the John Deere dealership in Bellevue," he admitted. "Pretty good pictures, too."

It was a rare event for Sarah to have an entire afternoon to shop for something other than groceries and livestock feed, so she took her time browsing the shops, bookstores and galleries until she thought she had seen enough for one day. She loaded Jack up like a pack mule with books, pictures, and souvenirs, and led the way back down the sidewalk in the direction of their hotel, happy to have been a tourist for a day.

Jack was relieved to unload his cargo of bags in the hotel room and have an hour or so to relax. It would be dark soon, and most of the stores would be closed, so he wouldn't have to endure any more shopping. He was already thinking about dinner, and Jack had drawn a mental map with the location of all the steakhouses they passed during his wife's shopping spree. Sarah was right about one thing—he *did* eat a lot, and shopping was hungry work.

"Did you see this?" Sarah asked, unfolding a local paper to read about an upcoming fall festival in Sun Valley. "They have a *Trailing of the Sheep* festival every year in October, and they trail a band of more than a thousand sheep right down Main Street behind a parade of kids and horses and wagons. Maybe we could come back and spend a few days taking in some more of the local color. They have lots of fun stuff to see and do."

"Yeah, Dan told me something about that," Jack answered. He was pleased that his wife was enjoying herself.

"They have Basque and Polish folk dancers, and the Boise Highlanders come down every year to perform with their bagpipes," Sarah read on. "An exhibit area for art and handmade wool clothing is set up at the community park in Hailey, and they give away samples of lamb stew and barbequed lamb cooked outside an old sheep camp wagon—you should like that."

"Sounds great," Jack said, pandering to his wife's enthusiasm. "I'm hungry already."

"Maybe Charlie would like to come up to see it, too," Sarah said. "He hasn't strayed off the farm much for the past year or so."

"Maybe," Jack replied. Their son was rarely inclined to take a trip out of town. Jack decided to leave it up to Sarah to sell Charlie on the idea. His mind was on getting cleaned up so they could walk across the street for a thick, juicy steak and a giant baked potato.

Jack and Sarah talked during most of the drive home, but they were also content to enjoy each other's companionship during the quiet stretches of miles when words became unnecessary. Jack was still feeling sluggish from the twenty-ounce rib eye steak he devoured the night before—and the baked potato that came with it was the size of a football. He wouldn't have to eat again any time soon. He could live for a while off the food that was still in his stomach.

Jack got lost in thought for awhile, and remembered a story his Grandpa Jake often told to a captive audience around the family supper table. Jack and his brothers had listened to the story of John Laidlaw at least a hundred times. Laidlaw was the biggest sheep rancher in Blaine County for many years, and their dad had even worked for him for a few months during the lean times of the Great Depression.

Jack remembered his Grandpa telling of how Laidlaw had been a multi-generational sheepman with real grit, and that his ancestors in Scotland had raised sheep in the highlands near Inverness. He had suffered through summer droughts and deep winter snows in Idaho, and was well-acquainted with the difficulties of ranching in the American West. He had been forced to stand his ground with persistent bankers on more than one occasion when the lamb markets fell and wool prices slid below the levels necessary to make a profit, or even to pay bills. Still, the tenacious rancher managed to build his herds to nearly a hundred thousand sheep before he was forced by weather and economic circumstances to sell off part of his land and much of his livestock.

It was rumored that the iron-clad rancher had been called onto the carpet by his banker in Boise and chastised for not being able to pay the interest on his loan for the year. The story had become legend, and was probably embellished with each successive telling.

"Do you have to be the biggest sheepman in the world?" Laidlaw's banker had admonished.

Laidlaw frowned at the aging banker in his poorly-fitted blue suit and slowly shook his head, then perked up again as a vagrant thought suddenly crossed his mind.

"No, sir," Laidlaw responded, triumphantly. "But if you foreclosure on me, you will be." Laidlaw left the bank victorious that day. His loan was extended for another year, provided the interest was caught up after the next sale of spring lambs.

"Where there's a will, there's a way," Grandpa Jake told all his boys, delivering the time-worn moral to his oft-told story.

"What are you smiling about, sweetheart?" Sarah asked.

"Sarah, did you ever hear my Grandpa Jake's story about John Laidlaw?" Jack asked.

"About a hundred times," Sarah said.

"Do you want to hear it again?" Jack offered, flashing a big grin at his wife.

Sarah reached into one of her bags and retrieved a gourmet cookbook she bought at one of the shops in Ketchum.

"Does this answer your question?" she replied, opening the cover to the first recipe.

"He wasn't always a sheep rancher, you know," Jack said. "My grandpa, I mean. He left the ranch for a few years to work for the Union Pacific and even got a job as a brakeman on the line that ran through

Green River and Rock Springs, Wyoming. He always wanted to be a locomotive engineer, but he never made it. Said it was one of the biggest disappointments of his life. He always told me that he considered himself an educated man because he finished the fourth grade, but the railroad wouldn't train a locomotive engineer unless he had a high school diploma. Or at least that's what he said. When he got married and started raising a pile of kids, he moved back to the ranch."

Jack tried to encourage Sarah to join him in a little more verbal thrust-and-parry, but she continued to browse through her book in silence and pretended not to listen.

"Are you ignoring me?" Jack asked, with contrived astonishment.

"Do you know we will be married forty-five years this October, Jack? Doesn't the time go by in a blink?" she uttered softly, dropping her magazine onto her lap.

Charlie Stewart bore an uncanny resemblance to his father—tall, square shouldered, and with the same steel-gray eyes. The only physical difference between the two men was that Charlie's dad bore the battle scars of life called age wrinkles, and the thick, dark hair of his youth had receded slightly and turned a silvery shade of gray. Otherwise, Charlie was his clone. He sat quietly next to his dad on the back porch and stared down at the floor as he studied his worn, unpolished boot toes.

"All I'm saying, son, is that you should show a little common courtesy when your mother offers some advice on life," Jack said to his only child. "She's right about divorce not being the end of the world—other people get through it. Just be glad you didn't have kids with her. It would have made it a lot harder for both of you."

"I've tried to push it out of my head, dad," Charlie said quietly, trying to show some respect for his father's advice. "But it's not easy. I thought everything was fine between us, but she came home from work one day and said she wasn't feeling fulfilled and that she wanted something more out of life that I obviously couldn't give her."

Jack wasn't comfortable giving his son advice on affairs of the heart. Besides, he had always believed that men were supposed to endure their emotional troubles in silence. It was part of the man code. Charlie was a stoic like his father, so he never asked for sympathy or understanding.

Still, Jack knew his son was depressed, and felt compelled to say something if it might help lift Charlie out of his sullen mood.

"Just because you waited until your late thirties to marry doesn't mean you were going to be given a guarantee of a happy life," Jack said. "Some people just aren't meant to be together, and you can't make a woman happy if she isn't already content with her life—and not if it means giving up your own happiness." Charlie didn't respond. He had heard all the clichés before.

The two men sat in silence for a while, then adjourned their man meeting when Sarah called them to dinner.

"I think it's time you found something to do that will get you off this ranch for a few days a week, Charlie," Sarah said. "It's just no good hanging around here all the time. You should get out and join the world again."

"Sure," Charlie replied, with an obvious twinge of sarcasm. "Maybe I could join one of grandma's quilting bees."

"Listen, you're not too old for a trip to the woodshed, Slick," Sarah cautioned her forty-year-old son. "I still know how to cut a willow switch, so you better think about that the next time you have the urge to get lippy with me."

Jack smirked, unable to constrain his amusement.

Sarah turned her attention to her grinning hubby.

"And you don't have to encourage him, big boy," she warned Jack. "You can both sleep in the barn and eat hay with the horses. Maybe you can practice your smart remarks on each other." Sarah was exasperated. "It wouldn't kill you to get off the farm and try to enjoy life once in a while, Charlie."

"Why don't you drive up to that construction site above Midway tomorrow and see if any of the contractors need some extra help, Charlie," Jack said, as the two men shared the chore of filling the horse stall feeders with hay. "I heard they were short-handed, and they have to finish that job before the snow flies. The winter Olympics start in January or February, I think. It'll give you something to do besides feed cows and watch television."

Sarah Stewart climbed the steep stairs to the attic and rummaged through all of the junk and heirlooms collected in the dusty storage room. She found the pair of old Hazelwood shepherd's crooks leaned up in a corner, covered in dust and tethered to the wall with cobwebs. She used an old bed sheet that was used to cover her mother's cedar hope chest to wipe the dust from the smooth staffs. They hadn't been used in at least twenty years—not since she and Jack decided to sell off all the sheep and run a small herd of Black Angus beef cattle. Sarah hefted a crook in each hand, inspected them carefully, then decided upon the longer staff her husband had used for guiding his sheepdogs around the livestock.

"Why don't you give this to your son?" Sarah asked, holding out Jack's old shepherd's crook as she descended from the attic. "Maybe he can learn to be as good as you were. There are plenty of border collie pups around—it's just a matter of finding the right one."

"I think you've got something there," Jack said, accepting the crook from his wife. "I haven't seen this in years, Sarah—where did you find it?"

"It was in the attic with everything else we don't use but still won't throw away," Sarah replied. "I called the secretary of the Utah Stockdog Association and got a few phone numbers and addresses of people who have border collie pups for sale. Maybe you could take your son and go have a look at a few."

"Charlie, come take a ride with me," Jack invited his son. "You've been an easy chair jockey long enough for one day, and that boob tube is just about worn out."

"Where are we going?" Charlie asked.

"Dog hunting," his dad said. "Let's go."

"You've got a dog," Charlie said, hauling himself out of the recliner.

"Kit's retired," Jack said. "He's almost fourteen. Doesn't even like to follow me out to the mailbox anymore."

"Why do you want another dog?" Charlie asked, following his dad down the back porch steps.

"It's not for me," Jack said. "It's for you."

Charlie stopped abruptly. "I don't want a dog."

"Yes you do," Jack corrected.

"No I don't," Charlie insisted.

"Just get in the truck, Charlie," Jack said. "We're doing this for your mother."

"I don't get it, dad," Charlie said, as he drove out the long gravel drive to the highway. "What's this about?"

"Remember all those times you asked me for a puppy of your own when you were a kid?" Jack began. "Well, now I'm getting you one."

"What am I supposed to do with a dog?" Charlie asked, as he drove out onto the highway.

"Feed it," Jack said. "Train it. What does anyone do with a dog?"

Charlie thought for a moment. "I like Dalmatians," he said, somewhat enthused at the prospect of having a more lively dog around the ranch.

"No good around livestock," Jack vetoed.

"How about a bird dog?" Charlie suggested.

"How about a stockdog Charlie—we live on a ranch, remember? Let's find a useful dog."

"You want me to herd cows?" Charlie asked, still unsure of his dad's motive.

"I want you to get off your butt, Charlie," Jack said. "You used to show some interest in the dog trials we took you to watch when you were little. I'm going to show you how much more fun it can be when you're the one at the controls."

"I'm not sure I want to be," Charlie said, his enthusiasm waning. "Sounds like a lot of work."

"It is, but let's humor your mother on this one, shall we?" Jack said. "If you don't like it after a few training sessions, you can call it quits, and Kit will have another dog to keep him company. At least then I can tell your mother I tried."

Charlie wasn't expecting to be hired the same day he showed up at the Winter Olympics site to look for work.

"What can you do?" the site foreman asked.

"Drive truck, operate a grader or a backhoe—most of the equipment that's not too complicated, I guess," Charlie said.

"Can you get yourself to work every day by six?" the foreman questioned.

"I always get up early," Charlie assured the man. "And I only live ten miles from here."

"That's good to know, but it doesn't answer the question. Can I count on you to get here on time every day?" the man repeated, actually relieved to have a local area job applicant who didn't have to drive for an hour every day to get to the job site. He was running out of time to complete the job before his deadline, and too many of his recent hires had quit on him because of the long commute to work from the Salt Lake Valley or because of the long hours—sometimes both.

"I can be waiting for you every day before you get here if you want me to," Charlie offered.

"No you can't," the foreman countered. "I've been sleeping in that temporary office trailer over there for the past three weeks," he added, pointing to a small grey mobile office that had been dropped in the middle of what appeared to be a large parking area.

"Well, I'll be here on time anyway," Charlie insisted. "And I'll stay until you tell me to go home."

"Good enough," the foreman said. "My name's Wayne Clark. You go down to the office and tell Carol that I sent you. She'll set you up with the forms you'll need to sign, and you'll have to get a physical and a drug test. Nothing personal—just one of the requirements for contractors working on the Olympics site. Oh, and they'll do a brief background check, but it won't hold you up from working. You'll just be on probationary status until all the results are in. Meantime, you can work. We have just four months to finish nine months of work, so expect a lot of overtime."

"Thanks Mr. Clark," Charlie said. "I'll be here first thing in the morning, then."

"Why, is today your birthday?" the tough foreman asked sarcastically. "You get back down here as soon as you sign your paperwork. We've got work to do."

Charlie steered the big diesel gravel truck down the hill from the hollow above Midway, strumming his fingers on the wheel and rocking back and forth in his seat to the freight-train rhythm of his favorite Johnny Cash tune. He sang along, a little off key, but he didn't think Johnny would mind.

I'm gonna break my rusty cage and run
Too cold to start a fire,
I'm burnin' diesel, burnin' dinosaur bones

He liked the truck driver job the foreman assigned to him—it gave him plenty of time to think during the hour long drive each way through Parley's Canyon and across the east bench to the mouth of Big Cottonwood Canyon where he took on a load at the gravel pit before making the return trip to Midway. He made the round trip four or five times a day, six days a week, and usually worked ten hours or more each day. He was always ready to go home at the end of the day, but never exhausted from physical labor. It was the perfect job for sulky Charlie, given his state of mind. There wasn't too much thinking involved, and he was able to work alone, so he didn't have to interact with others more than a few minutes at a time.

Charlie spent an hour every morning with the eight-week-old border collie pup that he and his dad picked up in Spanish Fork, and another hour or two every night after he got home from work. Two weeks earlier, he and his father had used up the better part of a Sunday, driving around the Salt Lake Valley to different farms to look at puppies, until finally they found one that they could both agree on. None of the pups they saw were pedigreed, but Charlie's father knew the breed very well and he insisted that owning a registered pup was not important.

They agreed on a little black-and-white male that followed Charlie around and pounced on his boot toe whenever it could catch up.

"Looks like he wants to herd something," Jack observed.

"Maybe he just likes boots," Charlie said. "Do you think he has the right look?"

"You're not entering him in a dog show, Charlie," his dad told him. "Border collies are working dogs. All you should care about is whether he can learn to herd, and that he's healthy and has a good temperament. Nothing else is important."

Charlie sat in a porch chair and held the smooth shepherd's crook across his lap as he inspected its fine workmanship. The likeness of a Scottish thistle had been carved into the tip of the ram's horn by a skillful crook maker, and was then painstakingly doweled into the top of the Hazelwood staff. He leaned the crook against his chair and bent down to pull on his boots as called to his little dog.

"Come on, Bone. Let's go have some fun."

CHAPTER TEN

A SEASON OF TRIALS

Evanston, Wyoming—2002

"It wouldn't hurt you to take a real vacation, would it?" Bev asked her husband. "We could do some sightseeing in England and Scotland and maybe go and watch the World Sheepdog Trials while we're there." She hadn't told him she was thinking of entering one of her own dogs in the competition.

"Nope," her smart-aleck spouse declined. "I severed my ties with England in 1776. Didn't leave anything there," he smirked, picking up his coffee mug.

"I suspected you lied about your age when you asked me to marry you, Don Thompson," Bev chided. "Now I'm sure of it. You're an old geezer."

"An old *American* geezer," he corrected. "I don't mind traveling, as long as I can stay in my own country. I went with you to the Nationals in St. Louis last year, remember? And I didn't have to bring my passport."

"It's not as if I'm asking you to go to France or Italy," Bev said. "You won't have to learn a foreign language."

"That's not what I heard," Don countered, unimpressed with his wife's attempt to reason with him. "And it's still a foreign country. Besides, I've already traveled to all the exotic places I ever wanted to see."

"Yeah, Laramie doesn't count." Bev went back into the house, determined to work on her husband a little more after he had some time to think about it. Sooner or later he was bound to come around. He had to eat, and he wasn't a very good cook, she thought, but she didn't want to resort to threats of starvation to get him to change his mind. It wouldn't help to stop his laundry service either—he would probably wear dirty clothes before he would try to figure out how the washing machine worked.

She was determined to take the trip alone if she had to, but it would be more fun if her husband came along, even if he behaved like a cranky old man on occasion.

Bev heard the dogs barking and altered her course from the direction of the kitchen and started toward the front door. She saw a familiar face through the glass panes and swung the door open wide to greet her visitor. "Well, Charlie Stewart, how have you been?"

"I've been okay," Charlie answered with a smile and a handshake. "Is Don at home?"

"Sure, come on in, Charlie," Bev invited. "He's just sittin' out on the deck, gettin' old. He'll be glad to see you."

She set her coffee mug down on the dining table as she led Charlie through the kitchen toward the back deck.

Charlie noticed Bev's china cabinet standing against one wall of her dining room, packed so full of trophies, ribbons and championship buckles from stockdog trials that there wasn't room for a single dinner plate or piece of glassware. Most of the winning memorabilia belonged to Bev, but a good share of the earlier trophies and ribbons had been won by Don. Framed photographs of their best dogs from the past twenty-five years hung on every wall of the living room, dining room and kitchen.

"Hey, Gulliver, look who's come to see us," Bev taunted her stay-at-home hubby as she showed Charlie out onto the deck.

"Well, Charlie, what a surprise." Don hauled himself out of his deck chair to shake hands with the younger man. "Don't pay any attention to Bev. She's just mad 'cause I won't go with her to the other side of the world. How are your mom and dad?"

"They're fine. I'm sorry I didn't call first. I was just hoping to find you at home."

"We're accustomed to unannounced visits out here, Charlie," Bev said. "And we don't need any advance warning from family."

"That's right," Don agreed. "We live too far out in the boondocks to be too choosy about our visitors. Bev once told me that she was thinking about putting up a sign by the front door that read *'If You Didn't Call—Don't Knock'*, but none of my friends know how to read, so it wouldn't have done any good."

"Dad suggested I stop in to see you the next time I was in Evanston," Charlie said. "He thought you might be willing to part with a few tips on training sheepdogs."

"I didn't know you were interested in working sheepdogs," Don said. "We never saw you at any of the events with your folks after you started high school and got your driver's license. The next thing we heard was that you had moved away We thought you had gone out to conquer the world."

"I did, but I was outnumbered," Charlie said. "I sure didn't expect to end up back at home after twenty years, though."

"So, how is it that you suddenly developed an interest in training stockdogs?" Don asked.

"It was Dad's idea. Or Mom's—I'm not real sure. I was turning into a couch potato and they probably thought it was the best way to get me out of the house. Anyway, now I've got this young border collie, and I'm trying to get him ready to compete in sheepdog trials. I don't seem to be very good at it."

"Did you bring him with you?" Bev asked.

"Yes, ma'am—he's out in the pickup."

"Well, let's go see him," Don said, hobbling toward the steps of the deck with a visible limp.

Charlie remembered hearing that Don had suffered a badly broken leg about four years earlier when his horse stumbled in a badger hole and rolled over on him. He had been alone, searching for stray cows, and he lay on the ground for nearly two days before anyone found him. His leg had never quite healed right. The doctor gave him a walking cane, but he refused to use it—said it made him feel like a cripple. He wouldn't even give up wearing cowboy boots in favor of something more comfortable for walking.

Charlie opened the truck door and let Bone jump down to get acquainted with three of the Thompsons' dogs that waited to greet their canine visitor with a couple of nice-to-meet-you sniffs.

"He looks young," Bev said. "How old is he?"

"Just over a year," Charlie answered.

"Why don't you bring him out back and let's see how he does on his outrun and fetch."

"There's a band of fifteen or twenty sheep at the far end of the field," Don said. It's maybe two hundred yards or so to the sheep. Send him out and let's see how he does.

Bone had already spied the sheep and was lying prone next to Charlie's side, quivering with anticipation.

"Bone, go!" Charlie sent the young dog across the field, and Bone flew in a wide arc to the right to get around behind the sheep without disturbing them. He slowed his pace as he neared the band of sheep, slowing his approach and crouching low in a classic sheepdog stance to avoid startling the sheep. He positioned himself on the opposite side of the sheep from where his master waited at the other end of the field, and began a slow and steady walk to lift the woolies from where they had been grazing to start them trotting toward his master. The sheep began to move too fast.

"Slow him down a little, Charlie," Bev said. "He's bringing them too fast. If the sheep change direction on him or decide to bolt, he may not be able to react quick enough."

Charlie cupped his hands around his mouth and called out to his dog. "Bone, get back!" Bone didn't react immediately. "Get back!" Charlie called again, louder and with more insistence in his tone. Bone backed off and allowed the sheep to slow down. He balanced the sheep between himself and his master, and kept them moving in a straight line toward Charlie. Whenever the sheep tried to drift off course, Bone flanked them to block their sideways movement and kept them on track in the direction of his handler.

"He has a pretty good fetch," Don observed. "Maybe a little too eager at first, but he settles down. He's still young."

Bev watched the dog carefully, making mental notes of Bone's strengths and weaknesses, and any handler mistakes that Charlie was making. She saved her comments until Bone brought the sheep in close and accepted his master's command to lie down, taking the pressure off the sheep just enough to allow them to relax, but not so much that they thought they had permission to wander off. Bone kept an unwavering stare fixed on the sheep.

"Bone's a nice dog, Charlie," Bev complimented. "I think you can train him into a decent trial dog if you spend enough time with him. He's got a good outrun and lift, but he is a little pushy during the fetch. That's easy enough to train out of him—much better than having to beg him up. Is he always this eager to work?"

"Every day," Charlie answered. "I have to bring him to the house and make him sleep on the back porch at night or I'll find him at the pasture fence. He's constantly watching his sheep."

"It's good that you don't give him too many commands," Bev said. "It's a lot for a young dog to think about when it's hearing commands yelled at the same time that it's trying to stay in contact with the sheep and follow its own instincts."

"I confused him a lot at first," Charlie said. "I was constantly barking commands at him until he got so frustrated and confused that he just quit. Dad finally told me to shut up and let him work. He said Bone was born knowing more about herding than I was likely to learn in a lifetime."

Bev and Don smiled and laughed. "That sounds like Jack talking," Don said. "He always said that over-handling a good sheepdog was the worst mistake you could make."

"I think the best thing you can do is enter a few sanctioned trials,

Charlie," Bev advised. "I've got this year's list of upcoming events in the Border Collie Handlers Association newsletter."

"I thought I'd just start him out on some arena work in a few of the smaller events first," Charlie replied. "Maybe it will build his confidence to compete in a few all-breeds trials."

"It might build your confidence, but it won't do much for your dog. The only way to get Bone ready to compete in an open trial is to sign him up and run him in a few open trials," Bev said. "What do you care if he doesn't do well at first? He'll have the experience of working the longer and more difficult courses, and that's exactly what he needs to compete in the big trials."

"She's right, Charlie," Don agreed. "Don't worry about finishing in last place—worry about finishing. It's the fastest way to get your dog ready to compete."

"Now, let's see how he does with his drive," Bev said.

Charlie spent the next half hour working with Bone while Bev offered her best instruction to help man and dog work together until they began to work as a team. It is an unnatural thing for a stockdog to drive sheep away when every instinct tells it to fetch them toward its master. It is one of the most difficult maneuvers to teach a dog, and one that requires patience, training and a well-timed command or two.

Bone had both the intelligence to learn and the desire to please his master. Charlie was happy with the small progress they made under Bev's tutelage. He was determined to go home and practice with Bone every day until his dog's driving skills were perfected.

"I can't thank you enough for this," Charlie said as he shook hands with the Thompsons and opened the passenger door of his truck for Bone. "Maybe I'll see you at the trials in Gillette."

"You will for sure if you show up," Don said. "Bev wouldn't miss it. She's already entered with two of her dogs. I'll probably go with her, 'cause I won't have to leave the state."

Bev shook her head. "Somebody put glue on Don's pants and he can't get up from his rocking chair," she said. "I'm having a real hard time of it trying to convince him to take a vacation to England with me."

It was Charlie's turn to offer advice. "Maybe you're using the wrong bait," he said. "Figure out what's most appealing to him and lure him with that—maybe he'll change his mind." Charlie climbed into the pickup cab next to Bone and slipped the key into the ignition.

"Thanks, Charlie," Bev said with genuine appreciation. "I'll remember that."

"Good luck," Don said, skeptical that anything would prompt him to reconsider. "Charlie, you tell your mom to give us a call once in a while. She needs to stay in closer touch with her Bradley family. We haven't seen her since your grandmother's funeral. Aunt Martha was a fine lady."

"Yeah, Grandma was real nice to everybody. And she was the best cook I ever knew," Charlie said.

Charlie waved back at Bev and Don as he turned the pickup around in the gravel drive and aimed it toward the highway.

The wheels were already turning in Bev's head as she walked back to the house ahead of her husband. I've got you now, Don Thompson, she thought. You have to sleep sometime.

Bev got most of her paperwork done after her husband went to bed at night, and it was also the time when she could place an uninterrupted phone call. Don adored his grandsons, but they rarely came to Wyoming for a visit since Don, Jr. took a job in Washington State three years earlier. The two boys were eight and ten years old, and growing fast. It would be good for them to get in touch with their ancestral origins, Bev thought. A trip to England for the whole family would be the perfect vacation. Bev picked up the phone and dialed her son's number in Seattle.

She broke it to Don over his morning coffee the next day. "Good news, honey," Bev announced. "I talked to Donnie last night and he's going to bring Marcie and the boys to England with us this summer. He was thrilled that you wanted them to come with us."

"You invited them to go to England?" Don asked, beginning to get the sense that he'd been had.

"Nope, you did," Bev said, with a self-satisfied smile. "I told

Donnie you didn't like the fact that the boys were growing up so fast and that you never got the chance to see them anymore."

She watched Don closely for any sign of a contradiction. He remained silent. "Oh, and he said to thank you for the plane tickets, and that he'd be glad to chip in for part of the hotel expense."

Don sipped his coffee and looked across the rim of his mug at his smiling, deceitful wife. He marveled at what a plotting, devious mind she had. There was nothing to be said. He lowered his coffee mug to the table and smiled back at her.

"It'll be great to tour some castles with your grandsons, won't it?" Bev said triumphantly.

"Yep, it will," the outwitted man confessed. "What's for breakfast?"

Charlie thought he was prepared for the competition in Gillette, but when the trial day arrived he was apprehensive. He worried that Bone might not do his best in unfamiliar surroundings and around so many other dogs.

"Don't fret over it, Charlie," Don said. "It's not like there's a big cash prize at stake. Just go out there and do your best. Bone will stay calm if you do the same. And remember not to over-handle your dog—let him work."

"It's hard to ignore the butterflies in the stomach, Don. I can't remember the last time I felt this nervous."

"If you stay calm, Bone will stay calm. Just relax," Don assured the younger man. "Let's watch some of the others. Bev is fourth or fifth in the order, I think, so she should be up soon."

Don and Charlie watched a couple of handlers work their dogs through the trial course. Bev was called up with her first dog and they made the course look easy. She always stayed calm and in control as she directed her dog through the panels and down into the shedding ring, where they worked together to separate five sheep from the rest of the band. Bev opened the pen gate and stood aside to give her dog room to coax the wooly animals into the small enclosure. She always remained patient and kept her dog calm during the process, no matter how many minutes ticked off the time clock. Any attempt to rush the sheep would only cause a wreck. A polite round of applause went up from the small crowd of other handlers and spectators when she closed the gate behind the sheep for a successful pen.

Charlie stood by the handler's post as Bone lay by his side, waiting for the command to begin his outrun. On the judge's signal, Charlie sent his dog on a wide arc, crossing nearly three hundred yards of field to get around behind the small band of ewes set out at the far end of the field. The sheep were sharing a tiny pile of alfalfa hay that had been dropped to keep them from straying until the dog arrived to lift them and begin the fetch toward its handler. Bone came in low and slow, and eased the ewes away from their mid-day brunch to start them on a line toward the gate panels. So far, so good, Charlie thought. The sheep hadn't been startled, and they didn't drift off course or attempt to make a dash away from the dog.

Bone kept the sheep bunched up in a tight packet and brought them in a nearly straight line through the center panels and kept them moving directly toward Charlie and the handler's post. Charlie was pleased. He held out his shepherd's crook with his right hand to send Bone counter-clockwise around the handler's post. "Awaay—waay," Charlie commanded calmly, directing his dog to steer the sheep around the handler's post and begin the drive-away to the next set of panels.

Charlie's hours of practice with Bone were paying off. His dog was moving the sheep directly away from him in a fairly straight line toward the panels set up on the right side of the field. The sheep stalled for a moment and started to turn to the right and make a run toward the exhaust pen. Charlie whistled his dog around to flank the sheep on the right and keep them on course. He over-corrected, causing Bone to miss the next set of panels and lose points in the process.

Keep going, Charlie said to himself. You'll only lose more points if you try to fix it. Just keep going. Bone kept the ewes moving and pushed them directly through the center of the next set of panels. Charlie whistled and Bone turned the small band of sheep around the other side of the panels and brought them straight back toward his master. Bone was a natural when it came to fetching. He had a knack for keeping the sheep on a good line toward his handler, and that meant fewer points lost to a tough judge.

More than five minutes were left on the time clock when Bone entered the shedding ring with the sheep. Charlie stepped away from his post to assist his dog. The large, circular shedding ring was marked clearly on the ground, and Charlie knew to stand just off the center to give Bone plenty of room to hold the sheep against him and still hold them inside the ring.

He stepped in sideways, careful not to disturb the sheep, as he reached in with his shepherd's crook to help Bone separate five sheep from the band. Two, then three, peeled off from the rest as Charlie spooked the unneeded sheep away from the others until only five remained. He still had enough time to complete the pen.

"Lie down," Charlie commanded his dog as he walked away from the shedding ring to open the pen gate. "Walk up," he called, after swinging the gate open wide and turning to face his dog. The tight band of five sheep stood frozen in place, watching nervously as the wolf-like dog kept his eye fixed on them.

"Steady—get back!" Charlie called out harshly. Bone was bringing the sheep too fast, and they would be too rattled by the time they reached the pen to go inside willingly. The animals felt threatened, and the urge to flee was overwhelming. One ewe broke away from the others and bolted toward the large exhaust pen where the livestock was kept after it was used on the trial course. Bone raced to get around the frightened sheep and bring it back, but his reaction time was too late. It escaped across the field, and the remaining four, released by the lack of attention from their canine warden, followed the first escapee toward the large holding pen.

Bone had to start again, rounding up the woolies and heading them back across the field toward the pen. He had already lost a few points for his error, and he was running out of time. He brought the sheep back to the pen, and heeded his master's command to lie down, allowing the sheep to settle before trying to push them inside. He stepped forward slowly, and the sheep matched his movement with a step or two toward the open gate. Another step, then another, and the sheep avoided the gate opening altogether and ran around the outside of the pen. Bone stayed with them, moving in a wide arc around the stubborn animals to hold them against the pen and bring them full circle, back to the open gate.

"Time! Thank you." The buzzer sounded and the trial judge ended Bone's attempt to complete the course. Charlie called off his dog. It was a disappointing day for Charlie after such a good start.

"It's frustrating, Bev," Charlie said. "Bone pens sheep at home all day long during our practice sessions. He never misses."

"Don't get too worked up over it, Charlie. He's working with sheep he's never seen before—and they haven't seen him. As dumb as they can be, sheep learn to recognize a dog, and they feel safer when they're being moved around the course by a familiar dog if it's not too aggressive with them—they're less likely to be easily startled."

"I guess we've got work to do," Charlie said with a sigh. "Bone is going to have to learn to stay back and give the sheep more room, and I'm going to have to learn to keep him there."

"Now you're getting it," Bev said. "Most of the time it's the handler's fault when something goes wrong. Listen, why don't you come stay at the ranch with us tonight. You can ride with me after breakfast in the morning, before you head home. Don doesn't like to get on a horse much anymore, and we have a mare and two geldings that see a lot of idle time in their stalls lately. They'll be grateful for the exercise."

"Sounds good to me. I'll hang around for the awards presentation. I think you'll have a ribbon or two to pick up, if I'm not mistaken."

Charlie saddled a big buckskin gelding while Bev readied a halter and lead line for the third horse and climbed aboard her tall bay mare. The horses all needed exercise, and she didn't have much time to ride when the sheepdog trial season was under way.

"Are you sure you don't want to come with us?" she asked her husband, as he swung the corral gate open for the two riders. "It's a gorgeous day."

"Don't forget to write," Don chuckled, reminding his wife that he no longer favored horses as his transportation of choice.

"I guess it's just going to be you and me, Charlie," Bev said, as she led out across the pasture. Three of Bev's border collies showed the way, running out ahead of Bone and the horses as they crossed the open field toward the sagebrush-covered BLM land. The Bureau of Land Management controlled much of the land that surrounded ranches in Wyoming, and if nothing else, it did provide a lot of room to ride without encountering fences along the way.

They galloped the horses across an open stretch of ground for about a quarter mile to let them blow off a little pent-up energy, and then settled into an easy walking gait. Bone and his new companions maintained the easy pace, detouring from time to time to sniff out all the enticing smells in the brush before racing to catch up with the horses and riders.

"Isn't that a beautiful sight?" Bev asked, as she reined in her horse to admire the view of the snow-capped Uintah Range in the distance and the Bear River winding its way across the basin.

"It's beautiful country, there's no doubt about it," Charlie agreed. "Don't you love living in this part of the world?"

"We wouldn't live anywhere else," Bev answered. "I have a hard time getting Don to go anywhere else, for that matter."

"Well, he finally agreed to take the trip to England with you, didn't he?"

"Only through trickery, thanks to your suggestion," Bev laughed. "You know, Charlie, you should start entering Bone in a few more competitions. He's not going to get better unless you give him a chance to work in unfamiliar surroundings and let him compete more often. You might want to think about signing up for the Big Willow trials before the roster is filled up, and I think there's an open trial in Cedar City this fall. You'd be smart to plan ahead for them. It'll do you both good, and you can learn a lot."

"I'll do that, Bev," Charlie said. "I have to admit that it's been a lot of fun."

A few yards off the riding trail, one of Bev's dogs gave a shrill yelp and jumped away from a sagebrush, then came rushing back toward the horses with its tail tucked between its legs. It stopped in front Bev and dropped to the ground, panting heavily and whining. It was Bev's little two-year-old female, Nell.

Richard Hooton

"Do you think she stepped on something?" Charlie said, concerned for the dog as it lay still, waiting for its human owner to come to its rescue.

"No, she isn't limping. She may have been bit," Bev said as she swung down off her saddle and kneeled down to inspect the young dog. Two tell-tale marks were visible on the dog's muzzle, and she was obviously in pain. Bev inspected the wound carefully, then picked up the dog and handed it up to Charlie. "Hold her for minute, Charlie, while I get mounted."

Bev climbed on her mare and reached over to take her dog from Charlie. "You ride back to the house on the run, Charlie. Tell Don to call Doc Nelson and tell him we'll meet him at his clinic. Nell's been snake bit—a Diamondback, probably."

Charlie didn't wait to ask questions. He kicked the big gelding in the flanks and took off at a gallop toward the ranch. Bone followed his master, and kept up with the horse and rider the entire distance back to the house. The big buckskin was lathered up with sweat and Bone's tongue was lolling out of his mouth from the exertion of the mile and a half run back to the house.

"Don!" Charlie yelled as he ran up onto the rear deck of the house and pushed open the sliding door. "One of Bev's dogs got snake bit. She said to have you call the vet and tell him to meet her at the clinic. She can't ride too fast with the dog, but she should be along in a few minutes."

"Go cool that horse down, Charlie, and get some water for your dog. I'll make the call first, and then bring the truck around. You watch for Bev and let me know when you see her riding in."

Charlie rushed to unsaddle the gelding and hose it down with cool water, keeping an eye on the field beyond the corral for any sign of Bev. He had forgotten about Bone in the excitement of the moment, until he heard the noisy lapping sound and looked over to see his dog standing chest deep in the horse trough, lapping up water like it was to be his last drink.

He spotted the riderless horse first, trotting across the open field toward the corral, and trailing its lead line to one side. He ran out to catch the loose horse, worried that something had happened to Bev, then saw her riding in from the far end of the field.

"Did Don call the vet?" Bev asked as she rode up with Nell cradled in her arms and handed the dog down to Charlie.

"I'm sure he did. He said he was going to bring the truck around as soon as he got hold of the doctor."

Don came out of the house, moving as fast as he could on his bum leg. "Dr. Nelson will be there in twenty minutes," he said. "He has serum, but he doesn't know how much he'll need. I'll get the truck."

Charlie took the reins of the mare and led it over to the corral fence to take the saddle off. He released it into the corral and hurried back to Bev. "How's she doing?" he said, then felt ridiculous for asking as he noticed the dog's badly swollen muzzle.

"She's bad, but I think she was only bitten once. We're going to have to hurry."

Charlie loaded Bone into the back seat of his pickup and followed Don and Bev out onto the highway, accelerating to keep up as Don raced ahead at more than eighty miles per hour toward town. He checked his rear view mirror, hoping that they wouldn't encounter any Wyoming Highway Patrol cars on the four mile drive into Evanston.

The trucks pulled into the veterinary clinic and Bev climbed out of the cab with her dog before Don could bring the truck to a full stop, leaving the passenger door open as she rushed to the front entrance. A young vet technician opened the door for her and led her back to an examination room. "The operating room is in use right now," the young woman said. "We'll bring everything we need in here. Dr. Nelson should be here any minute."

Nell's breathing became labored as the swelling increased in her tongue and muzzle and her air passages became more restricted.

"It's okay, Nell," Bev said to her young dog, in the most soothing voice she had. "We're going to help you." She stroked Nell's back and shoulder gently to keep her calm. Bev knew that dogs had the ability to withstand a great deal of pain, and she hoped that Nell would remain conscious and breathing until the doctor could treat her.

Dr. Nelson came through the rear door of the examination room with two technicians close behind. "Bev, what do we have here?" he asked, as he gently lifted Nell's head and felt around her muzzle to better determine the extent of the swelling and the severity of the bite. "How long has it been since she was bitten?"

"About an hour, maybe a little longer," she answered, not sure of how much time it took to ride back to the ranch from the place where Nell had been struck by the rattler. "I couldn't ride very fast with her."

One of the technicians assisted Dr. Nelson with the vial of anti-venom while the other rinsed and cleaned Nell's tongue and the soft, tender tissue inside her mouth. "Looks like it was a big one," Dr. Nelson observed, as he pointed out two distinct fang wounds more than an inch apart. "But it appears she was only bitten once, and that's fortunate. We'll have to administer a series of treatments. One of our technicians will stay with her at all times, so she won't be left alone. Why don't you stick around for an hour or so? You can go next door to the cafe or sit out in the waiting room."

"I'll stay with Nell if you don't mind," Bev said.

Dr. Nelson nodded his assent, looking up to make eye contact with his technician to let her understand that he approved. He had been the large and small animal vet for the Thompsons for nearly fifteen years, and he knew what a strong-willed woman Bev Thompson could be when the welfare of her animals was involved, particularly if it meant saving the life of a dog or a horse. It would take a swat team to get her out of the clinic, and even that wouldn't be a sure thing.

"We'll be at the cafe next door," Don said to the young receptionist at the front desk. "If my wife comes out, would you let her know?"

"I'll be sure to tell her, Mr. Thompson," the girl said. "I'm sure her dog is going to be all right. Dr. Nelson is very experienced with snakebite treatments."

"Has he ever lost one?" Charlie asked.

"Only once—it was an older dog that had multiple bites and they didn't bring it in until the next day. It was in really bad shape when it arrived. But, I wouldn't worry—Nell is young and strong, and you brought her in right away."

Don and Charlie settled into a booth at the café and ordered something to eat. "Bev won't come out of there all day unless she's satisfied her dog is going to be all right," Don said.

"I may have to leave the truck here for her, and ride back to the ranch with you."

"Do you really think she'll stay in there all day?" Charlie asked.

"You just hide and see if she don't. She won't come out of there until she's satisfied her dog is going to be all right," Don said. "She takes better care of her dogs than she does of me."

Charlie smiled. "You don't think she really cares more about her animals than she does about you, do you, Don?"

Don took a brief moment to ponder the question, and smiled. "It's probably a toss-up," he said.

CHAPTER ELEVEN

HIS MASTER'S VOICE

Carver Ranch, Meeker, Colorado

Instinct trumps training every time, and no one knew that better than Scott McKenzie. Constant training and practice were always important to prepare a dog for working a trial course, but when the time came for the dog to work with unfamiliar sheep, and in the excitement and tension that came with competition, Scott knew that it was a dog's breeding that took over. A handler can only give direction by whistling commands from a distance, but it is a dog's instinct that guides it the rest of the way. Often working out of hearing range, a skillful dog has to decide on its own how to overcome unforeseen obstacles and events. The most instinctive dogs were usually the ones that prevailed at a trial.

Scott conducted a number of sheepdog clinics every year in South Dakota and Colorado, as well as the daily training that he offered on his small farm in southern Alberta whenever he wasn't traveling to clinics or competitions. He was an accomplished trainer and handler, and could boast a number of wins at Canadian and U.S. National competitions.

Charlie first met Scott at the sheepdog trials in Gillette, Wyoming and was impressed by his performance. He never seemed to give a command unless it was necessary, and he often allowed his dog to make its own decisions. When he did give a command, he followed it with a strong correction in a harsh tone if his dog didn't respond instantly. Charlie remembered watching him tell his dog to get back when it was bringing sheep into the shedding ring too fast, and when the dog failed to give way, Scott raised his voice and growled "you-better-listen-to-me!"

His dog stopped and dropped to the ground, then came up again more slowly, acknowledging its handler's command, but without losing contact with its sheep. Charlie was impressed. He signed up for Scott's next clinic in Colorado.

"Bone is a lot of dog, Charlie," Scott said. "You'll have to keep a handle on him in tight situations. He doesn't want to take any nonsense from unruly sheep, and he's likely to get the urge to be a little rough with them at times. If you let him get away with it, he'll be hard to correct."

"You don't think it will break his spirit if I correct him too often?" Charlie asked.

"You don't have to be too harsh with him—but be insistent. Never let him forget that you're there, and that you're watching him. Show him that it's your way or the highway. This is one dog you won't have to beg up. His instincts will drive him to keep trying, and he's got a powerful eye."

Scott McKenzie always established himself as the alpha male when he began the process of training a dog, and training time was almost any time he was with them. He imparted that wisdom to his students and it proved to be an enormous help to them. All too often, it was a lack of respect for their handler that caused a dog to attempt to go its own way when it should be heeding commands.

"Don't try to use too many verbal commands, Charlie," Scott cautioned. As smart as they are, border collies still have a limited vocabulary, so even short sentences are just so much yakety-yak to them. They'll respond a lot better to the whistle or to one or two word commands. They can sense your mood and intent from the tone of your voice better than another human can, and they have an uncanny ability for reading body language. Use it all to your advantage, and you'll begin to work as a team."

"I hope so," Charlie said. "The way we've been working, I'd be happy with any decent finish right now."

Scott shook his head in disapproval at his student's lack of confidence. "You should always aim high, Charlie. Never go into a competition thinking about anything but a win. Shoot for the moon, and if you miss it and hit a star, then that's okay."

Charlie came away from the two-day clinic with a sense of accomplishment. Under Scott Mckenzie's expert guidance, he learned how to narrow the psychological gap between Bone and himself when they worked with livestock. When he applied the techniques he had learned, Charlie got a quicker and more effective response from his dog.

Understanding what was expected of him, Bone seemed to have more confidence when he worked with his handler to steer the sheep around a trial course, and when he heard a command he reacted instantly. Charlie was glad he came. He knew that he would need to gain an edge if he expected to compete seriously at the big trials.

He pondered the events of the past two years during the long drive home from Colorado, along Interstate 80 through Cheyenne, and westward toward the Utah border. He had never before felt such personal satisfaction with any endeavor he had undertaken in his life as he did when he worked with Bone. He had begun to appreciate the connection between man and dog that grew into such a powerful bond. It was an inexplicable feeling that could only be understood by someone who shared the same experiences with a herding dog. He was finally beginning to understand why his parents loved the breed so much.

Charlie glanced over his shoulder into the back seat of the crew cab where Bone lay on his side, sleeping contentedly as the hum of the engine and the gentle vibration of tires rolling along the highway kept him secure in his slumber. Bone loved to ride in the truck with his master no matter what the destination might be. He was just as excited to go for a ride to the local gas station as he was to take a drive into the mountains for a day of hiking and exploring. As far as Bone was concerned, every ride was a good ride—with the possible exception of the occasional trip to the vet for vaccinations and the uncomfortable encounter with that pesky thermometer.

The late fall colors of the Wasatch Forest were in full array as Charlie and Bone crossed into Utah and recognized the familiar landscape close to home. A light dusting of new snow was visible on the north side of Mount Timpanogas when they rolled into Heber City in the late afternoon. Tomorrow might be a good day for a hike before winter sets in, Charlie thought. He had taken a week of vacation time and still had a few days before he had to go back to work. He was enjoying the quiet solitude and the time alone with his dog—it was good medicine for his soul. He talked to his dog about what they needed to do to prepare for the next sheepdog trial as they drove up the highway toward the farm. Bone was a good listener, and didn't interrupt when Charlie was talking.

"How did the clinic go?" Charlie's dad asked when Charlie came through the back door into the kitchen, kicking off his boots in the mud room before he stepped inside.

"It was good, Dad. Even better than I expected, I think." Charlie unbuttoned his mackinaw and hung it on the coat rack by the door. "Did I get home in time for dinner, or am I on my own?"

"We may both have to fare for ourselves if your mother doesn't get home soon," Jack answered. "She's been gone most of the day, working on some volunteer project at the middle school to help kids with their reading."

"Well, we just might be reading a menu at the cafe if she doesn't get home soon—I'm starved," Charlie said.

"You'll live. She'll be home any minute now and you can take us all out for a steak in Park City. She'll probably be too tired to cook. You did just get a raise recently, didn't you?"

"Yes. Yes, I did."

Charlie was in a good mood as he talked with his parents on the drive to Park City. Life was treating him well, and he spent his time thinking about the things he had instead of the things that he thought were missing from his life. He had managed to save a pretty good chunk of cash while he was staying on the farm with his parents, and he was able to work a lot of overtime to keep busy. He helped out around the farm and even put a fresh coat of white paint on the house and barn on his days off in the summer.

"I learned a lot from Scott McKenzie's clinic," Charlie said, as he changed lanes to get out of the way of a big tanker truck. "Didn't do Bone any harm either. It's funny that I keep forgetting that most of the

Richard Hooton

trouble a dog encounters while it's trying to work comes from its handler and not from the livestock."

"Yep," Jack said. "I told you to leave that dog alone and let him work."

"I know, I know," Charlie conceded. "Don and Bev kept telling me that, too. I guess it didn't really sink in until Scott McKenzie showed me how many ways there were to communicate with a dog without barking commands at him all the time. He said that I'd learn more from Bone than he could ever learn from me."

"Sounds like a smart man," Sarah said. "You better listen to him."

Never—not even in his wildest imaginings—did Charlie ever think that at his age he would be living back on the farm with his folks and actually enjoying their company. The farm had become his refuge—a fortress to protect him from the outside world. It was a place where he could live among familiar surroundings and be comforted by knowing that each day would be much the same as the last. It would do for now.

"I thought I'd take Bone on a hike up the back side of Mount Timpanogas tomorrow," Charlie said. "I haven't been to the top since I was in Boy Scouts. We won't climb to the top, but there should be a great view from above the tree line, and Bone can explore to his heart's content."

"You better check the weather report first, son," Sarah cautioned. "They've been getting some rain and snow in northern Nevada from those last two Pacific storms. Maybe you should wait a day or two."

"I'm not worried. If I feel a temperature drop or see any dark clouds flying over the ridge we'll just get back down the trail as fast as we can," Charlie said. "I'll pack some cold weather gear in my backpack just in case," he added, seeing the warning look in his mother's eyes. She was pretty wise about the weather in the Heber Valley, and knew better than to get caught out in it when a storm broke over the mountains.

"Come on, Bone. Let's load up," Charlie said, as he opened the rear door of the crew cab and stepped aside to allow Bone to jump up into the back seat. "We're getting a late start. We better get a move on." Bone settled into his favorite riding spot, where he could move from the left side of the cab to the right and put his head through the window to see what was going on outside. He loved the feel of the wind in his face as they traveled down the county road toward the base of the mountains.

Charlie had rolled out of bed late that morning, feeling a little lazy after nearly a week of vacation that had given him time to sleep in almost every morning. It was nearly nine when they reached the end of the gravel access road at the base of the mountain. He set the foot brake and stepped out onto the damp ground, inhaled a deep breath of fresh mountain air, and lifted his backpack out of the truck bed. Bone jumped out through the open window, eager to begin whatever adventure his master had in mind for the day.

"Let's go exploring, boy," Charlie said, with eagerness in his voice. Bone barked excitedly, backing away from his master to show how ready he was for whatever fun was about to begin.

Charlie checked the contents of his backpack. He had a thirty-foot length of eleven millimeter nylon climber's rope, a rain poncho, matches, a rigging knife, and a water canteen. He pushed the ham sandwiches he made that morning into the top of the backpack, along with a large package of beef jerky he picked up at the gas station in Heber Junction the night before.

He pulled up the zipper on his mackinaw and slung the pack loosely over one shoulder as he started out toward a line of trees near the base of the mountain. There were sure to be a few trails that converged onto one main trail further up the mountainside. Bone was already running out in the lead, sniffing his way up the slope and marking bushes along the way.

"Stay with me, Bone," Charlie called out, not wanting his dog to get too far ahead, or to get distracted by the scent of a rabbit or a squirrel that might lead him far off the trail and out of sight. He was glad that Bone got to roam around without any fences or boundaries to constrain him.

There was something about wide open spaces that was good for the souls of men and dogs. Charlie paused to turn and look around at the Heber Valley. They were already high enough to have a great view of the central part of the valley. It was a sight that Charlie loved. Peaceful farmlands stretched out below, dotted with houses and barns and defined by fence lines that gave it all a sense of order. Everything looked better from a distance, Charlie thought.

"Come on, boy. You stay with me!" Bone came out of the trees and trotted down the trail to his master before making a u-turn and heading back up the mountain to resume his hobby of varmint tracking. "If I had your energy we could make it to the top before lunch," Charlie said, stopping to catch his breath. He was beginning to feel the effects from physical exertion and the change in altitude.

Charlie felt the sudden temperature drop as the trail led into a large stand of trees. The constant shade kept the warming rays of the sun from reaching the earth, and it felt as if it was at least ten degrees cooler in the forest. He paused to pull his woolen stocking cap down snugly over his ears and reached into his pocket for his gloves.

He hadn't seen Bone for a few minutes, and called out to him to come back. "Bone, where are you? Bone! Come on, boy." He kept climbing up the trail, anxious to see a sign of his dog and to get above the trees and back into the sunlight.

He could see more light up ahead, and quickened the pace of his uphill climb, panting and puffing and feeling a burning sensation in his thighs from the strenuous climb. He kept moving until he reached the tree line. "Bone! Here, boy!"

Charlie drew a breath and whistled as he walked out of the trees and onto an immense scree slope covered with years of rock deposits that had separated from the cliff walls high above. He was beginning to worry. It wasn't like Bone to ignore his call. He climbed higher on the rocky slope to get a better view of the tree line below him and called again in a louder, harsher voice. "Bone, you better get over here! Bone! Here, boy."

He began to traverse the rocky slope, slipping and falling on the unstable rock slope as he called down into the trees for his dog. He stopped and waited, wondering if his dog could see him from the shadows of the trees. Probably not, Charlie thought. He would have heard me, and come running.

A heavy gust of cold wind nearly knocked Charlie off his feet. He sat down on a large rock, opened his backpack and took out a canteen. He took a few gulps of water, caught his breath, and waited. There was still no sign of his dog. He reached into the pack for a sandwich and took a few bites. Charlie had a good view of the tree line below him and would have seen if Bone had crossed out of the trees and into the open. He scanned the rocks and trees for a long minute, looking for any sign of movement. Nothing.

It was just past noon and the wind was picking up. Dark clouds appeared over the mountaintops to the west and Charlie could feel the temperature dropping fast. He knew it was time to get off the mountain. He strapped on his backpack and started back down toward the trees. Looking back in the direction he came from, Charlie decided he must have come at least a hundred yards or so from where the trail emerged from the trees. He followed the tree line until he found a game trail, then he started down into the trees, calling and whistling for his dog as he descended the steep slope. With any luck, his dog might have found the same deer trail and followed the scent.

Another gust of cold wind hit Charlie in the face, this time with an icy blast of freezing rain. Within seconds he was caught in a downpour. He kneeled down under a tree and opened his backpack to retrieve the rain poncho. He was glad that he knew enough to pack rain gear, just in case. He was already wet by the time he got his poncho out of the pack and pulled it over his head. It didn't do anything to protect his pants, and it only took a few minutes for his pant legs to be soaked all the way through.

Charlie called for his dog over and over, frustrated and angry that he was getting no response. He was sure that Bone could find his way back down the mountain, but it was no good for either of them to be caught out in an early winter storm with no shelter. He suddenly realized that the game trail was leading across the mountainside rather than down slope. Deer weren't as concerned as humans were with reaching the bottom of the mountain. They simply traversed the slopes to wherever the best grazing was at a particular time of year, or to a safe place to sleep for the night.

Charlie didn't know how far he had strayed from the spot where he had emerged from the woods, but he was sure that he couldn't find his way back to the hiking trail in the sleet that was beginning to sting his face and build up on his shoulders and pant legs. He stopped and got his bearings. He was pretty sure of the way down, and just hoped he didn't climb down into a ravine that led in a direction he didn't want to go.

Bone came up behind Charlie in the dim light of the storm-shrouded forest and pushed his muzzle up against his master's gloved hand. Charlie nearly jumped out of his skin. "Yaaah! Bone! Don't sneak up on me like that. Where have you been?" Charlie kneeled down to brush off some of the sleet that was caked on Bone's coat. "You stay with me. What's wrong with you? You don't run off that way—do you understand?" Bone wasn't sure what his master was saying, but he knew it wasn't praise.

Charlie started down through the trees, stumbling over rocks and brush and downed tree branches. He couldn't find anything that remotely resembled a trail, but he knew he had to get out of the trees and onto the lower slope so he could see where he was going.

Sleet turned to wet, heavy snow, and Charlie was beginning to slip and stumble on the wet ground with nearly every step. Bone tried to follow, but the icy downhill slope made it difficult to maneuver, even for a dog. Charlie sat down and leaned against the trunk of a big evergreen to catch his breath. He quickly decided that stopping wasn't such a good idea—he felt the cold penetrate his wet clothing. His boots were soaked and he wasn't wearing long underwear. He suddenly felt woefully unprepared for what was supposed to be an easy day hike.

Charlie considered his options. It was starting to get dark and he had no sleeping bag or tent—not even a small tarp. He hadn't expected to get caught off trail and in this kind of weather. He could keep moving and risk a serious fall and injury, or he could stop and build a makeshift shelter from pine boughs and build a small fire. He decided to keep going for a little longer, while there was still daylight.

"Come on, Bone. Let's keep moving." Charlie grabbed at tree branches to steady himself as he slipped and slid his way down the mountainside. Bone stayed with him, picking his way cautiously down the steep slope to avoid losing his footing. They were closer to getting off the mountain with every step, and that was all that Charlie cared about.

Icy wind was biting his face and heavy snowfall was filtering through the tree branches—it would be much worse when they reached the open area below the trees. Charlie considered once more whether he should stop and build a shelter. He didn't want to wait until hypothermia set in or he could be in real trouble. It would be easier to find dry wood under the canopy of the trees if he didn't waste any more time. He knew that as soon as the heavy snowfall penetrated the tree branches and covered the ground beneath them, there would be no dry firewood or kindling to be found.

Five more minutes, that's all. Keep going for five more minutes and maybe we'll reach a clearing, Charlie thought. He sidestepped down a loose slope covered with small rocks and tree litter, feeling the wet ground give way under his weight as he went. He reached up to grasp a tree branch as he side-slipped underneath it and lost his footing on the wet pine needles, twisting his ankle as he dropped to the wet ground. He raised a forearm to protect his face from the tree branches that swatted him as he slid downward and banged into a fallen tree, bruising his ribs on the rough trunk. The wind was knocked out of him.

Charlie berated himself for not stopping sooner. What a stupid idea it was to keep going in such foul weather! He had learned the basics of survival years ago. Shelter first, then water, and then food. If he didn't have shelter, food and water wouldn't help him. He sat up, holding his rib cage as he drew in short breaths. It was too painful to take a deep breath, and he thought he had cracked a rib or two. He felt the pain in his right ankle and was sure it was only a sprain—but a bad one, nonetheless.

Bone scooted down the slope on his haunches and forepaws and hurried to Charlie's side. He sniffed all around Charlie's face and hands to be sure he was all right, and saw that he was moving and breathing, but Bone was no good at diagnosing sprains and bruises. He didn't know his master was in trouble.

Charlie tried to stand, but he couldn't put any weight on his right ankle. He looked around, trying to remain calm as he thought about what he should do next. Below him and to his left he could see an opening in the trees. Wind gusts were blowing blinding snow, so it was difficult to tell whether or not it was a large clearing. He decided to make one last effort to get out of the trees and try to determine his location on the mountain before resorting to building a fire and a lean-to for shelter.

He broke off a long limb from the fallen tree trunk and used his rigging knife to pare off the smaller branches. It was a crude walking stick, but Charlie was able to use it as a crutch to take the weight off his right leg as he traversed the slope toward the place he thought he saw daylight through the trees. If he didn't find anything, Charlie decided, he could lash his makeshift crutch between two trees about three feet off the ground and lay pine boughs against it to protect him from the worst of the storm. A fire would feel good right now, he thought.

A cold, wintry blast of snow hit Charlie in the face as he reached the edge of the clearing, blurring his vision temporarily. He blinked and wiped his eyes, trying to see through the heavy snowfall. It was almost invisible in the waning light, but Charlie thought he could see the outline of a structure below him on the open slope. He couldn't gauge the distance in the driving snow, but he was sure it wasn't more than fifty or sixty yards.

"Bone, stay with me," Charlie called as he began his gimpy, stumbling descent down the snow-covered slope. His left foot slipped from beneath him and he landed on his back in the wet snow.

"This isn't working, Bone," he complained with a brief burst of laughter, trying to keep what sense of humor he had left. "Let's get to that shed, or whatever it is." Charlie scooted on his rump, dragging his crutch along with him until the slope leveled out again. He could see it more clearly. It was definitely some kind of shed, he thought, as he drew closer to the structure.

Near whiteout conditions were setting in as the wind-driven snow blasted the mountainside and reduced visibility to only a few feet. Charlie kept going, calling to his dog as he hobbled downhill toward the shelter they desperately needed.

"Bone, you stay with me! Where are you?" Bone came up the slope through the blizzard toward Charlie. He had already gone ahead to sniff around the old wooden structure. Once he reached his master and nuzzled his hand to demonstrate his obedience, he turned and led the way downhill to the small shack.

Charlie reached the uphill side of the structure and saw a small window. He hobbled around to the front and discovered a small covered stoop and a door. Thank God, he thought. This beats a lean-to in the trees.

He pounded a couple of times on the door, calling out just in case someone was inside. He turned the rusted doorknob and pushed, forcing the old slat door inward and was struck with the musty, old cabin odor. It was a genuine refuge from the storm. It was heaven.

Charlie left the door open to take advantage of what light was left in the western sky and adjusted his eyes to the dim light of the interior. It was a tiny, one-room shack, not more than twelve feet wide. A small bunk was against one wall; its thin cotton mattress was rolled up and left atop one end of the wire and spring supports. A tiny wooden table and handmade stool rested next to an old cast iron wood stove. Charlie was relieved beyond words. "We've hit the jackpot, boy," he said to his dog. "We're going to be all right." Bone walked around the small cabin, inspecting every corner and crevice as he listened, comforted by the calming sound of his master's voice.

The old floorboards creaked under Charlie's weight as he hopped over to the wood stove and looked into the firewood box that lay on the floor next to the stove. The four or five pieces of dry wood that it held, plus a few kindling pieces and pine cones in the bottom, would not be enough to keep the place warm through the night. The shack was not insulated, and would barely keep out the wind, much less hold in any heat from the stove.

Charlie pushed the door closed, took the matches out of his backpack and started a fire, using most of the dry firewood in the process. There wouldn't be enough to make it through the night, he thought, so he would have to bring in whatever wood he could find and let it dry out next to the stove during the night. He left his backpack on the floor, picked up his hobble-stick and started out the door into the freezing snow and wind.

"Come on, Bone. Let's go find some more firewood." Bone didn't hesitate to follow his master out into the blizzard. It didn't matter that they had only gained refuge for a few minutes before giving themselves up again to the storm; he would go where his master called him to go. His temporary absence during his varmint-hunting excursion would be forgiven, and from now on he would keep closer watch over his master.

Charlie struggled against the wind, his rainproof poncho flapping wildly as he leaned on his crutch and limped toward a fallen tree that lay on the ground a few yards from the shack. His ribs still hurt, but the pain wasn't overwhelming. With any luck, he was just scraped and bruised. "This is our lucky day, Bone," he yelled to his dog through the howling wind. "It's a dead tree." He had no more worries for his immediate future as he began to break the brittle branches away from the fallen trunk. He had good shelter, and enough food and water to wait out the storm—even if it was a bad one.

Charlie gathered all the wood he could carry in four trips, resting long enough after each armload to warm himself by the fire for a minute or two before going back out into the storm for more wood. He spread the pieces of wood on the floor around the hot stove without stacking any of it in a pile. It would dry much faster if he didn't stack wet wood on top of other wet wood. He put another piece of wood in the stove and began to strip off his wet clothing. He had a difficult time getting his injured foot out of his wet boot, and he had to remove the laces altogether so he could open it wide enough to remove his foot without causing more pain.

Charlie and Bone shared some beef jerky and the rest of the ham sandwich Charlie had started to eat earlier in the day. He put the other sandwich and the rest of the jerky in the backpack for later. It could be a long night. Now that he and Bone were out of immediate danger, Charlie took a few minutes to think about his dilemma. His ankle was beginning to swell and the pain was intense. His parents would certainly be worried. Someone was sure to come looking for him if he was missing all night, but there was nothing he could do about it now.

It suddenly occurred to Charlie where he was. He was sure that he had stumbled down the mountainside onto the old homestead cabin site near the upper end of the hollow. It had been there since the time the U. S. Army soldiers had camped in the hollow in 1847, the year the government conducted its first survey of the region.

Nothing looked the same in a blizzard, but he was certain that it was the same old cabin that sat on the hillside above the cross country skiing area. It must have been three miles from where he had parked the pickup, he thought, but less than a mile to the parking lot for the resort. It might as well have been fifty miles. He wasn't going anywhere before morning.

He turned his pants and cotton pullover that hung over the wooden stool next to the stove so they could dry on the other side. His woolen sweater and parka were the only clothes than weren't sweat-soaked or covered with snow. He stoked the fire again, then unrolled the mattress on the bunk and pulled it closer to the stove. He covered himself with his parka and huddled under it to get warm. It felt good—not exactly a four-star hotel—but still good.

Bone was sound asleep on the floor next to the bunk, unconcerned with the howling storm outside and content with the Spartan accommodations he shared with his master. Charlie pulled his knees up under his chin to keep his entire body under his parka. He felt like a moron for starting up the mountain so unprepared and for getting himself into such a predicament. He was exhausted. The warmth from the wood stove put him to sleep.

Charlie woke up shivering. The fire had gone out and the wind was still blowing, but not as violently as it had been in the early evening. His ankle was more swollen and throbbing with pain. He groaned aloud and Bone came to his side, pushing his muzzle against his hand. "It's all right, boy. I'm okay."

He forced himself off the mattress and felt around for the stool. His pants and pullover were cold, but dry. He pulled them on in the dark and fumbled in the backpack for the waterproof tube filled with stick matches. In a few minutes, he had a big fire roaring in the stove again. Most of the wood he had gleaned from the dead tree was dry enough to burn, so he stoked the fire with enough wood to keep it burning for a few hours. He used the light from the fire to read the dial on his wrist-watch—just after two in the morning.

He knew his folks would be worried, but he hoped they would remember that he was resourceful, and that he had enough survival skills to stay alive if he was caught in a storm. Even so, he knew that he would have to listen to his mother's admonishments for the next few days—or weeks.

Charlie felt hungry, and he was sure that Bone would be happy to eat something. He broke out the last ham sandwich and gave his dog most of the meat before eating the rest himself. He chewed on some beef jerky while he waited for the cabin to warm up again. He gave another piece of jerky to his dog, then covered his bare feet with his sweater to keep them warm and curled up under his parka again.

When he woke again it was four-thirty and the early morning cold was bitter. The fire had nearly gone out again, but a few red coals were all that was needed to ignite a couple of dry pine cones, and Charlie stacked enough firewood on to get a good blaze going. He sat on the stool, close to the stove, and waited for the shack to warm up again. He didn't need anymore sleep. He set his boots closer to the stove so they would dry out a little better and peered out through the small window to see how much snow had fallen during the night. The snow had stopped falling and the wind had died down a little. It looked like more than two feet had piled up around the tiny cabin, but some of that may have been due to drifting, he thought. He decided to wait until first light before opening the door. He wanted to be ready to leave when the cold air rushed in again.

Charlie struggled to pull his right boot on over his swollen ankle. He laced it as tightly as he could to be certain it would give him some support, but it still hurt so badly he couldn't put any weight on it. He would have to wade through the drifted snow, but it wasn't more than a mile to a road. He could make it.

Karen Parker had spent nine years with Wasatch Search and Rescue. When she wasn't volunteering her time to help rescue cross-country skiers and backpackers, she worked as a nurse at the medical clinic in

Park City. She had seen every kind of skiing-related broken bone, and had helped to patch up hikers, climbers and snowboarders who had been brought in with cuts or head injuries. She was well-acquainted with the debilitating effects of hypothermia and frostbite, and was rarely surprised by the kinds of injuries that came into the clinic. She was an experienced cross-country skier and snowmobile rider, and a valuable asset to the rescue team.

Karen suited up in her snowmobile jumpsuit in the parking lot at the Zermatt Resort while she waited for the team leader to finish reviewing a geological survey section map of the area with a deputy sheriff and one of the search and rescue dog handlers. It wasn't unusual for them to see an October snowfall, but they couldn't remember the last time a storm brought in so much snow before November. It was still too early in the morning to see, but the storm had moved out during the night and the wind had died, so visibility would be good as soon as the sun began to rise.

Karen noticed one of the rescue dogs looking across the hollow, its nose lifted as it sniffed at the air. Karen turned her attention to the same area on the side of the mountain where the dog was looking and lifted her head to inhale deeply. She was certain she smelled a whiff of wood smoke, but there were no inhabited homes or cabins nearby. She walked a short distance across the parking lot from where the rescue team was gathered so she could get a better view across the hollow and up the side of the mountain. At first it looked like a wisp of snow, carried off a rooftop by the wind. She watched carefully for a few more seconds, and was sure that she was seeing smoke coming from the top of the old homesteader's shack high up on the slope.

Karen climbed on the big Polaris and fired the engine, then backed it down the ramp onto the snow-covered parking lot. "I'll be back in a few minutes," she said. "I want to check something out." She rode toward the lower parking area and crossed the small bridge that spanned the year-round stream that flowed out of the hollow. It took less than five minutes for her to reach the lower slope where she could see the old shack clearly. She was right. A faint trace of wood smoke wafted out of the old metal chimney. It was scarcely visible, but the unmistakable aroma of burned pine hung in the air.

Charlie pulled the poncho over his head, picked up his walking stick, and opened the door to meet the early morning cold. The temperature was below freezing and a thick blanket of snow covered the slope below him. He wasn't sure exactly how much snow had fallen during the night, or how much it had drifted, but when he stepped off the covered stoop, he was knee deep in it. This isn't going to be fun, he thought.

"Come on, Bone," Charlie said with an air of resignation in his voice. "No time like the present."

It was slow-going for Charlie as he planted the crutch into the ground for support, then vaulted forward, lunging through the drifted snow as he pulled his left leg up and out of the snow and hopped forward a couple of feet at a time. Every step was a major effort, and the exertion was causing him to huff and puff as he struggled to move downhill. Bone was bouncing through the snow and having a great time, savoring mouthfuls of the white stuff as he frolicked down the hillside ahead of his master.

Charlie stepped into a drift-filled gulley and plunged waist-deep into the snow. He tried to pull himself up and only succeeded in sliding further down into the small ravine until he was nearly up to his armpits in it. The sound of an approaching snowmobile raised his spirits.

"Hello, down there," Karen said, as she pulled her goggles away from her eyes and lifted them up to her forehead.. "Are you hurt?"

Charlie blew some snow out of his mouth and looked up at the young woman sitting on the snowmobile at the edge of the gulley. "No, I'm all right."

"Really? Silly me. I could swear you look like you're in trouble from where I'm sitting."

Karen dismounted the big Polaris and retrieved a short nylon line from the utility box on the back. She tied a loop in one end, secured the other end to the back of the snowmobile and tossed the line down to Charlie. "I'm gonna go out on a limb here and say your name is Charlie Stewart. Am I right?"

"Yeah, that's me. I wish it wasn't."

"Did you injure your leg?" she asked, seeing the crude staff he grasped with one hand.

"Well, my ankle was twisted pretty bad, but now it's mostly my pride that hurts."

"Your dog seems to be okay."

"I never saw him before in my life," Charlie said sarcastically.

"No? Well, he seems to know you." Bone stood at the edge of the gulley, his tail wagging as he watched his master flounder in the snow-drift.

"Yeah, well we're not talking to each other right now," Charlie said, as he slipped one arm through the loop and cradled his elbow snugly into it for support as he held tightly to the line with both hands.

Karen nudged the throttle until the slack was taken up in the line, then throttled up slowly and dragged her rescue out of the gulley.

"It doesn't look like you're too much the worse for wear," she said. "Did you spend the night in the old homestead shack?"

"Yeah, it's the last thing we could see before dark," Charlie admitted. "If we hadn't found it, I guess we would have spent the night under a tree." He struggled to his feet, wound up the nylon line and handed it back to Karen. She saw that he was favoring his right leg, and noticed how much wider the laces were spread apart on his right boot. It was obvious the ankle was badly swollen.

"Why don't you climb on behind me," she said. "There's room for your dog in between us. I'll go slow so you don't fall off."

Charlie felt emasculated. He swung his right leg over the seat and threw his crutch into the snow, then called Bone over to the snowmobile and coaxed him up onto the seat. He saw the bold lettering embroidered onto a large red cross on the back of Karen's parka that spelled out Wasatch Search and Rescue, and regretted that he hadn't told his folks he might be gone for more than a day.

Several members of the rescue team and a deputy sheriff were waiting in the parking lot at the Zermatt Lodge when Karen pulled up with her passengers. She had radioed ahead to let them know Charlie had been found, and to ask her team leader to get the emergency vehicle ready to transport him to the medical facility in Heber City, where they could x-ray his ankle and check him for hypothermia and dehydration. She was certain he would be all right, but they had strict procedures for handling rescues.

"Your parents have been worried about you, Charlie," the team leader said. "I have to ask you a few questions first, and then we'll get you on your way to the medical center so they can check you over and take care of that ankle for you."

The man turned away and radioed to the helicopter that was standing by at the lower end of the parking lot. "I'm sending two guys down for you to take up to the west side of the mountain to help look for those missing climbers who didn't get down yesterday," he said to the pilot. "They'll be there in five minutes."

Charlie was relieved when the team leader seemed to change his mind about questioning him, and instead told the emergency vehicle driver to take off for the medical center. It appeared that he had larger concerns than to learn why Charlie didn't get off the mountain immediately, once he saw the weather start to change. "Karen, get some details about his hike and his route. You know what to ask," the rescue leader said.

"I'll take your dog with me, Charlie," Karen said, as she constrained Bone from jumping into the back of the emergency vehicle with his master. "And I'll call your folks to let them know you're all right."

Charlie was relieved the focus of attention was no longer on him. It was bad enough being the subject of a search, and being carried out on a gurney with a sprained ankle was just embarrassing. Having to submit to a series of questions about how he managed to get himself into such a predicament would have been worse. It made him feel like an idiot.

"You don't look so bad," Karen said, as she walked up to Charlie in the emergency room of the Heber Medical Facility. "Are you sure you weren't faking it, just to get a ride on my shiny new snowmobile?"

Charlie grinned at the young woman's humor. "I probably would have," he said. "But this time it was real. It feels like they wrapped about fifty feet of Ace bandage around my ankle."

Karen pulled her woolen cap off and a blonde ponytail tumbled onto her back. "I called your folks and told them not to worry about you. I figured you were embarrassed enough without having your mom come here to look at your swollen foot."

"Thanks," Charlie said. "I owe you." He hadn't been able to see her very well through the big goggles and knit cap she was wearing when she found him half-buried in the snow, but her beauty was striking. She wore no makeup, but the fresh, rosy color on her flawless skin made her extremely attractive.

"I'll be happy to drop you off at your place if you like," Karen offered. "I've got your dog out in my Jeep, so you have to say yes or I'll keep him."

"He might be more trouble than he's worth," Charlie laughed.

"That's what I was thinking about you," Karen said. "But I'll take a second look after you get cleaned up."

Charlie didn't mind the wheelchair ride out through the door to the parking lot—in fact, he was beginning to like the attention he was getting from the young search and rescue lady.

"Bone is a border collie, isn't he?" Sarah asked as she wheeled Charlie over to the passenger side of her Jeep Wrangler.

"Yes, he is. He's starting to be a pretty good herding dog, too. I just need to get him entered in a few more trial competitions so we can both get more experience."

"I have a young black lab and border collie mix," Karen said, as she buckled herself in and reached into the back seat to give Bone a pat on the head. "Her name is Cricket."

"You named your dog after a bug?" Charlie said with a chuckle and a grin.

"You named your dog Bone, so you've got nothing to say," Karen defended. "Cricket was a rescue herself, and now she's starting her training to be an avalanche search and rescue dog."

"Really? I'm impressed," Charlie admitted. "Do you work full time at saving people from themselves, or is it just a hobby?"

"Neither—I'm a volunteer. I like it, though," Karen added. "I'm a nurse at the medical center in Park City, and it can be pretty boring except during ski season. Between ski injuries and mountain rescues, my winters are usually quite busy."

Charlie was pleased that she liked dogs so well—not to mention that it provided him the perfect excuse to see more of her. "I'm taking Bone down to Cedar City for a sheepdog trial in a couple of weeks. Since the ski season isn't upon us yet, maybe you'd like to come and watch."

"How are you going to manage that with a bum leg?"

"I don't have to chase after sheep. That's Bone's job. I get to stand in one spot and whistle—and I have a shepherd's staff to lean on."

"I don't know, Charlie. I try to make it a point never to go to a sheepdog trial with a guy on our first date. You'll have to take me out to dinner first."

Charlie liked Karen's flair for wit. He was glad he got stuck on the mountain in an early snowstorm. He looked across at Karen and studied her face as she drove her Jeep onto the slushy pavement.

"What?" Karen said, with a tone of amusement, when she looked over at Charlie and caught him staring at her.

Charlie didn't look away. He liked the way she looked, and he liked the way she talked. And she seemed to love dogs, which was even better. "You're really something," he said.

CHAPTER TWELVE

SOLDIER HOLLOW

Heber Valley, Utah

Tiny shoots of green meadow grass pushed upward through the sparse patches of late spring snow that clung to the ground along the highway, reaching for life in the bright sunlight of an April morning. There was hardly any traffic on the road, and the thirty minute drive into Park City promised to be a pleasant one.

Life was good for Charlie Stewart. He had everything he had ever wanted—a house, a dog, a loving wife, and a beautiful little girl—and a good-paying job so he could feed them all.

He left for work early on Saturday to get to the site of the new Park City condo project before seven. He was three weeks late getting the foundation poured, and failing to keep a job on schedule made Charlie's partner edgy. Charlie was meticulous with his planning, preparation and plans review, but once a construction project came out of the ground, it was Wayne Clark who took over and kept them on schedule. His years of experience, including the time he spent overseeing the construction of the cross-country skiing site for the 2002 Winter Olympics, had proven him to be a contractor who was capable of bringing in a quality job, on time and under budget.

"Hey, Wayne—how's it going?" Charlie asked, as he stepped out of his truck and walked over to where his partner was double-checking a set of foundation plans for the exact number and location of anchor bolts. Wayne had already been on the job for an hour or more, checking the level of the forms and making sure all the bracing and ties were in place. It was the kind of attention to detail that kept their little contracting company in constant demand with area developers.

"I'm good, Charlie. Cement trucks should have been here already, though," his partner said, without looking up.

"You want me to call them?" Charlie asked.

"I already did. Dispatcher said they were on the way. I'm not sure whether that meant they were on the way here, or on the way to get coffee and doughnuts."

Wayne Clark was never a man who tolerated laziness—or tardiness either, for that matter. He had learned his solid work ethic from his father, who always reminded him that there were only one thousand four hundred and forty minutes in every day. A man had to use every one of them wisely if he ever expected to accomplish anything in life. Charlie was lucky to have him as a business partner.

The morning went better than expected once all the cement finishers and trucks arrived. The pour went well, and by noon they were nearly done for the day.

"Wayne, I have to take off now," Charlie said. "I'm due at the house at two o'clock."

"What? You haven't been here four hours and you're already leaving?" Wayne complained. "I'm exhausted from working twelve hours a day all week long and you have to take off? Well, just throw me in my coffin right now and I'll be happy."

Charlie chuckled as his hard-working partner ranted. Wayne didn't know anything except hard work—he only wanted to be noticed and appreciated for it.

"I have to stop at Heber Junction and pick up a birthday present for Mary," Charlie explained. "My little girl turns four today, and if I'm late for her party, Karen will tear strips off of me for sure."

Wayne's demeanor softened. "Oh, well then," he said, in a voice that was quiet and understanding. He was a husband and father himself, and required no further explanation. "You give her a hug for me, and tell her I said happy birthday. You better hurry," he added.

Charlie stopped at the factory outlet stores on the way home and searched for just the right birthday gift for his little girl. After a few minutes of wandering through the store, he realized that he had no idea what a little girl might want, so he solicited the help of a young woman who appeared to be about the right age to be a mother herself. It paid off—the helpful clerk had two daughters of her own, and guided him to a section with children's books and play sets. He had to stop himself before he bought one of everything.

He arrived home with a half hour to spare—time enough to clean up and change his clothes. Charlie's mom and dad were already there. His mom helped Karen finish putting up the party decorations while his dad doted over his only grandchild.

"I never knew that having kids would be this much fun," Charlie said, as he walked up behind his wife and mom at the kitchen counter and reached between them for a cupcake. He got his hand slapped from both sides for the attempt. He retreated to the upstairs bathroom for a shower and a shave.

Mary's friends began to show up with their moms, and before long the house was filled with the sound of children laughing and squealing. Bone and Cricket sat outside on the deck with their noses against the sliding glass door.

Charlie talked with his dad while the birthday party went on around them, only pausing in their conversation long enough to acknowledge his little girl when she opened her present of children's books and came over to show them to her daddy and give him a hug.

"A letter came for you today," Karen said, after the ice cream and cake and kids were all gone. "Looks important."

"Was it fan mail or a draft notice?" Charlie quipped. "Otherwise, it couldn't be very important."

Karen retrieved the letter from the kitchen counter and brought it to the small dining table where Charlie sat with his parents. "Open it and see," she said, handing the envelope to him with a smile.

Charlie looked at the return address and tore the envelope open. He read the short letter twice; he wanted to be sure he wasn't seeing things.

"Well," Charlie's mom said. "Tell us."

"I can't believe it," Charlie said, looking up with amazement at Karen and then at his parents. "It's an invitation to compete in the Soldier Hollow Classic on Labor Day Weekend."

Charlie read it again. "I can't believe it," he repeated. "I must have had enough wins in some of the Utah area trials or I wouldn't even be considered for an invitation."

"You came in second at the Big Willow Classic in Payette last year," Karen praised. "And you won at the Sonoma Sheepdog Trials. I think that justifies an invitation."

"I'll have a lot of work to do to get ready," Charlie said. "I'll have to train with Bone almost every day. The competitors will be big trial winners and national champions from all over the world."

"Don't let it worry you, Son," Sarah Stewart said. "You're as good as the best of them, even if you don't know it."

"I don't know," Charlie said, somewhat skeptically. "Bev gets invited every year because of her top rankings at Meeker, Colorado and at the Nationals. Scott McKenzie and a woman by the name of Amanda Miller are top winners in Canada year after year, so they're sure to be invited. There's a guy from California who has a lot of wins, too—Bill Broderick, I think his name is—not to mention the champions from Great Britain and Scandinavia, and all the big names that get invited from the East and the Midwest. I've heard there are some tough competitors at the Bluegrass Classic in Lexington."

"Don't get yourself all worked up, Charlie," his dad said. "They're still just dogs working with sheep."

"Yeah, in front of several thousand spectators and one very critical judge," Charlie said.

"You've got an edge, Charlie," his wife said. "You and Bone know the terrain. You spent the night up there once, in the old homesteader's shack right in the middle of where they set up the trial course. Remember?"

"Oh, yeah. That should cinch a win for us."

"Don't be smart," Karen said. "Most of the other competitors have never seen the course or the terrain, and they don't get a chance to walk it before the trials. Besides, if you do poorly, you can always stay there and hole up in that old shack again to hide your shame."

Charlie and Bone trained with a small band of sheep in his parents' pasture almost every day after he got home from work. Jack and Sarah lived right next door to the home Charlie had built for Karen after they married. His parents had a five acre parcel of land surveyed out of their farm, and gave it to Charlie and Karen as a wedding present. Mostly, his folks had just wanted them to live close by, especially if any grandchildren were born.

Sarah had gotten along very well with her daughter-in-law from the first time they met, and she adored her granddaughter. Mary spent every day with her Grandma Sarah while Charlie and Karen were at work, and the dogs spent their days hanging around the farm with Jack and Sarah and Mary.

Charlie walked through the old screen door on the back porch of his parents' house and caught his little blonde-haired, blue-eyed daughter as she jumped into his arms.

"Hi, cupcake. Did you color with Grandma today?"

"Uh-huh. And we read some books. You wanna see?"

Charlie sat down at the kitchen table and paid close attention as Mary guided him through her favorite children's book, page by illustrated page, giving him a thorough explanation of all the pictures, characters, and story. As he listened to his little girl tell the story of the pig who learned to herd sheep, he noticed his mother's wooden carving of the sheepdog in the middle of the table.

"You probably shouldn't let her play with that, Mom," he said. "You won't be happy if it gets broken."

"Don't worry about it, Charlie," his mother said, dismissing his unwarranted concern over the family heirloom. "She's learning how to be careful with it. It's going to be hers someday."

Mary looked up from her book and smiled at her father, nodding her head.

"Let me get this straight. You're willing to trust a four-year-old with your precious wood carving, but not me?" he teased.

"Not yet. She'll get it when she's older. It usually skips a generation as it's handed down anyway. That's how we make sure it always stays in the right hands. Besides, girls take better care of their things than boys do."

"Can we eat over here tonight, Mom?" Charlie asked. "Karen called and she's going to be late. It's the last weekend of skiing and a bunch of broken bones and torn ligaments came off the mountain."

"We already ate, Daddy," Mary said. "You're too late."

"You sound more like your mother and grandmother every day, you little imp." He grabbed his daughter by her arms and blew a noisy raspberry into the side of her neck as she squealed and giggled.

"You can fix yourself a sandwich if you want," Sarah said. "Hot food's gone. Your father and daughter ate it all."

"I think I'll clean up and go into Park City and meet Karen at the medical center. She deserves a dinner out for being so patient while I've spent so much time working with Bone every day after work. Can Mary stay with you tonight?"

"Of course she can. Did you think she might wait at home by herself while her parents are out on the town?"

"There sure are a lot of comedians in this family," Charlie said, as he kissed his little girl on the forehead and left through the back door.

Charlie and Bone trained hard every day, and competed in two competitions during the summer in preparation for the September trials. He began to think about the big event every day as the Labor Day Weekend drew nearer, and hoped that he would be ready.

He didn't try to fool himself into believing that he could win, but if he could place in the top fifteen and earn the right to compete in the final championship round, he would be happy.

The summer went by so quickly that Charlie didn't think he had enough time to prepare for the big competition. It was two days before the big weekend, and he already had butterflies in his stomach. He lay awake every night, thinking about each voice and whistle command he would have to use to help Bone through the course.

On the first day of the trials, Charlie was out of bed and in the truck with Bone at five in the morning, driving up through Midway to Soldier Hollow to be sure he wasn't late for the handlers' meeting. He arrived at the event site with more than an hour to spare. Only the vendors were up and about, setting up their food tents for the day and getting ready for the first arrivals of handlers and spectators. Bone could sense his nervousness, and raised a paw to Charlie for reassurance.

As the other handlers began to arrive with their dogs, Charlie saw a few familiar faces and that helped him to relax. He saw Bev and Don Thompson before they saw him, and walked over to greet them. After a minute or two of family talk, Bev led her dog away and walked down to the judge's tent to get ready for the handler's meeting. Charlie decided to follow along.

Several other handlers were gathering, and he recognized a few more faces. Patrick Donovan was there from Idaho—he had taken home the blue ribbon from the Big Willow Classic on more than one occasion, and Julie Smith from San Diego—Charlie had competed with her once in Sonoma.

"Hello, Charlie," a familiar voice said from behind him. He turned and saw his former trainer who had helped him at a clinic in Colorado. "I heard you were on the roster this year. You've been doing well."

"Hello, Scott," Charlie replied, reaching out to shake hands with the affable Canadian. "I thought I'd see you here."

Scott McKenzie turned to another handler who was standing next to him and offered an introduction. "Charlie, this is Amanda Miller. She's from Canada, too. She's competed here almost every year, and has a couple of very good dogs. You have to be careful or you'll be eating her dust."

Charlie relaxed and laughed, put at ease by the friendly man from Alberta. "Hello, Amanda. It's nice to meet you. I think I'll be eating everybody's dust today."

"Oh, I'm sure you'll do fine," Amanda said. The short blonde woman was dressed in casual western wear and kept the sun out of her eyes with a broad-brimmed straw sunbonnet. Charlie thought she looked like Little Bo Peep in blue jeans. He knew her only by reputation, but he knew that she was a formidable competitor.

Charlie listened carefully as the competition judge explained the course and the rules, and answered questions from the handlers. The man was a transplant from Scotland, and now made his home in Missouri. He had judged many sheepdog trials, and had competed successfully in a number of events in Great Britain and North America in years past.

The crowd of handlers disbursed after the judge adjourned the handlers meeting, and the first competitors went to bring their dogs to the trial field. Charlie had already seen the daily roster. He was twenty-eighth in the order of a field of more than forty handlers and their dogs. It would be a few hours before it would be his turn to send Bone out to bring sheep.

He watched the first few handlers work their dogs. A few of them ran the course and completed the pen before the buzzer, but others failed to pen their sheep in the allotted time. He was beginning to accept as truth his mother's comment about being as good as the rest of them. Maybe he was, and just didn't know it.

The stands were beginning to fill up with spectators. It was a one hour drive up through the Heber Valley to Soldier Hollow from Salt Lake City, and that's where most of the visitors came from, arriving in larger numbers after ten o'clock. The bigger crowds always gathered by mid-day, and the numbers swelled on the last two days as the contenders for the Grand Championship round were decided.

Charlie walked behind the announcer's building, got Bone out of his crate, and led him down to the vendor tents to see if he could find his wife and daughter. Mary spotted him from a distance as they approached from the parking lot and alerted her mother. "Mommy, there's Daddy and Bone."

Charlie was on his way to get a shepherd's pie from one of the food vendors when Karen walked up behind him and grabbed a handful of extra fat that he had been carrying around his waistline. "I thought you were going to work this off this summer, Butkus," she teased. "Maybe you should let Bone wait by the handler's post while you run up the side of the mountain and fetch sheep."

Charlie just smiled in response and picked Mary up so she could get a better view through the gathering crowds of spectators and visitors. "Daddy, I want a snow cone," Mary cooed, as she spotted the colorful vendor trailer parked along the side of the promenade. Naturally, he gave in immediately. Karen had always said he was a big mush-puff when it came to giving in to their daughter's frivolous requests. A snow cone sounded good to Charlie, too, and it gave him something to do while he waited for his turn on the trial course. It was a warm day—the temperature had already climbed to more than ninety degrees, and it wasn't even noon yet.

"They have a tent down by the exhibits where they do face painting, and they have coloring contests for kids," he said to his wife as they slurped on the flavored icy treats. "Maybe Mary would enjoy it. She loves to color, and you could have your face painted like a raccoon or a panda while you wait for her." Karen punched him in the ribs, then closed her eyes and sucked in air through her mouth to alleviate the brain freeze she got from her snow cone.

"Did mom and dad ride up with you?" Charlie asked.

"Your mom said they would probably come up tomorrow," Karen answered. "Your dad wasn't feeling too well today. He's okay, but his blood pressure has been a little high and your mom doesn't want him walking around outside in this heat all day."

Charlie walked back down to the handlers' area and waited for his turn to work the trial course. There was only one more ahead of him before it was his turn. He picked up the shepherd's crook that his mother had given him five years ago, and got ready to walk out onto the field and take his place at the handler's post. He looked up at the big Olympic scoreboard and saw that several scores had been posted in the low eighties. A ninety-two had been the top score during the preliminaries, so they were all going to be hard to beat.

"Next on the field is Charlie Stewart and Bone," the announcer's voice boomed over the loudspeaker system. "He is working with a five-year-old male border collie, and he's had some good success the past two years in several western trials.

Charlie walked out to the post with Bone and watched for the judge to signal that it was okay for him to send his dog on its outrun. He waited until he was sure the sheep were all set out and held in place at the top of the hill. The judge nodded toward him and waved a hand to signal that he could send his dog, and Charlie released Bone to race up the trail to the left in a wide outrun. He waited and watched as Bone found his way above and behind the sheep, then cautiously lifted them from their spot next to a small pile of hay and began to move them down the slope and through the fetch panels.

Bone reached the handler's post with his sheep in good time, turned them and began his drive away without a hitch. He had a decent cross drive through the other two sets of panels at the lower end of the course, and brought his band of sheep back into the shedding ring with over four minutes to spare on the time clock. Charlie worked carefully with Bone to separate five sheep from the others and move them smoothly toward the small pen. Everything was going well so far. He grasped the rope on the pen gate and pulled it wide, then stayed to one side to give Bone plenty of room to work.

The problem with the big range sheep was that they didn't like being put into a pen. They preferred open fields and pastures, and had probably never been shoved into a pen that small. It looked like a trap to the uncooperative sheep, and they tested every direction to get away from the man and his dog without having to enter the pen gate. Seconds ticked away on the clock as Bone worked back and forth, lying down on his master's command to take pressure off and give the sheep a moment to reconsider their choices before moving stealthily back in to turn their heads toward the pen.

Bone finally nudged a couple of the ewes into the safety of the pen, and the other three backed up with them through the gate. It wasn't pretty, but they were in. Charlie pulled the gate shut behind them with a half minute to spare, and received polite applause from the crowd gathered in the stands. He released the sheep and took Bone over to the water-filled stock trough next to the judge's tent and let his dog jump in to cool down. He waited for his score to come up on the giant reader board—an eighty-six. Charlie was thrilled. It put him in second place for the day.

He took Bone down to the handler's area and got him a drink of water, then walked back up to the stands to find his wife and daughter.

"Daddy, Bone did good," Mary explained as Charlie walked up to where his little family was sitting. "Did you see him?" she asked, smiling up at her daddy with a little panda face.

"Yes, I saw him, honey. He did good, huh?"

"That has to take some pressure off, doesn't it Charlie?" Karen said, smiling proudly at her husband.

"It doesn't hurt," he answered. "As long as we can stay in the top scores, we'll be okay. There's still ten or twelve more to go today, so we'll know in a couple of hours. I see you decided not to get your face painted."

Charlie spent the next two hours going back and forth between the exhibit booths and the viewing stands, watching some of the other competitors and checking on the scores from time to time. He was still in second place and nearly all the dogs had run. He sat down next to a couple of other handlers and watched until the last one took her post. It was Amanda Miller from Canada. Charlie marveled at how smoothly her well-trained dog worked the course, and he left shaking his head in awe and admiration as she and her dog separated sheep in the shedding ring and penned them with more than three minutes left on the clock. She moved into second place for the day, and Charlie dropped into third place. It was still good enough to put him into the competition for the Grand Championship.

The next two days of trials determined more of the finalists, as each handler worked to move his or her dog through the course without giving up valuable points due to errors. Top handlers and their dogs had gathered from around North America and the world demonstrated their herding skills.

The final list of Grand Championship contestants was being filled, and competitors from Scotland, Switzerland, and South Africa were added to the short list of fifteen who would compete for the top three spots. Grand Championship Monday would be a day of keen competition.

The spectator stands were placed far enough back from the trial field to prevent the crowd noise from breaking a dog's concentration or agitating the sheep, but close enough to give the spectators an excellent view of the field, shed ring and pen.

Charlie arrived early on Monday, and sat in the stands with his family as the announcer called out the first handler and his dog. When the national anthem began to play, he stood and turned to face the Olympic bridge at the left end of the field and placed his hat over his heart as he watched Old Glory fly from the top of the last flagpole in a long row, along with the flags of all the countries that were represented at the trials.

The course would be much more difficult for the championship. It required a double lift—a fetch of two bands of sheep, one after the other, and a shed that required the dog and handler to separate only five sheep that were fitted with red collars. More time was allotted for the added difficulty of the course and the maneuvers, and it would be time that was needed.

Bill Broderick was the first handler to send his dog. He was last year's champion and had made it into the championship round for the third straight year. His dog completed the difficult course with time to spare, and completed a successful pen. He would post a good score.

Bev Thompson and Amanda Miller and another woman from Oregon had all made it to the finals, and both Bev and Amanda had posted high scores. They moved into first and second place in the standings. In a championship event that was designed to separate the men from the boys, two women and their amazing dogs were separating them all.

Charlie's turn came ninth in the order, and several good scores had already gone up on the board. Charlie and Bone worked like a team, heeding the training advice he had been given by Bev and Don Thompson, and drawing on the knowledge he picked up from Scott McKenzie at his clinic in Colorado. Bone relied on his own instincts as he drove the course and completed the shed with only two minutes left on the clock. Charlie felt the urgency as he rushed to the pen, pulled the gate open wide, and called Bone to bring the sheep. It was nearly flawless, but Bone sensed his master's nervousness and moved too quickly. He allowed the sheep to circle around the outside of the pen twice before he settled down on his master's command and dropped to the ground. Bone came up in a stealthy crouch, and inched forward with one paw raised slowly, then silently stepped closer to the reluctant sheep. He nudged the woolies into the pen with remarkable finesse, and Charlie closed the gate with three seconds to spare. The spectator stands erupted with cheering and applause. He took off his hat and waved it to the crowd, then kneeled to praise his dog.

Charlie walked Bone past the judge's tent and let him jump into the stock trough to cool off in the water. His score was announced—he was in third place. It was good enough for Charlie. He never expected to make it this far.

The announcer's voice rang out across the field and grandstands with the name of the next handler. "Next up is Red Chisholm, ladies and gentlemen. Red is the elder statesman of stockdog trials in America, and at the age of eighty-three, his name has become legendary on the trial fields. He comes from a long line of stockmen, trainers, handlers and dog-breeders who trace their family tree and their dogs' bloodlines from Texas to Missouri, and all the way back to the years before the Civil War. He'll be working with his ten-year-old border collie, Roy. Let's give him a big welcome." There was cheering and whistling from the large crowd as the old-timer in the Wrangler jeans and cowboy hat ambled out onto the field.

Charlie watched as Roy approached the post at his master's side and dropped to the ground, staring up the slope of the mountain with trance-like concentration. The black, rough-coated border collie waited until it heard the quiet command from its master that sent it streaking up the long slope to where the first band of sheep waited. It was like watching a ballet as Roy lifted the small band of ewes, fetching them down the hillside with instinctively-timed moves and pauses, wearing the sheep in a nearly perfect line through the fetch panels and around the post without a moment's hesitation. His cross drive was flawless and his return to the shedding ring took only a minute. He turned immediately on his handler's signal and raced back up the hillside to the right, searching for the next band of sheep his master had sent him to find. Roy couldn't yet see the sheep, but he knew they were up there or his master would not have sent him. In less than two minutes, he came down through the trees and onto the open field, pushing a band of ewes ahead of him in a straight line.

The crowd of spectators watched in awe and admiration as Roy and his master worked together to separate five of the red-collared ewes from the rest of the band, then release the remaining sheep to send them toward the exhaust pen.

Red Chisholm walked calmly toward the pen with plenty of time left on the clock, and slowly opened the pen gate. The man and his dog had performed the same routine a thousand times. Red gave no command. Roy simply waited until the gate was open and his master was in place, then brought the sheep forward and pushed them straight toward the open pen, keeping just enough distance between his nose and the sheep in front of him to prevent them from balking. The sheep turned and faced Roy at the gate opening, standing their ground momentarily. The ewe in front stamped a hoof in warning; perhaps meant as an alert to the others in her tiny band of sisters to be ready to flee, or perhaps in a feeble act of defiance in the face of the wolf-eyed dog.

Roy eyed the woolies in the same way his wolf ancestors had eyed their prey, and then slowly approached in a crouching, stalking movement that unsettled the sheep and caused them to bunch together more tightly for safety. His instinct for gathering and driving sheep was innate—written onto his brain from before the time of his birth.

It was something more than skill—something that could not be learned. It was an ability unique to border collies, and it gave them a power over other animals that no other breed of herding dog possessed. It was the raw instinct to gather and drive animals toward the alpha member of the pack that allowed the border collie to give man mastery over herds of livestock.

Roy eyed the red-collared band of sheep, crouching low with one front paw raised in readiness, and waited until they turned together and retreated into the safety of the pen. Red stood as still as the gate post

Richard Hooton

until the sheep were inside, then swung the gate shut and raised his shepherd's crook into the air in victory. The crowd cheered and whistled for a long minute, as Red held his crook high above his head to acknowledge the crowd's applause and admiration. Red knew that he and Roy had won the top spot, and it had to be obvious to anyone with a good eye for the scoring process. No other dog and handler team on that day had been able to deliver such a perfectly-executed run.

When the final scores were posted, it was Red Chisholm and Roy in the top spot by a wide margin. Bev Thompson and Amanda Miller held the second and third places with the well-executed runs by their well-trained dogs.

Charlie stood next to the stands near the announcer's booth and watched as the Olympics-style medals ceremony began, and the winning handlers and their dogs mounted the three-tiered medals platform. The wail and drone of bagpipes came from within the forest above the trial field as the kilt-clad Salt Lake Scots came marching out of the trees and down the mountain trail toward the stands, honoring the champion with a stirring fanfare of pipes and drums.

He had watched the Soldier Hollow trials in past years as a spectator, but he never felt such pride as he did today. It was far more than a competition—it was both an exhibition and a celebration of a way of life, passed down through generations of dogs and men. The winners removed their hats, and one by one, bowed their heads to receive their medals of gold, silver, or bronze.

After the ceremony, Charlie walked down to the handlers' tent to greet Red Chisholm and congratulate him. A large number of well-wishers were already gathered around Red and his dog, and Charlie waited patiently for the opportunity to talk with him. Red looked up and saw Charlie standing a few feet away, and pushed his way through the crowd toward the younger man, excusing himself as he went.

"You're Charlie Stewart, aren't you?" Red asked as he reached out to shake hands.

"Yes, sir, I am. How did you know that?"

"I watched your first preliminary run, and I saw you work the more difficult course with your dog today," Red answered. "I hadn't seen you work before, and I always like to watch the competition to see what we're up against. You were pretty impressive."

"Thanks," Charlie replied. "I just came down to congratulate you and tell you how much I enjoyed watching Roy work today. I didn't get to see him work in the preliminary trials. He's an amazing dog."

"He is remarkable, isn't he," Red agreed, looking down at Roy with pride as he stroked his head.

"Well, I better be going," Charlie said. "I just wanted to stop by and congratulate you on your win."

"Hold on for a minute, Charlie. I want to talk to you."

Red said his goodbyes to several of his old acquaintances and fellow handlers, then went back to join Charlie near the side of the tent. "Why don't you walk down to the motor home with me, Charlie," Red invited. "I've got something I'd like you to see."

"Sure, Red—we were headed in that direction anyway."

"Your dog did real good today, Charlie," the old Texan said as the men walked across the bridge to the parking lot. "You can be proud of him. I noticed he got a little excited on the second day of the preliminary trials, but that can happen to anyone."

"Yeah, he got past me at the pen and gripped a sheep on its hind leg. It was my fault—pilot error, you might say. I got too cocky after our good showing on the first day," Charlie said. "I should have kept a better handle on him when he was working in close. Scott McKenzie warned me about Bone having an aggressive streak, and told me I'd have to keep an eye on him."

"Don't feel bad, son," Red comforted the young man. "It's happened to me. Disqualifications and losing the race against the time clock are just part of trialing, but there's always a new day."

"We'll keep working at it," Charlie said. "I think we'll both get better with time and experience."

"Has anyone else in your family trialed dogs in the past?" Red asked.

"Both of my parents handled sheepdogs quite a few years ago. Their families have been sheep ranchers for generations—all the way back to England and Scotland. This is my dad's crook, in fact. He gave it to me five years ago and encouraged me to get a dog and start training it for competitions."

"Have their families always lived in Utah?"

"No. My dad's great-grandfather came here from Scotland originally, but he moved up to Idaho not long after he arrived."

"The Chisholm family has managed to keep pretty good records on our dogs' bloodlines over the years, Charlie. We've maintained the same line for close to a hundred and fifty years. It was a man named Stewart who gave my great, great-grandfather his first border collie back in St. Louis, Missouri."

Red unlocked the door to his motor home and Roy leaped up into the interior and found a comfortable spot to settle. Red opened a crate and freed a small black pup, not more than three or four months old. The eager little dog bounded down the steps of the motor home onto the grass and greeted Charlie and Bone before turning its obedient attention back to its master.

"This little guy is about three and a half months old now. Sometimes I bring my new pups along to the trials, just to get them accustomed to the surroundings and excitement," Red explained. "I've bred Roy to a female I bought from Ian McGregor last year. He's bred some of the best border collies in Great Britain for years. Ian is a two-time Scottish National Champion, and represented Scotland here in the trials last year. I kept all of the pups except for two that Ian came to take back to Scotland with him a month ago. We're going to share in a solid breeding program that should insure the preservation of our dogs' superior herding instincts and endurance."

Charlie admired the little black pup with its white-whiskered nose and narrow white collar that ringed its neck in a perfect circle. One pricked ear gave the little dog the appearance of possessing a constant alertness to the sounds around it. "He's a fine pup, Red. I don't know if I've ever seen one so alert."

"I want you to take this pup and train it, Charlie. If you're going to keep trialing, and I'm sure you will, then you'll need to always keep another young dog in training. You work with this pup for a few months—make sure he gets training almost every day. I think he'll make an excellent herding dog."

"He's a beautiful pup, Red," Charlie said, shaking his head. "And he looks keen, but I don't have the money for a dog like this right now."

"You take him, Charlie. If he works out for you, then you can pay me for him the next time we see each other. We'll work something out on the price."

Red had begun to think about getting one of his pups into Charlie's hands after watching him work with his dog on the first day of the preliminary trials and seeing the young man's natural handling ability. He didn't know if there was a chance that he came from the same family of Stewarts who gave the Chisholm family their first stockdog, but it was worth a shot, Red decided. It would be a debt repaid.

Charlie kneeled down next to the little bright-eyed pup and looked him over carefully, then smiled up at Red with gratitude. He was pleased that such a dog would be entrusted to him. "I won't forget this, Red," Charlie said as he stroked the little dog's head and ruff. "I think I'll call him Ring."

Charlie loaded his dogs into the truck, revved the engine and pulled the gearshift into drive as Bone settled into the back seat of the pickup cab. The traffic on the two-lane road that led from Soldier Hollow down through Midway toward Heber City was beginning to thin. He accelerated to the speed limit, anxious to get home to his family.

Ring curled up on the front seat next to Charlie and felt his new master's comforting hand on his head. The stirrings of an age-old bond began to rise, causing the young dog to tremble slightly. He relaxed and lowered his head onto Charlie's leg, released a little sigh, and closed his eyes.

EPILOGUE

The love and appreciation of herding dogs is shared by countless numbers of admirers the world over, and will insure that the tradition of trial herding competitions will be kept alive for many years to come.

The Dogs of September

The bagpipes played for Roy
One bright September afternoon,
Amid the Wasatch forest that
Would change its colors soon.

Through the trees the kilt-clad pipers
Came, all marching to the tune, as
The bagpipes played for Roy
On that September afternoon.

Forty dogs and forty handlers
Stood to meet the judge's test.
With keen instincts and hard training,
Reached down deep to find their best.

Crowds were cheering, children laughing,
Dogs and handlers plied their skills.
Dog and sheep collided gently in a
Solemn test of wills.

"That'll do, Roy," spoken softly,
"That'll do," whispered again.
The handler knelt to praise his dog
And felt a glowing pride within.

One dog ran its finest run,
Thus the glory had been earned.
Roy's good master wore the medal
For the skills that Roy had learned.

What a glorious summer day
Beneath a daytime Wasatch moon,
When the bagpipes played for Roy
One bright September afternoon.

Richard Hooton

ACKNOWLEDGEMENTS

Mark Petersen and Howard Peterson
Founders of the Soldier Hollow Classic
Heber Valley, Utah

John and Diane Peavey
Founders of The Trailing of the Sheep fall festival
Sun Valley, Idaho

Hank Cartwright
For his encouragement and wit

Debra Semone Gell
For the border collies and support

Randy and Carol Heuther
For the gift of Archie the Wonder Dog

Jaime Green
For her patient and capable dog training

J. Michael Oakes and Peter Wagner
For their honest critiques

Chris Millspaugh
Regional History Librarian
The Community Library of Ketchum, Idaho

Tracy Martin
My dear niece, for her
valuable contribution to my historic research

See 1stWorld Books at:

www.1stWorldPublishing.com

See our classic collection at:

www.1stWorldLibrary.org

Printed in the United States
203242BV00010B/27/P